The
Testing of
Luther
Albright

The
Testing of
Luther
Albright

A N O V E L

MacKenzie Bezos

Fourth Estate
An Imprint of HarperCollins*Publishers*

HarperCollins books may be purchased for educational, business, or sales promotional use. For information, please write: Special Markets Department, HarperCollins Publishers, 10 East 53rd Street, New York, NY 10022.

FIRST EDITION

Designed by Jessica Shatan Heslin

Printed on acid-free paper

Library of Congress Cataloging-in-Publication Data is available upon request.

ISBN 0-06-075141-X

to Granyan

and to Jeff,

for similar things

Contents

The
Testing of
Luther
Albright

1 The Research Topic

THE YEAR I LOST MY WIFE AND SON, MY SON PERFORMED NINE separate tests of my character. One night during *Mutual of Omaha's Wild Kingdom*, the sofa tipped beneath us, and this is how it began.

"Whoa," he said.

His palms were flat on the sofa cushions. Liz was sitting cross-legged on the floor, and before I could think to stand, she had taken him by the wrist and led him to the shelter of the door frame. She reached to place a hand on his shoulder, and although he was fifteen, this was all it took to get him to follow her into a crouch. In a second, I had joined them there, and as I kneeled, I had to grasp the door casing for balance. Now I noted objects in the room by weight; our distance from windows. I became aware of sounds—a quick pop that could have been wood or glass; three dull thuds from different corners of the house—all of it muffled by the persistent rattling of our things: of flatware in drawers and knickknacks on shelves and pills in their bottles.

When the room stopped shaking, we uncovered our heads, and

Liz's eyes, which normally ignored the television, turned immediately to it. Jim Fowler was rappelling down a cliff face toward a nest on a narrow ledge.

Elliot stood.

"We should wait here a minute," Liz said.

He crouched again. "It didn't feel very big."

"All the same . . ."

When the condor saw Jim Fowler, it spread its wings, a span the length of a man. Jim wrapped his arms around it from behind, folding them in. His boots dangled in the air. He tagged the condor's ankle, and then opened his arms wide to release it, a burst of feather against the blue sky. As he was hoisted away by the helicopter, the head and shoulders of a local newscaster replaced him.

"We interrupt your regular programming with a special report. An earthquake was just felt in the greater Sacramento area." Her eyes flitted offscreen and back. "We do not yet have any data on the magnitude or the epicenter of the disturbance, but, here in our studio, objects dropped from high shelves." She touched her ear and paused. "The sensation was reportedly felt as far away as Redding, as this caller describes. . . ." From an invisible speaker in the studio came the voice of a Citrus Heights woman explaining that she had been talking to her sister in Redding on the telephone when it happened; her sister had been carrying a mug of hot coffee at the time, and at the exact same moment that the caller heard the tinkling of wind chimes on her own porch, her sister screamed because her coffee had soaked the front of her blouse.

Liz stood and crossed the living room. She had a beauty so striking even I could not recall it fully from morning until nightfall. She was over forty by then, and still people spent the first moments of any encounter with her as they would in a hospital room or a cathedral, their eyes locked first on one feature and then another, trying to decode their composite power. She bent at the waist and picked up a set of proof Kennedy half-dollars that had fallen from the shelf and fingered a crack in the clear plastic case. She and I had met twenty-two years earlier at the Wells Fargo Bank on J Street; she monitored access to the safe-deposit boxes, where I appeared weekly to deposit coins of dubious value. She had thought me an inheritor or a man in the midst of a legal battle until one day she stepped into the vault while I was pulling a small tin of wheat pennies from my coat pocket.

Now she set the cracked case back on the shelf and looked at us, two men she had left in the safety of a door frame. "Come on," she said. "Let's go make sure nothing else is broken."

Elliot led the way. He had grown so much in the last month that from behind he was like a stranger: a thicker trunk, and also a change, from loping to shambling, in his gait. We followed him into the kitchen, and we all three surveyed the room with a sensitivity to disorder we had not felt when we cleared the dinner dishes an hour before. Elliot stooped to pick up a ballpoint pen that may well have been dropped that afternoon. Liz righted things on the counter: a cookbook, an orange that had strayed from an overfull basket of fruit. We had heard no noise that could have come from the direction of the kitchen except that pop, and now I opened cupboards trying to find it. The dishes sat stacked behind smooth oak doors I had purchased twenty-two years ago and waxed with a T-shirt. Little felt pads I had glued to their inner corners let them close without sound.

When Elliot's patience with the normalcy of things ran out, he passed back into the hallway, and again we followed. In the hall above us was a small antique table that I had bought for Liz last fall when Elliot began high school. On it, she kept a potted jade plant, a framed photograph of the three of us in the shadow of Mount Rushmore, and a souvenir core of bedrock, which had rolled from the table to the carpeted floor. We found the other thuds without trouble: a thick book on gardening Liz kept on her small nightstand, and a five-pound hand weight she had set on an ottoman in our walk-in closet. This left only the pop.

When I built the house, I'd left the attic unfinished, and over the summer, Elliot and I had made a project of its completion. I had done some of the prep work for this during original construction—installing a subfloor; fitting extra collar ties between the rafters to take a ceiling—so that when I described the job, he was disappointed by how easy it would be. I tried to explain that nothing about our job would be easy—we had to install a knee wall, and just getting the studs properly bevel-cut to fit the sloping roofline would take a lot of care and time—but secretly I was moved by his ambition. He wanted to add dormers, something that altered the exterior of the house as well, and so that's what we did, kneeling on the scaffolding we had built together and snapping level chalk lines to mark space for them—the two sharp changes in topography they would be. Now the space was a sitting room where he did all of his homework, and as I watched him crest the stairs, I was frankly worried that one of these windows he had framed with such care had cracked under the strain of the earthquake. But the windows were fine. When we caught up with him, he was kneeling on the floor over the three large shards of a broken drinking glass.

"Sorry, Mom," he said.

She laughed. "Who are you: Mother Nature?" She reached out for his shoulder—he was at that age when he would shy from my touch, but not from hers—and gave it a squeeze.

I tore a few blank sheets from one of his notebooks and crouched next to him. By folding it, I made a sort of catcher's mitt. "Here," I said. He hesitated. The pieces were sharp and curved, like licks of flame, cloudy with fingerprints and the residue of soda. They clinked as he laid them on the paper, and this raised an odor—not soda: beer.

Liz put her hand out to lead him; "Besides, it's only a glass," she said, and he followed her, as he had to the door frame, down the stairs.

In the living room, he settled next to her on the couch. I sat alone in the armchair, and although the news of the earthquake was riveting in its way, now my son was his own quiet spectacle. The birth of one's first child is supposed to be a joyous occasion; so my initial assessment of what those nine months of waiting had yielded was a surprise. At first a lump of flesh. At worst, a stranger with needs so many and so persistent it was difficult not to resent him. I would go to his room at night to watch him sleep because, although by day I bent over his basket to make sounds, secretly his clear, dark, stranger's eyes watching my face so intently gave me a hollow feeling that scared me. I tried to make it go away. I lifted him in my arms and put my mouth to his soft cheek and walked him around our yard. I bundled him in blankets and made myself change his diapers, thinking the intimacy this would force might eventually overwhelm this sense of mine that I had invited a stranger—a tiny, judgmental intruder—into our home.

But then one day a change. I had his basket on the bathroom counter. Strands of Liz's hair had clogged the sink drain, and I had brought him in with my toolbox so she could sleep. I was about to crouch to open the trap, and when I switched my flashlight on, he tracked the bright beam on the wall with his eyes and then looked, God bless me, at my hand holding the flashlight. I released a laugh of pure astonishment, and at this, this single laugh, he gave me his first smile.

After this it was different. His body felt firmer in my arms, less precarious, and his face, once (forgive me!) a threat, seemed full of acceptance and promise. Instead of leaving the house to escape my feelings, I sometimes asked to take him with me when I ran errands. Without my noticing, his frightening, fragile neck had strengthened, and one day I found I could carry him down the aisles of a hardware store sitting up on my crossed arms. A damp heat rose from his hair, and I smiled first at a beautiful woman whose eyes I normally would have avoided on fearful principle; next, a one-armed man sorting through a box of nails. Something about Elliot's company: his head rested against that low spot at the center of my chest where, in their first pictures, children will draw the heart.

On the couch next to Liz now, he snorted at the television. Newscasters had taken over the programming completely, but mostly with interviews of people who had been no more than frightened. They had several good shots of shattered windows, and helicopter footage of a pileup on I-5. They reran this clip countless times, ending with a two-minute spot on what we could all do to make ourselves safer in the event of an aftershock: bolt tall pieces of furniture to the wall, hang pictures on tremor hooks, and remove sharp or heavy objects from high shelves.

"How about padding non-upholstered furniture?" Elliot said.

"Or wearing a helmet around the house," I said, and he laughed.

There was some real damage. In the days that followed, scaffolding appeared downtown on buildings that had dropped bricks to the sidewalks. On the right shoulder along Interstate 5 where that ten-car accident had killed two people, commuters slowed and rolled down their passenger windows to drop bouquets of flowers. But newscasters undermined solemnity with exaggeration. Local stations floated banners in the upper-right-hand corner of the television screen: "Uncovering the Damage," "Aftermath," and even "Sacramento Under Siege." For a full week, Channel 3 ran a nightly story about one of the injured: a waitress with a broken leg; an air-traffic controller with a neck brace; a schoolteacher with a sprained wrist, the camera zooming in dramatically to catch her writing on the blackboard in her shaky left hand.

I joined in the joking about this, but secretly I felt a sense of foreboding much deeper and more troubling than anything the media tried to stir. I tried to trace it to its source. Late one night, I reviewed our wills for oversights, but this did not make it go away. On my lunch hour, I mapped and then test-drove four separate routes from my office to Elliot's school for emergencies, but the next day in the kitchen as I filled our tumblers with orange juice, my pulse quickened in a way that I could neither suppress nor understand.

Finally, alone in my car on the way to work, another explanation occurred to me. I worked then as a civil engineer for the California Department of Water Resources. I had done so for twenty-three years, longer than Liz and I had been married, and in that time I'd seen the arrival, installation, and departure of three Principals above me as I rose from checking shop drawings to supervising a team of as many as twenty-eight in the design of dams. At the time of the earthquake there were three other Supervising Engineers in our division, and we reported to Don Moraine, a slight man with yellow teeth who touched his temple and looked sideways when he laughed. He was shy, but competent, and above him was our Division Chief, Howard Krepps.

Back in 1957, when I took my first course in Civil Engineering, water resources planning had a mystique in California that anyone now would have difficulty imagining. California is an important state, with an economy larger than all but six countries in the world, and its prosperity is largely dependent on the reorganization of its waters by engineers. This is not why I picked CE as a major—I picked it because the jobs were plentiful and stable, most of them state jobs where hours are reasonable and benefits good. But it is also true that in spite of myself I was enchanted by certain facts. Engineers had made whole rivers flow backwards. The California Aqueduct is one of two man-made structures visible from space.

It hadn't been difficult for me to get a job within the Department of Water Resources, but not long after I did, the climate changed. In just a handful of years, a complex set of political forces reduced the projects we were asked to design to a fraction of what they had been before. Between 1960 and 1973, sixteen dams had been built, and since then only one. I had done well during this period, surviving the cutbacks, and remaining part of a team that, as might be expected within a government agency, even after the trimming, was larger than it needed to be. Just months after the deepest cuts had been made, Don asked me to propose a design for a large earth embankment dam a mere seventy miles outside of Sacramento. It was a plum project, not only because we all sensed the change that would make it the last large dam constructed in over two decades, but because of the visibility its location would give our work in the local news. A photograph of Governor Brown cutting the ribbon on North Fork would appear on the front page of the *Sacramento Bee*.

Driving past a block of scaffolding on L Street, it came to me that it was only a matter of time before this coveted proximity made my dam an object of scrutiny again. There was a division within the Department charged with reevaluating dams when new data made better assessment of risks possible, and an earthquake of this size would almost certainly trigger one. Maybe this had been the root of my vague apprehension. I thought about it. Although these investigations were legitimately important and the dam safety engineers just as smart as any in our division, supporting the reevaluations was tedious and unrewarding work under any circumstances, and at the time I was wrestling with the design of Governor Brown's big geothermal project. But try as I might, when I dwelled on the implications—the time wasted rechecking old design assumptions, the traction lost on a technically challenging project—I could muster nothing more complex than irritation.

Which is honestly all I felt a few mornings later when we passed the newspaper to each other sheet by sheet, looking at more photos of fallen bricks and people covering their heads on the steps of the capitol, and Elliot said: "Do you think they'll investigate your dam?"

I said, "They'll at least explore it within Safety of Dams. Whether they hand it to us to look for deficiencies depends on what they find."

"Would it annoy you if they did?"

His spoon hovered over his soft-boiled egg. When he was four, he had come to the kitchen smelling of my aftershave. Last month, Liz had shown me a video of the two of us working on the attic together, and when at the end we both walked towards the camera with identical slope-shouldered posture, heat gathered beneath my arms. She rewound and showed it to me again, laughing sweetly, but still I felt the solemn press of responsibility that haunted every moment of his scrutiny or emulation.

Now he held his spoon steady, waiting.

I wrinkled my nose and shook my head almost imperceptibly, a look conveying good-humored dismissal. "Nah," I said. "Benign distraction."

Fear did not seize me then—not right away—but it's telling that I can remember so vividly the way he looked at me when I said this. The bright window behind him furred his head with a corona of sunlight, like the head of a martyr in some old painting, and gave his features a dark quality that matched the intention forming inside him. He watched me; he did not break his gaze when he lifted his juice glass to his lips, did not stop studying my face even when Liz showed us a photo in the paper of a man standing next to a doghouse he had reinforced with steel.

I forced myself to glance at the picture. I forced a laugh. "At work they distributed an Earthquake Evacuation Procedures memo."

Liz said, "At the supermarket they're selling flashlights and first-aid kits near the checkout."

Elliot took an orange from the fruit basket. "Mrs. Parks changed our research assignment. Now we have to do it on an ancestor instead."

Liz cocked her head. "I don't get it."

"Someone in Mr. Delmonico's class lost an uncle in that pileup on I-5."

He cupped the orange in a napkin and began to peel it. When he was small, I had taught him to eat fruit wrapped in a napkin. Citric acid brought out a fine rash on his skin that never burned or flared, but lingered for hours and had nagged me with thoughts of small dangers that might befall him.

Liz said, "I don't mean to belittle his death, but that seems a little extreme. You've already started. You've read two books on automotive history."

He shrugged.

She said, "So who are you thinking of doing? My Great-Uncle George would be good. He was a coal miner. Or kooky Cousin Lisa."

He pulled a strip of peel from the orange. It made a ripping sound and the kitchen filled with a sharp smell. In my exhortations on the use of a napkin, I never mentioned the rash, but instead talked of courtesy. The juice also left a brown stain on upholstery, and I wanted him to learn respect for his mother.

He glanced at me. "I was thinking of your dad, maybe."

Liz said, "Dad's dad?"

"If it's okay with him."

And finally a stab of the anxiety I had been feeling all week shot through me. Elliot's thumbs were poised to split his bare orange into sections.

"Of course," I said. "I think that's a wonderful idea."

That night, while I was brushing my teeth, Liz opened the bathroom door. She had already changed for bed, a pink T-shirt so worn from sleep and laundering, fine holes rimmed the letters: Davis Women's Fun Run '61. She pulled down her underpants and sat on the toilet, and I listened for the familiar sound of her pee in the bowl. She said, "So what do you think that's all about?"

"What's what all about?" I said, although of course I knew what she meant.

"Him picking your dad."

I cocked my head slightly to indicate thinking. She stood and flushed. The water would pass through the fixture trap, down the branch drain to the soil stack. From there, it would fall twenty feet to a pitched run that would carry it under our lawn to the city sewer. She stepped beside me and washed her hands in the sink, watching me in the mirror with a patient, open look I still picture for strength when I try to strike up a conversation with someone in the coffee room at my golf club. Clear water swirled in the basin and down under the stopper.

I said, "He's curious, I guess."

She picked up her toothbrush and wet it under the stream, her eyes still on me in the mirror.

I said, "I can't blame him." I picked up a bar of face soap. "He never got to meet my parents."

I lathered a long time, and then rinsed with cupped hands, and dried with my eyes closed, and although at the time it was blind instinct born of a tightness in my chest that made me do such things, in retrospect I see what a transparent discouragement such evasions must have been to her. When I opened my eyes to hang my towel, she was already in bed, and when I joined her there, she smiled and turned to switch off her lamp. I switched mine off as well, and before the cover of dark could restore her courage, I pulled her toward me in the sole gesture of intimacy that never leads to conversation.

I slept quickly after this, but woke within the hour. I was flatly afraid, and with the earthquake as scapegoat I again allowed my fear of loss to gather, not around my wife and son, as it should have, but this time around the fragile workings of our house. In the trace of moonlight, I glanced at the corners of the ceiling where I had coped the moldings to fit them flush. The following morning when I ran a faucet to wash my hands, I listened for water hammer. Although for some of these things I could not even use the earthquake as justification, I began my annual maintenance tasks early. On Monday, I flushed the drains with baking soda and hot water. On Tuesday, I emptied the sediment from our water heater. On Thursday, I vacuumed our smoke alarms. And on Saturday, six days after the earthquake, I asked Elliot to help me check for cracks in our foundation.

He followed me around the perimeter with the caulking gun. Since his early boyhood, I'd involved him in household maintenance, and the reliability of my program made him itchy for signs of failure. We had reviewed three sides of the house when I found the first: a six-inch fissure wide enough at its center to accept a nickel. At first the quickening of his attention gave me a sudden empty feeling, but as he leaned close and brushed my shoulder, I chided myself: anything unusual is intriguing. Then he turned to me. He wanted to know how wide a bead of caulk he should pull, and although I'd been watching the changes in him for several months, I have to say that it wasn't until that moment that I noticed the beginnings of a mustache. The sun was bright, his face no more than ten inches from my own, and the hair was blond and so fine it was almost transparent. A sprinkler ticked at the far end of the lawn. Somewhere in the neighborhood, a car door slammed. "Don't worry," I said finally, but in this context, perhaps because of the surprise on my face, he didn't understand me. He waited, as if I might say something he had been waiting years to hear. A better father would have thought to speak a word of affection or wisdom into that silence, but I did not. "Just pull the trigger," I said; "I cut the nozzle to a size that will determine the bead," and when I said this—maybe it's hindsight that colors my memory, but I do not think so—something like disappointment overcame him. His head dropped at my words, so slightly I never would have noticed it had it not been for the faint mustache. At this new angle, the light left it, and the fine hairs disappeared in shadow. Then he shifted slightly on his haunches—I remember that his weight crushed a sweet smell from the grass—and drew a thin seam of caulk along the crack.

That afternoon, he worked upstairs in his bedroom, typing an outline for his report on my father. As I changed out of my work pants, long pauses fell between each strike of type ball against ribbon. I went downstairs to the kitchen and poured myself a glass of milk. Liz was in the living room, labeling the leaves of a photo album from our trip to the Grand Canyon. I had planned, for my part, to spend the rest of the day on interior weatherproofing, checking for drafts by running a dampened hand along the edges of our windows and doors. But now I was distracted by thoughts about my son. How would this go? *I have some extra razors, if you ever need them.* Or this: *Would you like me to teach you to shave?*

Outside, a squirrel backed up the trunk of our elm tree, its small hands gripping the furrowed bark. Elliot's typewriter sounded upstairs, six hesitant strikes, and then silence. I took a wheat cracker from a mason jar on the windowsill and rubbed the salt from its surface with my thumb. I set the cracker first untouched on the countertop, and then in the waste can beneath the sink where the evidence of my indecision could not be detected.

Under the drain trap was a wire basket of new yellow sponges.

Inside their cellophane wrappers, they were already moist. I took one into the entry hall. My front door is a two-inch plane of solid oak, weather-stripped with spring copper and strips of felt. But one never knows. Houses settle. In earthquakes, they move. I pressed my palms against the sponge and traced the door frame as I have seen mimes do, without touching it, a pantomime of escape, checking for drafts.

2 The Razor

BY MY OWN ESTIMATION I HAD BEEN A DECENT FATHER, IN every way a better father than my own, but the fact was that over the summer I had suffered one small failure of composure with my son.

It had happened in the attic.

Every year, I had given Elliot the option of going to camp, and every year, to my quiet gratification, he had chosen to pass the long hot months with me, improving something in our home. When he was younger, I'd picked the projects myself and kept them small—painting the exterior of the garage; installing a new washer and dryer in the basement—but as he got older, I tried to win another year of his company by inviting his suggestions. When he was thirteen, he drew a sketch of the tables and cabinets that became a custom workshop in the basement. The following summer he brought home a book from the library on installing central air-conditioning. And in April of that year, he led me up the narrow stairwell to my unfinished attic.

It had started well enough. I am a careful man—to a fault, I see now—and although by the standards of the average boy, Elliot had always been hyper-responsible, he had a boy's overconfidence in his own abilities and ignorance of the dangers of the world, and sometimes this made him hasty. I'd done an excellent job, I think, over the years, of hiding my judgment of this. When, after several respectful hints from me about tensile strength, he'd whittled a good eighty-five percent off the body of his car for the Pinewood Derby, I suppressed my criticism and complimented him on the boldness of his experiment. When in an eight-year-old's show of finesse he had insisted on carrying all three of our plates from the dinner table at once, I crouched to help him clean up the broken pieces and told him gently that more balance would come with practice and time.

But that year it had been harder. He was an adolescent, and maybe it is not so strange that some of his behavior had begun to bother me. Little things. Although I bought him a thermal cup with a flip top, he opened can after can of 7-Up and left them open and sweating on the plywood subfloor next to absorbent bats of insulation. Each day at the slightest rise in temperature, he took off his shirt and walked around the attic bare-chested, heedless of the raw boards certain to scrape his lean torso as we worked. When he was younger, he had listened to popular rock with Liz, upbeat songs that made her sashay across the kitchen, but now he set a boom box at the top of the stairs and played something so malevolent and percussive it was a menace to concentration.

To my small credit, I recognized these irritations as petty, and I knew better than to give them voice. A teenage boy is hungry for approval, especially from his father, and in the forced ease of these liberties, I thought I recognized a clumsy stab at the air of authority that flows from the unstudied habits of a man. As far as the carpentry went, he did a decent job, but not always with the method I would have chosen. He hammered in a stylized, self-conscious way that resulted in a lot of bent nails, but they were only nails, and I never corrected his form. I let him work for hours each day without my supervision, and even in cases where the cost of repairing an error would have been significant, in time and effort as well as money, I had done no more to assist him than review his progress when I got home from work. The plan was working well, and I'd felt certain he would leave the summer burnished by success and paternal praise, until in July he'd floated the idea of adding a bathroom.

I should pause here and explain that all of the pipes in my house are copper. Copper pipe is lightweight, strong, and more resistant to corrosion and scale than other metals, but it's also the case that it's difficult to install correctly. Before soldering, a substance called flux should be applied to remove surface oxide, but too much flux can cause corrosion and too little will create gaps in the integrity of the connection. Overheating will do the same. And then there is the danger. The flame on a propane torch is soundless, and, in light good enough to do the work, it's invisible, too. If you char the wood on rough framing even slightly and don't wash it down with water, the embers can linger for hours inside the wood and come to blaze in a breeze while you're taking a break. After seeing my son's pride at two months of largely solitary work on carpentry, I didn't want to undermine his sense of competence with a month of micromanagement on a plumbing project.

For this reason, perhaps I can be forgiven for the small deception my misguided instincts supplied when he suggested the bathroom addition. I said, "Great idea. We can plumb it with plastic pipe."

I still think, despite all that happened, that this was a good decision. He got started right away, and his surprise when I handed him the schematic and told him he could do all of the joining himself seemed well worth the lie my show of interest in trying plastic pipe represented. Although back then many people were excited about CPVC's potential, I myself was skeptical, and despite what I'd implied, it offered me no mystery or challenge whatsoever. Joining plastic pipe is done with solvent cement that sets in thirty seconds, and you can cut some grades with nothing more aggressive than a sharp, sturdy knife. But I was banking on the chance that the very simplicity that secretly made it seem crude to me would allow my son an ego-bolstering success with installation.

And I was right. He had always been a hardworking boy, but the trust I granted him seemed to inspire him. Each evening when I got home from the office, he called me up to check his work. To my great relief, the joints appeared to be clean—with a steady bead of solvent rimming each one—and at my exclamations of pride at his craftsmanship he'd had to work hard to maintain his teenager's air of bored composure. He roughed in a toilet bend, a drum trap for the bathtub, hot and cold water supply lines, a plastic revent. He installed the toilet, then a pedestal basin, and, after I helped him heft it up the stairs in my tie and suit pants one morning, even a prefab fiberglass tub. By the end of August, the only job that remained was joining his new plumbing to my old system.

It is a little hard to remember, honestly, what our relationship was like by that point in the summer without coloring it with hindsight. As I said, his impulsiveness had grated on my nerves some, but by and large I think what passed between us was fairly simple. He told me stories. He ate food from my refrigerator. He fell asleep at my side on the couch. In other words, he was a boy, and I assumed my company did not make him think too deeply. But perhaps this is just an example of my being less sensitive or observant than I should have been because when I followed him up to the attic with the propane torch, I was not yet looking for his words to mean any more than they said.

I sweated the first joint myself, and I worked slowly to make a point, but all the while, he kneeled beside me, leaning forward in a way that made it seem he was impatient to take over. I held the spool of solder steady, moving it around the pipe, and watched as the bead grew shiny and began to stream. Then I turned off the flame and set down the torch.

"Can I try?" he said.

His easy eagerness made me nervous, and I felt a quick rise of irritation, but I did not show it. I handed him the gloves and goggles, and I reminded myself that he was anxious to become a man. And the truth is, he followed my example almost flawlessly. He removed dirt from the inside of both fittings with gentle twists of a wire brush. He wiped the surfaces down with a cloth and applied a thin film of flux. He was quiet during all of this, asking no questions, and I can say honestly that at the sight of his competence what little irritation I had felt was displaced by genuine pride. It was not until he finished his prep work and picked up the torch that I felt it return. He flipped the switch and held the flame up to the pipe. "So where did you learn to do this?" he said.

It's worth pointing out that, initially at least, very little of my stress was caused by the substance of his question. At that moment, it stemmed almost solely from the challenge of suppressing my shock at the fact that he would consider his first novice seconds manipulating a blowtorch inches from the tinder-dry framework of our house an appropriate time to strike up a conversation.

"Easy there," I said. "Hold the flame back or you'll burn away the flux."

He moved the flame higher.

He said, "Do you remember who taught you?"

"Excuse me?"

His tone was casual, chatty. "Do you remember who taught you how to use a soldering iron?"

"Propane torch," I said pedantically; then I pointed at it: "Don't forget the other side."

He moved it around the pipe. Without my reminding him, he also eased back the flame and touched the thread of solder to the seam above the fitting. Capillary action drew it swiftly into the joint.

"That's perfect," I said.

"Was it your father who taught you?"

"Now just wind it around—"

"He was a plumber, right?" he said, and he turned away from the flame to face me.

In fairness to him, he had already withdrawn the torch from the pipe, and he was holding it very steady. He was in danger of burning nothing, not even the flux, but the fact remained that he was working with an open flame for the very first time without paying full attention, without appearing to worry, without even keeping his eyes on his work, all while trying to carry on a conversation, and I guess after a summer of watching the seeds of boyish impulse threaten to flower into the habits of a reckless man, all of this simply overwhelmed me.

I said, "Jesus Christ, Elliot, what the hell do you think you're doing!?"

I can still remember the look that came over his face. He was surprised, his face drained of color and tensed in a way that is hard to describe except to say that now he looked guarded. He was not wearing a shirt, and I could see in his thin chest the undeniable but poignantly slight outlines of pectoral muscles he had been working with a set of dumbbells in the privacy of his room. All at once it seemed painfully clear to me that in raising the subject of my own apprenticeship he had been struggling gamely to transcend the adolescence that had been drawing my secret reproach all summer long.

Right away I did some damage control. "Actually it looks like you're better at multitasking safely than I'd be," I said. I had to force myself not to reach and switch off the propane torch in his hand. "I was just worried about you looking away from that flame."

"That's okay," he said.

He turned back to his work, and he passed the torch near the pipe to regenerate the heat that had dissipated during my outburst.

I said, "It just scared me for a second."

He drew the flame away and touched the solder to the last gap in the seam.

I said, "I forgot how capable you are."

There had been other moments when I'd lost my temper with him—when he was a toddler and ran into a busy parking lot; the year before when, without calling home, he had stayed out well after dark. Standing there in the sudden quiet of the attic, watching him wield an invisible fire, I'd reminded myself of these, but two months later, as I tried to decipher the strange runes of his piercing looks and choice of report topics, it occurred to me that this flash of anger had been different in a small but important way. It was the first that revealed feelings I'd been trying to hide.

A FILM REEL OF CLIPS FROM OUR PAST TOGETHER MIGHT MAKE my apprehension in the wake of the earthquake seem strange. Since his early boyhood, the first weekend of every month Elliot and I had gone out alone together for an activity of his choosing, and although I always worried as he grew older he would begin to postpone these dates, so far he had made careful plans for every one. In the evenings, when I settled in the basement fixing our toaster oven or cleaning the contacts on our water heater, he often slipped onto a stool with a stack of comic books to share my space in a silence so full of quiet affection, I was afraid to rupture it with speech. Even that Friday, the week I first noticed signs that things were changing, he phoned me at my office.

"It's me," he said.

In the background, boys were yelling. Car doors slamming. Three fifteen: he was just getting out of school. There was a familiar rustle that meant he was holding the receiver against his T-shirt, talking to a friend. I looked out my window. On the street below, a fat man in a suit dropped his keys and stared at them where they glinted. Elliot took the receiver away from his shirt; child noise replaced the static. "So there's this great-sounding party tonight."

"Wonderful."

"Lots of guys from school are going, and Antonio's mom can bring me home. Can I go?"

"Of course," I said, and braced myself.

He said, "Why not?"

He had grown skilled at this. There was a sharp note of irritation in his voice that I never heard from him except over the phone, when he pretended I would not give him what he wanted. Behind him, I could hear a boy's voice say, "Told you." Another said, "Man," an expletive among them for complaint. I'd found through experimentation that at this point it was best to remain quiet. I used to worry that he just hadn't heard me correctly, but reiterating my consent sometimes confused him and made his act difficult. Once I'd tried speaking nonsense to him between his complaints, a private joke between us: "Mercury vapor," I had said. "Rings of Saturn." But the pause this engendered made me think I had upset his rhythm, and I didn't want to risk embarrassing him in front of his friends. And the few times I had considered participating in his act, making up reasons why he could not go, I began to sweat. In the end, my silence seemed to work best for both of us.

Now he let it last, allowing time for a tirade of parental insensitivity. Then this: "You never let me do anything!" and the clatter of the phone in its cradle.

For over a year, Liz had assured me that this refusal of invitations to parties was born of a misconception about the after-school world of his peers that he would soon correct on his own. It was out of the sight of adults, she said, in fast-food parking lots and converted basements, that children forged their adult identities, and they did this by testing out views and postures more extreme than those they felt. Elliot would start going to parties when he figured out his friends were just exaggerating the secret feelings he was wrestling with himself. Until then, adults would seem safer. He would seek the stability of a world he felt he could predict and understand.

It assuaged my fears—both the plausibility of her explanation and the sound of her voice when she made it—but tonight for the first time I suspected him of an ulterior motive as well. When I got home, he was already there, sitting on the kitchen counter. Every Friday night, Liz experimented with a new cuisine, and that week she had asked Elliot to choose. The kitchen smelled sharply of fresh pineapple. She had cut one down the center, spilling its juice. Don Ho was playing on the stereo, and she had tucked a blossom behind one ear. As I came through the door, she was laughing, and immediately I was struck by the strange thought that he had been making jokes at my expense. In all honesty, in almost every case entering a room and catching a glimpse of the intimacy between my wife and son in their shared laughter or silence made me feel a large-hearted satisfaction, but from time to time I feared without proof that what drew them together was commiseration about me.

"Tell him, Luther," Liz said. "Men hula in Hawaii. They do warrior dances, a high-stepping kind of thing. It's not only for girls."

Elliot grinned. Now that I had noticed it, I could detect his mustache in any light.

She said, "Big musclemen with swords. Sometimes they do it with fire sticks. Really, it can be very tough."

He turned to me, and in a show of ignoring her, slipped for the last time into one of our old routines, one he'd picked up proudly years ago from listening to banter between me and Liz. "How was work?" he said.

"Excellent."

"Move any mountains?"

"Just some rivers," I said, but we both looked at the floor. In fourth grade he had learned that the California Aqueduct was visible from space, and for the first time my job had appeared heroic. A small part of me had panicked every time I fueled this fire, but then I thought it's not so bad for a boy to lionize his father.

"Hey," Liz said to him. "Hey, you." Her hair fell over her shoulders, the iridescent blonde that lines the inside of some seashells. She enjoyed his show of neglect for the adolescent affection it was, but as he drew it out, spots of red appeared above her collarbone. His love meant too much to both of us. "What about my dance?"

Elliot slid off the counter and put his hands together, tracing waves to one side and then the other, shaking his hips. Her hand dropped from her chest to her waist. Don Ho started a new song, "Ain't No Big Thing," and Elliot shook faster. Liz laughed out loud, her short laugh of surprise, all air, eyes wide. Elliot high-stepped over to her and took her free hand, and when he bumped his hip to hers, she beamed and set down her knife.

During dinner, he told us stories: a split lip on the soccer field; a teacher who had conducted class in whispers to avoid waking a sleeping student. For a moment, they lulled me, but when Liz got up to go to the bathroom, he took his notepad and pencil from his back pocket and laid them next to his water glass.

"What's the most surprising thing your dad ever did?" he said. Then he took a bite of his pork.

"Let me think about that," I said, and I leaned away from the table into the rungs of the ladder-back chair to make it clear that this was what I was doing. Yesterday, we had spent an hour going over those facts that would form the bedrock of his report: date of birth, siblings, occupation. Now he was moving into what Mrs. Parks called Theme Development, the distinguishing feature of quality biographical research. He had explained that it was a long project, divided into three six-week segments: research, rough draft, and revision. I understood immediately that he would be interviewing me aggressively until Thanksgiving and peppering me with clarifying questions until well after the New Year, and lying in bed later I had settled on a strategy: I would tell no lies, but would rely heavily on omission.

I should pause here and say that I wasn't so blunt-witted that I was incapable of connecting the dots. I knew there was more to his choice of subjects than an interest in pleasing his teacher. The problem was that to reveal why I always avoided talking about my father—to share the ways in which he failed my mother and me, the neat and inevitable unfolding of events from the tiny wellspring of his flaws— would be to repeat his mistake myself. In other words, to do so would be to infect my family with my old wounds and sorrows, and, unlike my father, I'm a man who chooses not to burden those he loves. Some might argue that if honest anger is what a loved one seeks, then it can only do more harm to withhold it, but I can say from hard witness that airing one's baser feelings is a very slippery slope.

So now I was stalling. Elliot watched me and chewed. Liz had glazed the pork with pineapple, but she and Elliot had danced three songs before the high from his flirtation faded and she remembered to check the oven. By the time she returned from the bathroom, he was still working over the same bite.

She said, "The powder room sink isn't draining."

"Really?"

"Well it is, but slowly," she said.

Across the table, I could see Elliot finally swallow. I raised my eyebrows at him. "I guess our services are needed," I said.

He and I had removed tangles of Liz's hair from the trap beneath my bathroom sink half-a-dozen times, and at this point he could do most of the work without me. Without having to be asked, he wrapped the jaws of the wrench with electrical tape to keep from scratching the copper pipe. When he backed the slip nut up the drain and swung the trap free, I shined the flashlight down it, and, as I suspected, there was nothing but water.

"Weird," he said.

"Not really," I said. In a sink used only for washing hands, a backup was more likely to be caused by something deeper, and I said so. But as he reattached the trap, I saw him roll his eyes. I had designed and built the house myself, included him in years of improvements that were integrated seamlessly into systems that had never failed in any way, and still this show of skepticism. He emptied the bottle of Drano into the basin and then leaned against the windowsill to wait. Liz appeared to fill our silence with a story about a friend of hers whose newly declawed cat had disappeared and barely survived a seven-day odyssey in the dog-filled wilds of their suburban neighborhood, and Elliot watched the basin full of chemicals as she spoke, his little mustache catching light from the frosted glass fixture above the mirror, until finally the mouth of the drain released two silver burps of air and swallowed the reservoir of Drano.

After dinner, I went outside to replace the spent bulbs that lit the leaves and tree trunks at the outer boundaries of our yard. I could see Elliot through the windows of my house, first at the kitchen sink rinsing dishes, and next huddled at the small desk in his bedroom over notes about my father. I watched him for a while, holding his head in his hands in a posture of sorrow or concentration, and suddenly my wife was beside me in the grass. My pulse leapt, not, I'm ashamed to say, out of love or even animal surprise, but out of a sense that she'd come for something I was afraid to give her.

I'd designed our house before I met Liz. It was a common floor plan, with a bedroom I referred to on blueprints as "Child's," but this was an act of optimism almost no deeper than the purchase of a lottery ticket. I hadn't dated at all in high school, and my experiences with women in college had been unsatisfying. I'd been looking for something specific, but as so often happens, I was wrong about what I wanted. In my first semester, I sat down at the desk in my cinderblock dorm room and drew a matrix. Along one axis, I listed those attributes I felt would make a good girlfriend for me (quiet; patient; not too pretty), and along the other, the names of women I could not take my eyes from: a thin, freckled woman who wore a beret and an apron at the deli where I bought my sandwiches; a woman in my calculus class who picked at the chapped skin on her lips in a way that left them a deep, unlipsticked red. In almost every case, there was no intersection. I tore a fresh sheet of notebook paper, but, staring down at its whiteness, I was distressed to discover that I could not really think of anything these women held in common.

Nevertheless, I invited a long succession of them to my room. I had a routine. Before I left the dorm for a party, I took some clothes from the lidded hamper in my closet and scattered them around the room. Then I set a portable fan on my desk chair so that the only place to sit was the bed. This always worked perfectly. I poured us red wine from a jug into Dixie cups and initiated a discussion about the quiz show scandal or the Kennedy-Nixon debates. Although people spoke passionately about these topics in the halls and cafeterias, I myself did not have very strong feelings, but once I discerned my date's, I would join in enough to get her talking. Then at a certain point, I'm sorry to say more out of boredom and grim purpose than affection or longing, I would pluck a few items of stray clothing from the surface of the mattress and say, "What do you know, there's a bed under here!" Almost invariably, she would giggle at this, and I could place my hand at the small of her back and lower her down on the bed among my musty laundry.

I didn't understand any better what I wanted after these episodes, and, more uncomfortable still, I didn't like myself much. In the spring of my junior year, I woke up next to a woman with a bandage over one eye whose name I couldn't even remember and lay awake next to her for an hour with an overfull bladder, smelling her sour breath, as a sort of penance. When I moved to Sacramento after graduation, I hadn't invited a woman to my room in almost six months. I rented a small apartment on Marconi Avenue, went to banks in a tie, bought a piece of land, and began building a house. I did not think of my father in any direct way when I did this, but it is easy to see now that the way in which I researched the neighborhoods—through process of elimination picking the suburb and then the cul-de-sac and the plot and the design that would allow me to build an unimpeachable home for a hypothetical family I did not even really expect to have—stemmed from a desire to conjure a different possible ending to a family story into being. Every day after work, I changed into coveralls, and on weekends I spent whole days at the site with a cooler full of sandwiches I had fixed in my kitchenette at the Sunny Pines Apartments. I had no free time to date, and, to my surprise, standing next to pretty mothers at the grocery store, only the weakest flares of desire. It's probably silly, I doubt this is actually the case, but I have sometimes had the thought that I might have spent my life alone had it not been for a strobe of red lights on my ceiling one night in my apartment. I drew back the thin curtain and saw a police cruiser idling in the parking lot. A burglary had taken place in the room next to mine. The next morning I took my valuables from a duffel bag in my closet and drove to the Wells Fargo Bank downtown to open a safe-deposit box, and it was Liz who issued me a key and led me into the vault. She wore low-cut blouses, and although I'll admit I deposited items more frequently because of this, the truth is her conspicuous beauty made me nervous, and it was she who finally had to suggest I take her out to dinner.

I didn't really expect anything to come of this. When I returned to my apartment that morning, I examined myself in the mirror. I am not an ugly man, but neither am I particularly attractive, and so I fall in with the majority of people whose fairly neutral looks become defined largely by the personality that filters through them. By then, I had been in Sacramento three months without talking to anyone but my coworkers, and in the evenings alone in my apartment I would spread a towel on my bed and eat a cold dinner in front of the TV. In my visits to the bank to deposit coins, I was sure I had revealed myself to be nothing more than lonely and strange, and Liz—well, she appeared to be something else altogether. She wore short skirts and shiny blouses and teased the men who stood in her line by slyly questioning their motives for opening accounts. With an alchemy of calculated looks and behavior I have only seen her use a handful of times since, she could draw all attention in that vast open lobby—men, women, children—even when she was doing nothing more remarkable than picking slowly through her big ring of keys.

But she surprised me. For that first date, I had taken her to the Coral Reef. She used a maraschino cherry to stir her rum and Coke, holding it by the stem. "Tell me about your family," she had said, a date question. "Well," I said. Three other couples sat around the hibachi table, obscured by steam. The chef's knives were flashing. Little pieces of shrimp and steak flipped from the blades and sizzled fiercely. It was a sound I would have to speak over. This too was inhibition. I looked at her. She was wearing a necklace with a cluster of amber stones that were probably plastic, but it was beautiful. I kept my eyes there. I said it again, "Well," and her cool palm covered my mouth completely. When I met her eye, she smiled and waited for me to absorb the strange comfort of this. Two seconds; maybe three. "Tell me about your job," she said finally. And then she let her hand fall.

Within three dates, I had told her about the time as a boy I had watched a dog die without trying to help or kill it, an act that had filled me with so much horror, I had crept into the Episcopal church on a weekday and left with a leaflet on Guilt in my knapsack. Then other things: a lingering look at my aunt stepping out of the shower; the comics I stole from a grocer who gave me pieces of gum for free whenever I stopped by his store. In each case she listened with a bright intensity to disclosures at the periphery of my deepest fears, and although at first her interest in such a plainly uncomfortable man was a bafflement, one night it dawned on me that it was these uneasy confessions themselves that were drawing her to me.

At the time, I could not explain the certainty I felt about this—it was intuition—but after joining her for a family dinner, I felt I understood. Liz was one of five sisters, the youngest by six years and, it turned out, the most attractive by an unnatural margin. She met me at the door to her oldest sister's house wearing a matronly gray dress and lipstick so pale it almost matched her skin, and led me to the living room where plain, dark-haired women and their husbands and half-a-dozen small children were packed in a confusing jumble. She introduced me to each of them with a small bit of description, Charlotte, "the doctor," Eleanor, "the schoolteacher," Pam, "mother of four out of six of the children in the room," and Trish, whose engagement was the occasion we were celebrating. After an awkward flurry of handshaking, one of the husbands said, "We were just talking about the situation in Cuba, Luther. I polled everybody on what they think Kennedy should do. What's your vote?"

When all of them looked at me for an answer, I turned to Liz and said, "Interesting. What did you recommend?"

Liz blushed, and an awkward silence came over the room.

"That's a good question," Charlotte's husband said. Oddly, instead of addressing Liz, he turned to Pam. "What *did* Lizzie say?"

"I don't remember," she said, frowning.

"We skipped her," Eleanor said. "Trish was bending her ear about bridesmaids' dresses."

"She's the fashion expert," Pam said kindly.

"Not the foreign-policy expert," Eleanor added wryly.

"She's always had the best eye," Charlotte offered.

"Yeah, that," said Eleanor, holding up her wineglass and winking, "and Trish wants to get her buy-in early on a frumpy tent so she doesn't steal the show."

Everyone laughed, including Liz, but by the end of the evening—

an evening in which we talked about health care and public education and finished the debate about the Cuban Missile Crisis—it was not so difficult to imagine how she might have grown up believing her looks were her only power. In the end, I sometimes wonder if I owe my good fortune to nothing more than this: I was the first person who responded as attentively to her character as to her beauty.

I asked her to marry me after two months of dating and ten days later she had done so. At first she had sketched out a large Sacramento wedding, but one evening she knocked on the door to my apartment and told me she wanted to be married with me alone, in the house I was building near the river. I'm not sure which ardent therapeutic motive drove this—to shield me from social awkwardness, or let me live vicariously through her impulsive nature, or spare me the guest-list tabulation of what she had begun to suspect was my sheer, empty-handed lack of family and friends—but it was clear from the moment I arrived that she had done it for me. She stood alone with the minister, unflanked by guests or flowers, on the exposed earth in front of the frame of our house, and she had tethered helium balloons to the studs and window casings. When I stepped next to her, she brushed the hair from my forehead with an expression of joy I already recognized as the unambiguous, sure-footed pleasure she only seemed to feel when she had spared me some kind of pain. The day was breezy, and as we said our vows the taut skins of the balloons bobbed against each other with a solemn dun like struck drums.

But even women who fall in love with their power to soothe a crippled man find after a time they have only so much patience.

Now she followed my gaze up to our son's window. "Penny for your thoughts, Inspector," she said.

"A penny? I wouldn't dream of overcharging so steeply."

"It'd be a bargain, I'm guessing." She glanced at the box of lightbulbs in my arms and raised her eyebrows, smiling. "Whatever it is, it's fueled a week's worth of obsessive maintenance work."

"We did find a crack in the foundation," I said.

"The earthquake, no doubt." She looked at my mouth, my fore-head, my hands. "I'm sure every house suffered some minor damage."

"Probably."

"More than ours."

"Maybe."

Above us, Elliot ran a hand through his hair at his desk. Crickets pulsed. From down the street came the sound of someone emptying trash into an outdoor can. Finally she said, "What is it, sweetie? What's been bothering you?"

"Robert Belsky asked me to go to Shipley's with him," I said, and my chest filled like a flight of birds. It was something that had been on my mind, something I doubtless would have shared anyway, but it was not what had been bothering me.

Robert Belsky was a peer of mine at the Department of Water Re-sources, and Shipley's was a topless bar in a bright pink building vis-ible off Highway 50. A month ago, word had begun to spread that the Principal in our division would be retiring soon, and Robert and I were the only two engineers eligible for the promotion. Although we had both survived the cutbacks of the last decade, when there was not enough work to go around I was assigned the bigger projects. His strange way of equalizing the power between us in the face of this competition was to invite me out to a bar at times when he seemed to know I would refuse. He usually did this with other coworkers standing behind him in the hall, and when I took a rain check, he would joke that I was too good for him, or that I "didn't like to mix with the hired hands." It was an obvious manipulation, but it worked. Over time, the sheer number of refusals had filled me with a desire to accept.

I said, "He stopped by my office and said something like, 'So, you ever going to say yes?' and when I said, 'How about tonight?' he said, 'Great, I'm meeting a couple guys at Shipley's in half an hour.'" Al-though what I should feel when someone manipulates me is anger, my first feeling is an annoying flare of desire not to shame them.

I took Liz's hand and led us silently across the lawn to the house, and briefly, opening my front door undercut the tension this conversation was stirring. The thick slab of oak is so perfectly balanced on its well-oiled hinges that despite its colossal moment of inertia I can push it closed by touching it with my pinky.

In the warm glow of our front hall, I crouched to set the box of lightbulbs at our feet and then stood to face my wife. Her arms lay still at her sides; the muscles in her face relaxed. A look of patience and attention. Sometimes now I conjure her limb by limb. It gives me peace, but it's not the same. Since her first miscarriage, she had toyed almost annually with the idea of becoming a volunteer counselor on a call-in line, and at times like this it always struck me that she would be extraordinarily good at it. Although these were precisely the moments when such an observation might have given her confidence, instead I found I could only bring myself to say it other times—counting out flatware for dinner or unlocking the car—when the compliment would not call for demonstration with a frank discussion of my fears.

"So what did you say to him?" she asked.

"I told him I'd pass. Then he said, 'Mr. High and Mighty,' but I didn't take the bait."

"You didn't say anything?"

"No."

"What bothers you so much about him, do you think?"

There were so many safe answers to this question—that he was rude, that he was talented but irresponsible, that he was difficult to work with—but already the familiar mix of tenderness and well-veiled impatience with which she was focused on my lie was making me feel guilty for distracting her from the truth.

"I don't know," I said.

She closed her eyes—a kind of reflexive wince at this answer that she had developed over the years. This always bothered me some, but more troubling was the look she wore when she opened them: forgiveness and resolve, as if she'd decided one more time to wring satisfaction from helping me with the shallow fears I was willing to share. "He's harmless, Luther. It's mostly habit for him, that style, but he's probably also trying to knock you off your guard a little. There's that rumor about Don retiring, and didn't you also say Howard's assigning new offices next week?"

I nodded.

She said, "He thinks you're about to get the nicer office *and* the promotion, and he's probably right. He wants to punish you a little, but I wouldn't be surprised if he's also just curious. The two of you are so different."

There were two light thuds above us, Elliot kicking off his shoes and letting them fall from his bed to the carpet. I felt a prick of heat beneath my arms, and a coolness on my forehead that meant moisture there: beads I knew she could see. She put her hand out to me. It was a foot from mine, but she did not reach to bridge that distance. It was different—better somehow—to make me take hers. She pressed each of my knuckles with her thumb. I suppose this was another moment when I might have told her what was really troubling me. But seconds later there was a rumble of footsteps on the stairs behind us, and she looked past me with the uncomplicated smile that sometimes graced her face in rooms with our son.

The following morning, I drove to a commercial plumbing-supply store where I had purchased all the pipe for my home. I told myself I was driving there to replace the empty jug of Drano, but I had no immediate need for more, and anyway Drano was something I could have bought at any grocery store. What I really wanted to do was talk to Larry Briggs. He was soft-spoken and knowledgeable, and even when five years had passed between my visits, he called me by name and offered me the contractor's discount. As he rang me up, I could say something about Elliot's reckless ways and my flare of temper, and Larry would laugh: because he'd worked with a blowtorch, because he had his own sons, and because my mistakes with Elliot could not hurt him.

I might have recognized this agenda in the sharp pang I felt when I entered his store, but I did not. I like to think that this was not because I was incapable of the kind of self-examination that might have spared me my losses, but because I was so surprised that Larry wasn't there.

In his place was a woman in a white tank top watching a small TV and eating a bear claw. She did not look up at me when I entered, and while I walked the aisles she answered the TV's false surges of laughter with her own. Only when I set the jug of Drano on the counter did she finally turn. She glanced at the jug and started to punch the register keys.

"I have an account," I said.

She looked up at me. Although later I would learn she was only my age, she looked older. Her blonde hair was dry and her skin wrinkled from the sun. "What's the name of your outfit?"

"I'm not in the business, but the owner gives me the discount because I bought all the pipe for my house here."

"I do, do I?" She was the kind of woman least noticed: neither beautiful nor ugly.

"You're the owner?"

"Afraid so." She was grinning.

"What happened to Larry?"

"He had a heart attack last year. I'm his wife."

"I'm so sorry."

"That's okay. I was home with our kids, and I can tell you this is a big step up."

Some measure of my shock and discomfort must have shown on my face.

"Joke," she said. "That was a joke." She turned back to the register. "Anyway, I'll give you the discount on principle. Do-it-yourselfers are great repeat business." She punched the keys. On her television, an angry woman was sending her husband downstairs with a pillow and blanket to sleep on the living room sofa. This caught her eye. "Doghouse," she said.

I handed her a five-dollar bill.

"Have you tried a plunger yet?" she said.

"Actually, I don't have a clog."

"It's nothing to be ashamed of."

There was a small purple stain on the front of her tank top. It looked like grape juice. Something about her was infuriating. I might simply have ignored her baiting, but she was staring at me, holding on to my money, not opening the register waiting for me to respond.

I said, "I'm just stocking up."

"Sure you are."

"I don't need any tips on how to clear a backup."

"Right."

"I designed and built my plumbing system myself."

She winked. "My point exactly."

I have come across so many people like this in my life that sometimes I am ashamed I have not numbed myself to the way they court confrontation. Maybe it is because my father was the first of them that they strip me of self-control.

I said, "You don't know what the hell you're talking about."

"Whoa!" She laughed and raised her hands in the air. "You're the boss."

She opened the register drawer, and I made a business of looking in my wallet: a sheaf of bills, some credit cards and a picture of the three of us at the Grand Canyon. I had taken it a few months ago. I had stood them at the observation wall and set the timer for thirty seconds, and captured a look on their faces that made me feel a lucky pressure in my chest, like the downward weight of hands. I am not proud of what I did next, but suddenly I had the impulse to take the photo out of its sleeve and hand it to her, not because I wanted her to know me, but because I wanted to show her what she didn't have.

It didn't have the effect I was expecting.

"Your family?" she said.

"Yes."

She studied it a moment, smirking, and handed it back to me between two fingers, so that I had to reach for it. Then she took some change from the register drawer and extended a closed fist across the counter. Her knuckles were chapped, and she was still wearing a wedding band. She would hold her hand there forever, I thought, to force mine beneath it. Finally I extended my open palm and she dropped my change into it—a single penny I would have left without had I known this was all that held me hostage. She laughed. "See you soon," she said. Then she turned back toward her TV.

It was absurd to put off such a trivial paternal duty; I knew this. The following night after dinner, I went into the kitchen and offered to dry.

"Thanks," he said.

He took a serving dish from the sink and handed it to me. Thus far the physical changes he was going through had passed largely undiscussed. Six months ago, he had hefted a set of dumbbells into Liz's shopping cart at Kmart, and since then each morning I had listened to his fierce breaths between lifts through the vent in the wall of my closet as I dressed. Now in his back pocket, I noticed the small notepad he had been using when he questioned me for his biography on my father. In these conversations, the deepening pitch of his speech was undermined by breaks into his old register at the ends of questions, and his hands, particularly at moments when he lost control of his own voice, trembled slightly, the way children's never do. Water streamed out of the tap into the sink below, and he scoured the bottom of the saucepan with a square of green plastic wool. He never complained of chores, never complained, really, of anything, and although in the past this had filled me with a sense of accomplishment, more recently it had made me afraid. He inhaled sharply through his nose, as if to clear it, and I started where I stood.

"Jeez," he said.

"Sorry."

He dumped the water from the pan into the sink, and it splashed both of us. I did not flinch, but this time instead it was stillness that seemed awkward. I groped for the resolve I had felt before I entered the room. I was careful not to look at his face so that scrutiny wouldn't lace my mention of his new mustache with a sense of invasion. I would like to say that when he finally broke the silence I myself had been seconds from speaking, but the truth was it had taken me less than five minutes to let go of my intentions completely. I was refining a plan to cut myself shaving the next morning, appearing at breakfast with a conversational dot of Kleenex glued to my chin by blood when he shut the water off and drew his notepad and pencil from his pocket.

"Quick: what's the one adjective you would use to describe him?"

"Meticulous."

He wrote this down.

"And what would your mom have said?"

"Perfect."

And briefly the strain of answering newspaper questions about my father excused me from my resolution to talk to him about shaving.

In the beginning at least, it was not so hard to stick to my plan; the early stories about my father were so free of omen. I told him that my parents had met at the Metropolitan Museum in New York in 1938. My father was a plumber from Hoboken with a high school equivalency and a lone magazine photo of the Hoover Dam taped to the wall of his basement apartment, but he was a smart man with exacting standards, and it had occurred to him that this might be an excellent place to meet a woman. This is the way my mother always told the story. On Saturday afternoons when his friends were running combs through their hair in preparation for a night out in bars, my father was riding the Hudson Tubes into the city. He slipped the recommended donation into the admission box and picked a different exhibit each time. He had been doing this for six months when he saw my mother in the costume gallery in the basement. She was the first woman he had bothered to speak to. He liked the way she held a finger up to the descriptive copy on the tiny plaque beside each display. That, and she was wearing a bright red dress that was a little bit shiny—she was killing time before a party. He came up to her and told her the casework had been installed poorly. If it were level, a tube of lipstick set on top wouldn't roll its length, and he waited for her to take hers from her purse to let him prove it. He was like a peacock, arraying his feathers. Or the frogs that puff up their throats to make an impression. When her lipstick dropped off the end, he caught it in his calloused palm. She was an hour late to her party.

All through my early boyhood, I was daily witness to a love between them that I took for granted. On the living room sofa after dinner, my mother might read a book of poetry while my father filed the metal burr from an imperfectly molded washer he had bought at the hardware store, not because it was necessary to the function of the washer, but because it bothered him in a way I grew to understand was both aesthetic and moral. The combination of ire and resourcefulness it ignited in him was the object of my mother's passion. She left broken things out on the countertop—a kettle, a wristwatch, a jacket zipper—just to watch him take out his pocketknife and curse the manufacturers. She did not begrudge him swear words, even in front of me. He was a man of fire and impulse and she a woman of introspection and restraint, and I would learn that she loved him for the long reach—for better or for worse—of his frankness and passions.

Elliot took careful notes, and I talked continuously to discourage questions about the years I did not want to discuss. I kept shifting the focus to things like what he'd owned or the map names of places he had traveled, and just when Elliot appeared poised to interject, I wandered off toward the living room to find a book called *America at War*. "Historical context is essential to good reporting," I said, and out of an impulse I imagine must have been born more of weariness than interest, he thanked me and took it up to his bedroom for the night.

But the following morning, he had a second wind.

"What did you admire most about him?" he said.

We were tucked in a booth at the International House of Pancakes. Liz was wiping down the syrup carafes with a paper napkin she had dipped in her tea. Elliot's notepad was covered in words I could not read. With the advent of puberty, his handwriting had grown scratchy, indecipherable.

I sipped my coffee. "His exacting standards," I said.

"Like on construction?" We had talked about this already.

"Yes."

"Something else."

"His resourcefulness then."

Liz said, "What about that time he took apart the door at Macy's?"

At Macy's in New York one winter, my mother left us to go to the ladies' room in the basement, and when she returned, she asked us to follow her back down to look at toasters. This alone should have aroused my curiosity. That fall my aunt had given her an electric mixer, and she had turned it on and then off just once before setting it at the back of a cupboard. But at six, I lacked this kind of suspicion. "I was thinking I might invest in one of these," she said, and I leaned in to help with her decision. She pressed a chrome lever down. Beyond a pyramid of stock pots was a group of customers standing inside a small glass-walled room full of crystal. One of them rapped on the door. A manager in a suit and tie rushed over and put his mouth close to the crack so he would not have to yell. "The repairman will be here any moment," he said, and when he left them to return to the telephone, my father shook his head and crossed the floor between the appliances. The plate-glass door was stuck shut, its hydraulic closing mechanism broken. In under five minutes he had removed the four screws that held the bracket to the door and pulled it aside. He moved us toward the Thirty-Fourth Street exit quickly, his hands at the smalls of our backs, and over my shoulder I caught sight of the manager scanning the floor in confusion. On the sidewalk my mother applauded. My father crossed his hairy arms. He was often in shirtsleeves, even in winter. It was not until I heard my mother retell the story for the third time that I realized she had lured us down there just to watch him rescue a group of strangers with his pocketknife.

I told a quick version of this story.

"Was it hard?" Elliot said.

"No. That's what irritated him about the manager."

"He was irritated?"

"I think so."

"What did he say?"

I thought about this: on the way home in his service van, his voice rising. "I can't really remember. But it was the kind of thing that annoyed him."

The waitress brought our pancakes and sausages on platters and little side plates, all balanced on her forearms and splayed between her fingers. Elliot moved his notebook aside for her and kept scribbling.

"What didn't you like about him?" he said.

Liz cleared a space for the food, repositioning flatware, moving packets of jam.

"He was my father," I said.

Elliot said, "Well maybe once he irritated you or disappointed you or something."

When I was twelve, I had won first prize in my school science fair, and then in my county, and went on to the state competition. I took my place there between two people whose display hinges were attached crookedly to boards that had not been beveled or sanded, and I made a note of this to point out to my father when he met us there after his morning service call. At two o'clock the judges came to shake my hand and examine my project. They made notes on clipboards. My mother looked at her watch. By four o'clock they had announced me the second-prize winner over a squeaky PA. They gave me a ribbon and people took photographs. Those who had won nothing began taking their boards down and carrying them out under their arms. We drove home in a car my mother had borrowed from a neighbor in exchange for a chicken casserole. Rows of poplars receded over the hills. Factories began to pop up and then again to disappear. When we got home, we found my father playing solitaire, a half-eaten sandwich on a plate in the sink.

Elliot's pancakes were steaming. In a minute he would pour too much syrup on them and eat them.

"He was my father," I said.

THAT WEEK, ELLIOT BEGAN RESTORING THE FIVE-HORSEPOWER engine from our old push mower in the basement. It was his idea, and immediately, I assumed an assistant mechanic's role. He cleaned and gapped the spark plugs, tinkered with the throttle, tightened the manifold screws and gasket. Now and then I went up to the kitchen for cool cans of soda and set them sweating on the pressboard where he bent over a plate of chrome, his breath clouding the surface. I handed him tools, and without turning, he checked the supervisory aspect of my assistance. "Not yet," he said, and dawdled over the last moments of his task.

I learned a new rhythm. I searched for ways to help that did not seem to irritate him, and soon found the boundaries of his patience. Advice was acceptable only in the form of stories about a centrifugal pump I had tried to build when I was his age. Offerings to his cause were accepted as well. I brought him an engine compression tester and a three-gallon can of gas, and when after four days it was still stalling out, I went to the library.

I browsed the stacks for the manual with the most technical tone, one that appeared to have been written for mechanics themselves. This was all I had come for, but when I stepped up to the circulation desk, an onion-scented girl with an opal at her neck slipped a card into its pocket. She wore brown lipstick and her hair tight at her neck in a bun and a watch too large for her slender wrist. "Good day," she said, and suddenly the plea implicit in these talismans of maturity moved me. I pictured my son beside me, our faces overlapping in his mirror, his face covered in foam. A towel swaddled his shoulders, making him look small. A conversation outside the bathroom would allow him more dignity. I thanked the girl and went back into the library.

There were a number of books in the young-adult section, but I spent an extra ten minutes searching the card catalog to find one in General Interest: *The Gentleman's Guide to Grooming*. Shaving technique was tersely reduced to its essentials. "To begin, soften the beard." "Address difficult areas last." There were diagrams to clarify the orientation of the blade. By copying these onto the back of the text, I was able to fit it on a single page. The photocopy machine bulb flashed like sheet lightning, and I pictured myself mentioning it in the basement, maybe as he fitted his safety goggles over his head. *I have a description somewhere that might save you some nicks. The physics are actually sort of interesting.* His eyes would disappear behind a dull plane of reflected light. *Metal contracts when it's cold, as you know. A cold blade will give you a closer shave.*

IT IS A SIGN OF HOW SUCCESSFULLY I HAD MISLED HER ABOUT my worries that that night after dinner, Liz suggested a neighborhood walk. We had begun them before Elliot was born. They'd been Liz's idea, at first a way of learning about my interest in construction and later of working on what she had probably come to explain to herself as my insufficient store of self-esteem. After Elliot was born, they stopped, until he was of an age when she knew my knowledge would seem a kind of magic trick to him. We had not taken one in a long time.

Now the moon was nearly full, and the sidewalks, slick with late rain, were alive with lamplight. She wore a lavender windbreaker with its hood raised and the drawstrings pulled close across her bangs and beneath her chin and somehow still looked lovely; her beauty was that bright. Elliot's jacket was open and caught gusts of wind. Years ago, Liz had purchased Thermos mugs with lids for these walks, and we each carried one filled with hot chocolate. When we got home, Elliot would open his to spoon cool marshmallows from its bottom.

"Find a really bad one," Liz said to me.

"We're coming up on one of the worst."

"Oh goody," she said.

I stopped in front of an older shingled rambler that had sold, I guessed, on the extravagance of its landscaping. Plum trees flanked the sidewalk, and the lawn was hemmed in by a series of carefully tended herb and flower beds. Wisteria vines overhung the front door, and the house itself seemed to rest on a foundation of enormous, dark-leafed camellia bushes. I said, "This garden is beautiful, but the house will have dry rot problems. The bushes will trap moisture against the shingles and breed fungi that will feed on the wood. Eventually, it will turn brown or white and crumble to the touch."

The moonlight cast shadows on Elliot's face. When I got home from work, I had given him the mechanic's manual, and he had examined it silently in the basement, his arm touching mine once and recoiling. I had not mentioned the physics of shaving.

He sipped his hot chocolate.

I said, "The one next door will have rot problems too." It was a new ranch house with a swing set in the front yard. "What's causing it?"

Elliot said, "The gutter is blocked."

"How can you tell?"

"Puddles next to the foundation."

"And?"

"Those dirt stains under the downspout."

I couldn't help myself; I touched his hair.

Typically we stayed within blocks of our own home, but now Liz led us the quarter mile along the river to the new development that fronted onto the golf course. All of the houses were large, four thousand square feet or more, with Jacuzzi tubs sunken into their rear patios and flagstone driveways, but their unfortunate secret was that they were built on a site of soft clay. Clay drains poorly. In wet weather, it can compress unevenly, placing stress on the foundation. A contractor can reduce the risk of this by sinking the footings more deeply. It's what I had hoped for when I saw the bulldozers pushing elm stumps and licorice weed across the field towards the access road, but the footings on these houses were not even as deep as those on my own.

When we passed between the lantern posts onto its wide streets, she led us downhill towards the artificial lake on the ninth hole. Rows of saplings with root-balls wrapped in burlap sat waiting in the muddy yards.

She stopped in front of a big one on a corner lot. "This is it," she said.

"This is what?" I said, although suddenly I knew just what she meant.

"The house Robert Belsky bought."

The house was huge, the largest we had yet passed, with a three-car garage and two-story columns flanking its front door.

She said, "What do you think?"

"It's pretty," I said.

"About the design, I mean."

It was dark, but by taking a step into the yard, I could see that holes had been drilled around the base of the columns for drainage. A copper roof edge glinted along the eave, and a flat of clay tiles lay neatly stacked in the street.

"Not bad," I said.

"But there are things, aren't there?" she said. "Things any engineer worthy of promotion should have been able to see?"

Sometimes I think helping me must have been a very difficult calling.

I led them onto the unlandscaped lot. Gravel crunched beneath our feet. From the front, it appeared to be only two stories, but the property sloped to the rear, where the developers had included a day-light basement. The backyard half of the lot looked level, but if you walked north, you could see that it sloped slightly towards the house.

"It will have drainage problems as soon as the rain begins," I said, and she leaned over and kissed me on the shoulder.

But in bed that night, she did not fall asleep. My wife's sleep was distinguished by a slight sound she made with her tongue against her soft palate, as if she were tasting things in her dreams; and tonight, when I woke in the dark, she was silent. Downstairs in the living room, the grandfather clock I had built from a kit during her first pregnancy tolled the half hour, a single, muffled bong. The sheets tingled beneath my arms. My ears buzzed with the effort to hear her breathe. It was a shock when she spoke. "I can't sleep," she said.

"Neither can I."

"I thought so."

"What's on your mind?" I said.

"What's on *your* mind," she said.

"Is that a question or an answer?"

She laughed, but still did not move.

When we were first married, she had wanted to get pregnant, and I had wanted to wait. After five years, I finally conceded, and then we had trouble. She kept a small calendar to keep track of her ovulation, then an extra pillow to slip under her hips after we tried, and she had two miscarriages, children we had already named. When we over-heard those names in public, she was careful not to look at me. At first I made sure to mention these episodes later, in the car as we stared at the road ahead, or in the bathroom at night as we washed our faces, and she would kiss me in a spot more tender for its remote-ness—at my jawline, or on the crown of my head. After a while, though, the repetition of these exchanges seemed painful in itself, the familiarity of the words and actions freighted with sadness, and I stopped. Elliot had no name until after the nurse took him down the hall to bathe him. It was the first time we had discussed it. We both suggested names far less popular than the ones we had chosen be-fore, and it was clear from this to both of us that we had separately planned for disappointment.

The pause had lasted twenty seconds now, too long for a change of topic, and finally in a way that might have passed for answer to her question but was not lying, I reached under the sheet and drew her towards me in the dark. But this time I couldn't silence her so easily. Each day her patience was thinning.

She said, "Is that meeting on Monday?"

"Which meeting?"

"New office assignments."

"Oh yeah," I said. Her grasping shamed me. "Nothing too exciting, I'm sure."

I think on some level she may have known this was not at the core of my worries, but because I had given her nothing else to work with, she laid a hand on my chest and said this: "No, nothing too exciting. Just a high corner with a view of the capitol dome." She talked about other favors I had been shown—invitations from Krepps; briefings with politicians—whispers between soft touches of her lips and hands, and afterwards slept soundly, making that sound with her palate, the savor that told me she was asleep.

To my small credit, I did lie awake for a time thinking maybe I should wake her and try to undo it. Say, "I think I may have hurt him." Or even just this: "Sometimes I think he wishes I were a different man." But there were things—the sad reckoning of our history together—that filled me with hesitation. After all my years of withholding and all her years of giving, the fact that I feared I might fail the only child my stalling had allowed her seemed an unfair burden to share.

Instead I tried for sleep—a little exercise I had been doing since I was a boy. When I was fifteen, I had worked for my father for a summer, and in early June, I had gone to the library and checked out a book. This alone should have been a clear sign to me that he was really changing. A few years before it never would have occurred to me to rely on anything but his tutelage, but already a mistrust of his word had crept into my thinking. Alone in my room in Trenton, I had read the introduction dozens of times, until I could see the pages long after I switched off my light. The publisher's medallion with a hammer at its center. Then the dedication: "for Gladys," who I had decided was the author's wife. And finally the introduction: "Behind the walls of a house," it read, "pipes do not always run straight. They curve, branch off, and may have to be connected to other pipes of different diameters or dissimilar composition. It is the design plumber's duty to ensure that these awkward turns and connections are made cleanly and quietly. For example, because stopping the flow from a faucet causes a shock wave that may bang loudly and with enough force to damage the system, he must install capped pipe extensions that create a cushion of air to absorb these sounds and preserve the peace a family holds dear. Although plumbing in essence is not a difficult trade, it requires careful planning to build and maintain a properly functioning water system, by which I mean to say, one that is invisible to the residents of the house."

Somehow the silent recitation of these lines never failed to soothe me. That night, when I'd finished them for the third time, I gave up the idea of waking her to confess my worry and resolved to seize the next good opportunity to talk to our son.

THAT WEEKEND, IT CAME. IT WAS THE FIRST SATURDAY IN November, and when he slipped into the passenger seat, he told me to drive to the Arden Fair Multiplex. Standing in line for tickets, I made guesses—comedies he had mentioned; things his friends had recommended—and he smirked at me, passing a hand over his mouth when I looked at him, a new gesture. In the last week, the roots of the hair above his lip had darkened. Now it was visible in moderate light.

"Dad?" he said.

"Yes?"

"Can I ask you a question?"

The skin on my neck tingled. "Of course."

"Did you ever see him really angry?"

"Sure I did."

"When?"

"That centrifugal pump I built. I let the parts start to rust in our backyard."

Now his eyes fixed on mine. "What did he do?"

"He told me to finish it."

"But what did he say?"

And all at once, the price I was paying for my outburst seemed unfairly high. The idea that Elliot might be wondering if he would have found a more temperate parent in my father was more irony than I could suffer without correction.

"He said, 'Finish that pump by Friday or I'll take the belt to your ass.'"

Elliot's eyes widened. I had spanked him only once, when he was a toddler, for running into the street outside a grocery store. I still thought of this whenever he turned his eyes away from me, but I realize that probably he did not remember it.

"Was he kidding?"

"No, he wasn't kidding."

"What did you do?"

"I finished the pump."

"I mean when he said that."

"Which movie?" a voice said then, and instead of answering my son, I turned to it. We had reached the front of the line.

He bought tickets for *On Golden Pond,* a movie about a boy hungry for connection with a father, and the clumsy bluntness of the message in this choice made me feel ashamed of my feelings of persecution. I sobered myself with thoughts of the duty I'd been avoiding. In the last three days, I had been to the drugstore twice. The first time, I bought a packet of disposable razors and a canister of unscented shaving cream. The next day I went back and bought one with an odor, something called "Sport," because I did not know what he wanted. Now in the darkened theater, the film's bittersweet music moved me, and words began to take shape in my mind. But they soon left me. He stirred in his seat, glancing at me during scene changes. During one of these glances, I saw that his cheeks were damp, and—God forgive me—I kept my eyes fixed on the screen. He sniffled, and I leaned forward a bit, so that his face was outside my peripheral vision. But after a few minutes, he whispered to me. "Dad?"

On-screen, the boy and the old man were clinging to a rock in the darkening water.

"What?" I said.

"Want more popcorn?"

"No thanks." I thought he would leave it at that, but soon he tapped my arm where it lay between us on the armrest, forcing me to turn. His face glistened in a flicker of light from the screen.

"What is it?" I asked. Perhaps it sounded sharp in the sudden quiet.

"Nothing," he said, after a time.

In the car, he sat beside me, his eyelashes dark with dried tears. We drove along Sunrise Boulevard with its signs like beacons: Plexiglas hamburgers and neon car keys; a hot tub filled with turquoise spangles. He asked me how I had liked the movie, and I told him I had found it very moving, sort of heartwarming, really very stirring, hinting at the emotion I had felt without referring to his own. In my own adolescence, my father had waited long enough that my first few beard hairs grew half an inch, fine like baby's hair. It was winter in New Jersey, and I felt the sparse mustache when I licked my lips to soothe their chap. I had thought of taking his razor or buying my own, but I knew he would notice that I had shaved, and in the last two years I had learned that his reactions were unpredictable. Instead I waited. In the end, he called attention to it at the dinner table in front of my mother in an exchange whose retelling would make him look worse than I'm willing to. But the memory of it troubled my plans. Now I could not imagine a conversation that would have made me comfortable.

When we got home, Elliot went downstairs to reclaim himself with work on his lawn mower engine, and I went to my bedroom and took the photocopied sheet from my pocket. In my medicine cabinet, I had stored the two cans of shaving cream and the small packet of razors. Beside these was a spare aluminum-shafted model I sometimes took to the office to prepare for a late-afternoon meeting, and what I thought then was that this one would better communicate my respect for him. There was ceremony in the gift of such a razor. I crept into his bathroom.

It was as the bathrooms in motels appear. His washcloth folded on the towel bar. His toothpaste and comb stored behind his mirror. I set the two canisters of shaving cream next to the sink and the razor beside these. I took the folded instructions from my pocket and laid them on the counter. The corners were turned up from the curve my hip had forced in the theater, and I smoothed them out against the tiles. I set the cans of shaving foam on opposite corners. I tried different arrangements and avoided my reflection in the mirror. In the end, I refolded the page and left it next to the razor, cupped in the shape it had taken in my pocket, and went back to my room.

THE NEXT MORNING, LIZ GOT UP EARLY AND SHOWERED BEFORE us. I found her in the kitchen, wearing jeans and a fawn-colored sweater, and the bright red sneakers she wore in the evenings when we toured our neighborhood looking for weakness. As she peeled white from a section of orange, I almost told her what I had done. I was sure this would be his first morning to use it, and it seemed our shared anticipation might offer some small consolation for all I had withheld.

"Today's the day," she said, and for a moment, it confused me. But it was my meeting she meant. "High corner office, for sure," she said.

Then we heard his footfall on the stairs.

For many years I would tell myself that, at least in the most immediate sense, it didn't matter; that telling her would not have prepared her for what happened anyway. Our son was fifteen years old, wore twill pants she bought at back-to-school sales each September, and had been on the honor roll every year since the third grade. He told long stories at dinner, holding his knife and fork suspended above the table, and would still fall asleep open-mouthed on a sofa beside us. Sometimes I came home from work to find him standing shoulder to shoulder with her as she sautéed a pan of onions in an intimate silence that she would describe to me with grateful wonder after we switched off our lamps for sleep. Although she was a mother, and over the years she had shared a thousand worries, it seemed to me that until what I drove him to that morning she had no real cause for concern about our son. The evidence must have seemed sudden. The night before he was complimenting her cooking and taking out the garbage unbidden, and twelve hours later he arrived at breakfast: clean socks, pressed shirt, pants and belt, and his scalp shaved to a waxy smoothness that gave off the scent of artificial pine.

In case you're assuming that baldness was a fashion then among children in California, I can assure you it was not. We lived in a suburb of Sacramento. Sacramento itself, like the capital cities of most states, is a small town, not cosmopolitan, where ticket lines and traffic flows at four-way stops are negotiated with the halting civility of legislature. The suburbs of such cities have the safe, unchanging magic of a village inside a snow globe. The children at his school, at their most radical, wore their sneaker soles down to the canvas and the fine welting on their corduroy pants to the sheen. Some boys persisted with the long hair that had been popular over the last decade, but by far the most common form of rebellious expression was the dirty T-shirt. His appearance could not have been more alien.

"Good morning," he said, slipping into his chair.

Liz was at the stove, spoon poised to pull a soft-boiled egg from its water. When she turned, her lips were already parted, but her greeting died there, and map shapes of color bloomed at her neck. Elliot looked at me. He had nicked himself slightly, to the right of the crown. Although I was by any measure surprised, I immediately decided that to express this would be a grave error.

"I like your new look," I said.

He had shaved his mustache too—it had taken me that long to notice this—and the bright pink of the tender skin there called strange attention to his mouth. Before I spoke, his lips had been slightly parted, and they remained so. He did not smile, or furrow his brow, or, as he often did when he was nervous, grasp his glasses delicately at the hinges and set them back on his ears. The egg water spurted and bubbled on the stove. He said, "You don't think it's too shiny?"

"Not at all."

Liz recalled herself. "No, sweetie."

"It's very sleek," I said.

"Yul Brynner," said Liz.

"Kojak." This bit of television knowledge had come to me unbidden, and I was grateful for it.

Liz's spoon dripped water on the tile. In the weird, slow time of shock, it occurred to me that our eggs would be overcooked. Elliot ran a palm over the top of his head. Back and forth. Watching us. "Here," he said finally. "Feel it."

And so I did. It was smooth and still cool from the moisture required to shave it bare. Liz crossed the kitchen and laid her hand next to mine emphatically, with a light slap, as if she feared too tentative a touch would betray her alarm. I thought about meeting her eye then, but I did not. I kept my own on the tiny, cold-shrunken pores of his scalp, and a vein there, snaking like a river through difficult terrain. The nick was to the left of this, and small. And there was a flat spot, just behind the crown, that a brief review of his early falls did not account for. I can mark the moment when Liz saw the flat spot with a hitch in her breath like the one that precedes tears of confusion. He looked so vulnerable. What I wanted to do was bend down and kiss him there, but of course I did not. Instead, I broke the silence we had let fall by removing my hand and remarking on how difficult it must have been to achieve such a perfectly close shave. Liz did the same, saying certain parts must have been like shaving a knee, only without being able to look. Or like buttoning a shirt in the dark. But more dangerous than that of course. The nervousness was rising in her, like a bubble, and she turned away from its object, toward the stove.

We ate our eggs hard-boiled, each handling the untested mechanics of this differently but discreetly, I pressing mine between two pieces of toast, Liz stripping the shell over the sink and slicing hers into rounds before she came to the table, and Elliot peeling his over his plate, chips of shell falling like ceiling plaster onto his toast crusts. Inside my shirt, a single drop of perspiration ran down my side and struck my shirt where my belt cinched it close. Instead of his scalp, it was those bits of eggshell that drew my eye. I had built that house twenty-two years before, and you could lift a roof shingle today and find the sheathing beneath dry as paper. Pipes never leaked, or knocked; my floorboards and hinges were silent, but still this misperception held: a snow of ceiling plaster on his breakfast leavings. He ate his egg from the fingertips on one hand, like a small piece of fruit. We turned newspaper pages. We offered to pass each other things across the table, and I left the house for my office as was my custom, at twenty minutes to eight.

3 The Drink

It's worth pointing out that although Robert Belsky had been on my mind, at this point he still wasn't very high on my list of preoccupations. Mostly I felt sorry for him, and irritated that he was, from time to time, able to make me feel awkward in front of my peers about something as trivial as not being free to accept a last-minute invitation. But never had he risen above the level of sideshow curiosity or puzzling case study in human nature. Liz and I had talked about him a few dozen times over the years as we brushed our teeth or fixed breakfast in the kitchen, more often than we talked about any of my other coworkers certainly, but not in the hushed tones and private places we reserved for topics like a bad homeroom teacher or a neighbor who, six years ago with a letter delivered by courier during dinner, had claimed that part of our swimming pool was in his yard.

When I drove to the office that morning, then, my sense of foreboding was attached not to the meeting I was about to attend, but instead to the pure surprise of my son's behavior. In my car on the

Sunrise Boulevard Bridge, moving my foot from gas pedal to brake to keep time with the traffic, the music on the radio became so unsettling, I turned it down first to low and then to a murmur before turning it off altogether. In the river, what at first appeared to be a dog swimming for shore turned out to be a branch. Although I didn't really need to, I stopped for gas so that I could try calling Liz from a pay phone. Elliot would most likely still be in the kitchen with her, but I might be able to gauge something about her state of mind from her tone. Answering machines were new then, and novel, and when after the sixth ring, her recorded voice came on the line, my chest filled with a mixture of relief and apprehension, and I began to interrupt. But even as I did so, I realized I was alone there on the phone, and that complex of feelings was replaced by embarrassment. I hung up and got back into my car.

In the parking garage, I returned to the car twice—once to retrieve the envelope of papers I'd forgotten, and once to make sure I had remembered to lock the doors—and in the polished granite lobby, I had to remove my suit coat to check the beginning of a sweat. I stepped into the elevator behind my secretary, Elena. She was a pretty Puerto Rican woman who by some harsh chemical process had dyed her black hair an unnerving red. She did not look up from her paperback until we passed the fifth floor, and then she did so abruptly, as if she had detected me suddenly, by smell.

"Up we go," she said. She reached up and patted a button on her polka-dot blouse. She began every conversation by checking for some unknown humiliation: a missing button, a static-churned skirt front, a run in her hose. "Up, up. Up."

"Yes," I said. We shifted our eyes to the lit numbers above our heads. Nine. Ten. Eleven.

She smiled slightly. "The penthouse, maybe?" Word of today's meeting had traveled among the secretaries, and it was the surprise of this small detail that recalled me. This meeting, I thought suddenly, was unlikely to go well.

We had them once a month. The four most senior engineers in our division, our manager, Don, and Howard Krepps. Don asked us questions to give Howard an overview of our progress and to demonstrate to Howard that he was doing a good job. Other than this, it served mostly to heighten the competitive feeling among us. Some projects were very obviously more important and interesting than others, and as each of us was questioned about our work, the other three had lots of time to consider this inequity. The effects of this lingered in the air as we slogged through a list of administrative details. With new office allocations and the rumors about Don's retirement, today's was likely to be particularly tense.

Lately we had been meeting in a windowless conference room down the hall from Howard's office. It was small and dark, with a poster of chickens from when the floor had been occupied by the Department of Agriculture, but it had its own kitchenette where Howard could disappear for refills of coffee. The building had recently passed a new policy against smoking, and he was trying to quit altogether. Caffeine was one of the instruments of his new discipline.

When I entered the cramped room, everyone but Don was already there. Howard clapped his hands together. "Okay, Luther, why don't we start with you?"

I glanced at the door.

"Don couldn't make it today," he said.

Robert fixed his eyes on me and winked; he had been the chief circulator of rumors about Don's retirement.

I sat down and took a file from my briefcase. "Okay. Fire away."

"Where are you on Bottlerock?"

"Still working on the turbine pedestal design."

"What about South Geysers?"

"About fifty thousand cubic yards of earth are already out, and Lacey said they haven't seen anything so far that will indicate major changes on the plans for the well pads or the plant foundation."

In the seventies and eighties we were doing a lot with California's plans for conversion to alternative energy. The geothermal power plants in Lake County were the highest profile of our projects, and when they'd been assigned to me, I'd felt a rush of excitement I'd tried to hide. This lasted about six months, and then what I found myself trying to suppress instead was a sense of foreboding. The Geysers Known Geothermal Resource Area is the largest geothermal field in the world. Among its hissing fumaroles and boiling springs, there are three hundred productive wells, but back when we arrived to start developing, PG&E and the municipal utilities had already acquired the best sites. The county balked some and required mitigation for wildlife habitat loss. Our plans were mildly contested during certification review—by Camp Beaverbrook, which objected to the impact of heavy construction equipment on the campers who walked along Bottlerock Road, and by an adjoining landowner whose case was argued on the basis that after many millions of dollars in design and construction, we wouldn't have enough steam to run it anyway. Although it was relatively easy to overcome all of these hurdles, in the end, the landowner's lawyers were right. We would operate Bottlerock for five years before admitting that although the steam field had been licensed at fifty-five megawatts, it was really only capable of producing fifteen, and we would abandon the steam wells at South Geysers before we even finished construction.

But at the time of this meeting, it seemed that everyone but me was sure that I would be able to tap the source of unlimited power trapped hundreds of feet beneath the surface.

Howard had more questions for me, during which he emptied his coffee and was too focused to rise for more. At one point, he encouraged the others to ask questions as well, but due to some combination of boredom and misplaced envy, no one took him up on this. Ken took out a file for his own presentation and reviewed it. David went to the kitchenette and returned with cocoa in a paper cup. Robert flipped through a long memo from the Personnel Office on changes in health benefits. It was forty minutes before we moved on.

The discussion of everyone else's work combined took less time than Howard had allotted to my project. Ken was working on some hydroelectric power plants, David on an early proposal for the expansion of the California Aqueduct, and Robert, because he had finished a big project just a few months ago, was left with reviewing shop drawings for a new visitor center. The contractor had prepared them, and it was Belsky's job to count and verify, for example, that the number of pieces of reinforcing steel intended in our design were actually in the contract submittal. This alone was not enough to fill his time, and so he was also working on a cost estimate.

"Robert, how are the drawings from Cooper?" Howard said.

He sat back in his chair. "Every bolt accounted for, sir." He tried to smile.

"Seriously. They're good, but they've changed the specs before. There's nothing missing?"

"No, no. They did a fine job."

"How about the cost estimate?"

"My son's fifth-grade math class has it all figured out. If we have to remove three thousand cubic yards of soil, and each truck has a carrying capacity of ten . . ."

All of us laughed, including Howard, but when we stopped, he said, "I'd like to see a copy of it when you're done." Then he closed his notebook. "Okay, just some administrative details left. Safety of Dams called to say they've been looking at North Fork since the earthquake—no surprise—and they've decided to go ahead and ask us to investigate for any deficiencies."

I picked up my pen to appear receptive, but my pulse quickened.

"No, Luther," he said, "you've got too much on your plate with Bottlerock and South Geysers. Bob, you do this one. You can go to Luther for backup materials if you need them."

"No better man to check up on Luther's work," Robert said, but he closed his eyes a second too long. Despite the false power it would allow him to feel over me, it was another bad assignment.

After a discussion of budget issues, during which Ken's eyes actually drifted shut, Howard unfurled a plan of the building on the laminate conference table. The coveted vantage in most office towers is south and west for the light and the sunsets, but in ours it was north and east for the view of the park and the capitol dome. We leaned in, doing our best to pretend we were only interested in gathering the information so we could dispense it to our teams. Howard pointed with a pencil and read off the office numbers without emotion, assigning Ken and David to center offices with views of the park. Robert and I were both assigned corners, but only mine had the view of the dome.

"Come again?" Robert said.

Howard repeated himself.

"Jesus!" He stood, setting his chair teetering on its legs. Howard glanced at his notes, as if Robert's expletive might have been scripted there. His hand trembled, but this could just as easily have been caffeine or nicotine withdrawal as nervous tension. Ken coughed. David sipped his cocoa, and Howard let the plans roll shut on the table.

Robert picked up his papers to prepare for an exit, but in the heat of his anger, he stormed into the kitchenette and slammed the door. We could see him clearly through a pane of glass, no more than three feet from David's chair, pretending not to notice his own mistake. He turned the water on.

"Personnel issues, anyone?" Howard said.

Ken cleared his throat and began softly with the latest installment on a strange junior engineer who had been coming to work sometimes as late as two o'clock and did not seem to respond to any of his warnings. It was difficult to fire people inside the agency; Howard recommended Ken talk to the Personnel Director and find out exactly what kind of documentation was required for his file. We all stood and began gathering our things. Robert slammed a cupboard in the kitchenette, and we left him there, the short boar bristles on the back of his neck standing out as he leaned over the sink.

I won't try to claim that any sympathy for Robert kept my thoughts from returning quickly to my family. I could see how the favor I'd been shown would be an irritation to him, but I had no respect for the self-indulgence involved in storming out of a meeting. Although I'd felt a pressure in my chest even before Howard had read the full list of reassignments—somehow I'd known mine would be better than Belsky's—this empathy was quickly overwhelmed by irritation, and, I'll admit it, a ghost's trace of embarrassment. Somehow it shamed me to see another man giving way so easily to his own worst impulses.

On my office wall were five pictures, framed by Liz one birthday, of the rivers I had helped dam. When I started a new project, I began by visiting the site. In some cases I might have let this task fall to someone else and spared myself the packed suitcase, the wait in the airport, and the oppressive quiet of a hotel room, but I liked walking the ground myself. Some of this was practical—there were things I could glean that reports and photographs might not tell me: the depth of weathered soil to rock; the steepness of the abutments—but there was also the pleasure. Before I left, I always took a picture from some point downstream of where the dam would be, picturing the accumulation of earth, the size and shape of the change I might make as I looked through the viewfinder and snapped the photo.

It is in one of these that I am featured, blurry and incongruous, in the foreground. When I was asked to evaluate the North Fork dam site, I had decided on impulse to take my family with me, and on the shoulder of the road, Liz served sparkling cider out of Dixie cups. Elliot was six then, and he touched his cup to mine and congratulated me. He stood there a moment looking proud of the gesture, his blown hair dark against the pale gray sky. Then he set off ahead of me to climb the steep hill beside us. I left Liz—pregnant one last time—by the car and followed. Stiff shoots of sagebrush broke against our pant legs and released a spiced smell. His breaths were short and determined by my side. At the crest, he asked me for my camera. He positioned me above him, with the gap of the canyon I would seal off behind me, and took this picture. In it, I am smiling in surprise at his request, and my hair is lifting on the wind.

I took a deep breath and moved to the window. My current office had a view of the I Street Bridge over the murky water of the Sacramento River, and although I'll admit I looked forward to the stately view of the capitol dome, there was something here that soothed me. Cars drove slowly across the bridge, one east, and then one west. I could look straight down out my window, at the tops of the buildings below, little antennas and ducts and maintenance doors and patches of tar, all of it hidden from view as people walked through the clean white seat of our government, and somehow, no matter how anxious I was feeling, each time I did this my lungs would fill fully of their own accord, and I would turn back to my desk, momentarily relieved.

I tried to get some work done, but every fifteen minutes or so, I picked up the phone to see if I could reach Liz. I wanted badly to tell her I wasn't worried about Elliot, although in fact I was. Why did I want to do this? She was a strong woman, stronger than I was in almost every way, but when I looked at her, even her unusually muscular arms or the set of her jaw when she confronted an unscrupulous salesman (aloud!) about what he was trying to put over on us, somehow all I wanted to do was protect her. As I've said, she was the youngest of five sisters, the only one without a job and the last to have children, and while mostly her insecurities only made themselves plain in an excessive attention to my needs, in that last year before Elliot was born, they seemed to consume her. One memory that stands out is the night of a black-tie fund-raiser Trish and her husband were hosting for the Cancer Treatment Center at Children's Hospital in San Francisco. We hit bad traffic coming over from Sacramento, and all through the drive, Liz was sitting up very straight to keep her white taffeta dress from wrinkling, but shortly after we arrived, she disappeared into the kitchen to sit on a stool and play Candy Land with two nieces in velvet dresses. I tried to tell myself she was having a good time, until just before dinner, when her sister took the landing on the stairs beneath a crystal chandelier and toasted the bravery of the children they were supporting, and I saw Liz glance at her own reflection in a gilt mirror. Later I woke in the guest room alone, and I went downstairs to find her sitting on the bottom stair beneath that same mirror. She looked up at me, her cheeks shiny with tears. "It's just hard being here," she said. "I'm so glad for her, but it's hard seeing what she has."

I think I did a reasonable job of hiding it for her sake, but the truth is the words stung me. The fact that I had not yet managed to get her sustainably pregnant was making me feel more than a little inadequate, and I had begun to fixate irrationally on the other things I could not give her. Across the street, for example, our new neighbor was building a mock Tudor house with a three-car garage, and this had moved me to repaint our house and dig a swimming pool in our yard. After her second miscarriage, although her Ford was only five years old, I had traded it in for a new station wagon that simulated movement toward a future with children. So when the *San Francisco Chronicle* ran an article about Bay Area philanthropy featuring a picture of Trish standing between her two daughters on the porch of their hilltop Victorian and I saw Liz pinning it to our refrigerator, I guess something boiled over inside me. I said, "Is it really so disappointing, what we have?"

She looked genuinely confused. "What do you mean?"

"No black-tie fund-raisers. No big house. No girls in velvet dresses."

"Oh, Luther," she said. "I don't envy Trish because her life is fancy. I envy her because she's so important."

"Who cares about the society pages?"

"That's exactly my point." She opened the refrigerator and took out a package of ground beef.

I said, "You said she was important."

"Yes I did." She took a frying pan from a drawer beneath the stove. "Because she's a good mother and an activist, not because her name is in the paper." She peeled back the plastic on the package of meat. I watched her shape it into three hamburger patties. Finally, she shook her head and turned. "I didn't say she seemed important to other people, Luther. I said she actually is important."

It was a few hours before my ego receded enough for me to recognize the self-criticism at the heart of her envy, and although at the time I still felt too implicated by the general dissatisfaction it implied to feel any compassion, now whenever I looked back on this moment, my breath caught for her. Occasionally this came mixed with a selfless courage that almost moved me to ask her if she still felt that kind of jealousy, but more often it only made me feel a vague desire to give her something large, like an oven or a sapling, although at times like this—at most times, truthfully—I was at a loss to imagine what she might need.

My afternoon at the office passed with very little work. I did some filing I normally would have given Elena, because after a while the accumulation of minutes I passed picturing Liz emptying the trash can full of Elliot's hair instead of finishing the memo I had to write was making me feel the beginnings of self-loathing. The filing was easier. I was bending over a drawer when Robert Belsky appeared in my doorway.

"Hail to the Chief," he said.

"Come on in," I managed.

"Can I? The inner sanctum?"

He looked up at the ceiling tiles, making a quick count. "Your new one's not just the view corner, it's bigger too."

"More space for you and the investigators to sit."

He smiled; I had won something with this. "We can set up the polygraph next to that big window," he said.

"Right."

He stepped into my office. When I first met him, he had told me he didn't like my shoes. *Never trust a man in Hush Puppies,* he had said, laying his brain bare. Now he reached for my desk and picked up one of my family photographs: the three of us in front of our house in the late sixties, Elliot seated on my joined hands and gripping my arms like a boy on a swing. There is a quality to a child's use of you when he is young: your lap a stepladder, a desk, a drum. Belsky's thumb pressed on the glass would leave a mark.

He said, "Come out with us tonight. Buy a round of drinks for the losers."

"I'd like to, but I can't."

"We're government employees. Take off half an hour early. Who are you kidding?"

"Actually, I am leaving a little early, but I've got another commitment."

He grinned. "And with a wife like yours? You dog."

I tried to imagine what turns of life produced someone like him. It made me angry. Instead of expressing this, I said, "Maybe another time."

"Sure, sure," he said, and he set the picture back on my desktop.

As soon as he was gone, I stood and gathered my things, because now I had my lack of social courage to add to my list of distractions. It was almost four thirty. I might as well go. I got into my car, and although I had resolutely avoided thinking about it—there was a vague embarrassment in the predictability of what I would do—when I headed across the river toward Arden Fair Mall, the shame of this was muffled under the familiar excitement that made this kind of errand a habit. I tried to think about what recently had seemed to absorb her, what she had pursued with energy and confidence to the unarguable benefit of her husband and son, and by the time I pulled into the parking lot, I had already decided. Ken's Cameras was on the east side, near the food court, and as the salesman showed me three different models, his showroom floor smelled less of photo paper and camera plastic than waffle cones. I pretended to listen to his pitch and then settled blindly on the one with the most features. It had a remote control and a screen that collapsed for storage in a metal tube, and I drove home listening to a traffic report to avoid examining my own behavior—the strange impulse to reassure my wife of her worth and purpose with the gift of a slide projector.

When I pulled into the cul-de-sac, they were in the front yard, loading the first leaves of fall into a dark plastic bag. They looked up when I pulled into the cul-de-sac, like a pair of deer alert to the breaking of twigs, and immediately I was struck by the familiar feeling that they had been discussing me.

As I got out of the car, Liz waved.

"Aren't you industrious," I said, my heart racing.

"It was Ellie's idea. He came home and wanted to rake and bag."

I had been thinking about it all day, but still the stark expanse of his scalp made me feel the pulse in my neck. In the periphery of my vision, I could see a pink-brown worm writhing, exposed by their work. Damp elm leaves were around our feet. I could not look down, the energy between us was so electric. Liz was wearing a yellow-flowered sundress and my hooded sweatshirt and a pair of green rubber boots. For three or four seconds, she was able to hold my gaze, but finally her eyes slid toward him, and I wonder now if already she understood how thoroughly I would disappoint her.

I said, "Is there something I can do to help with dinner, or should I take over here?"

She handed me the bag. "I know what's cooking. You two finish up."

The storm had pulled enough to fill two bags, but it was only the first week of November, the tree above us still dense with yellow leaves. We would do this work half-a-dozen times before the season was over. His head rose and fell in front of me, and the leaves made their papery sound. When he was only two years old, he had insisted, one day, on helping, and I saw how one of the pleasures of parenting is the simple lesson that humans are born with a yearning to be of use. He had taken the rake from me, the handle a wild and unwitting weapon in his hands, and I forced myself from warning or assistance. And then again, another pleasure: the surprise of his competence. Within four or five attempts he had the hang of it, gripping the handle low and dragging the leaves with the rake's big scraping hand.

I said, "We had our senior staff meeting today."

"Oh yeah?"

"You were right. Safety of Dams decided to ask us for an investigation."

He stooped again for another armful of leaves. "Is it going to be a hassle for you?"

"No. They assigned it to Robert Belsky so I can keep working on the geothermal project."

He snorted and released an armful of leaves into the bag, waiting for me to ask him what was funny.

Finally, I did.

He said, "I just hope you like him."

"I like all of my coworkers."

"Yeah, but this guy's looking for mistakes in your work."

He stooped for more leaves. He'd reached the end of the pile, and what remained was dark and sodden. I watched him draw the wet leaves against his sweatshirt.

I said, "There's a great deal of trust between good colleagues."

"I'm just saying it could be pretty tense."

"We're all on the same team."

"Whatever you say."

"We're practically like family."

The bag was too full for this last armful, but he straightened and forced them in anyway, making a sloppy job of it. Then he looked at me. "Then how come I've never met any of them?"

"What?"

"If they're like family, how come I've never met them?"

"It never occurred to me that you'd like to."

"Well, I would." He blinked at me. There was a dark circle on his sweatshirt where he had pressed the leaves to his chest. "That is, unless you wouldn't want me showing up at your office."

"Of course I would."

"Sure—"

"I'd be proud to introduce you around."

He snorted. "Take me out for a drink with your boss . . ."

"Why not?" I said.

When I was fourteen, my father began to test my mother's patience just like this, abruptly and roughly, like a firefighter sounding a roof for weak zones. Elliot tied off the bag without answering my question and then stooped to tie his shoe, and the view of the pink crown of his head filled me with an uncomfortable mixture of anger and compassion. I closed my eyes.

During dinner, he was quiet, but Liz enjoyed an ease with this she only exhibited in the wake of a frank conversation, and in imagining the uninhibited give-and-take about his haircut that had probably punctuated their half of the raking job, I was forced to acknowledge that his silence now was triggered solely by me. She steered us deftly through conversations about Michael Jackson's new video and the Falkland Islands and a woman she had seen that day driving in a car filled with live geese. Elliot and I both ate more than we otherwise would, hiding behind the mechanics of chewing and swallowing, but in Liz the tension between us only brought out grace. She served him a second potato and told a joke that made him laugh, and when she did so herself, I could tell that for a moment, in rising to the occasion of our father-son crisis, she had forgotten its burden. The laughter was genuine. She sat back in her chair; her eyelids fluttered; and in the pocket of ease this created, Elliot and I both set down our forks.

In bed that night, she sat cross-legged on our bedspread, sorting nickels into paper sleeves. A textbook on gardening lay open beside her, and as her fingers combed through the loose change, she glanced at it. In twenty-two years with me, she had mastered a posture of easy, indifferent patience. I stepped in and shut the door.

"Well," I said—a complete sentence.

She laughed, but for the first time that night there was something nervous in it.

I laughed too and then said, "For the record, I'm not worried about it."

"Me neither," she said.

"He's a happy boy, and the evidence, however weird, is still consistent with this."

"You're right."

I said, "He seemed fine tonight."

She nodded, searching my face, and it is hard to remember if my pulse rose then due to excitement about my surprise or a sudden sense of shame about the sleight of hand it represented.

"I have something for you," I said.

I had left it behind me in the hall, and I did not wait to check the look on her face before I turned. I opened the door and slid the boxes in and when I stood up to explain she was already blushing. "Oh, Luther," she said. She wore an expression that used to pass across her face both when Elliot drew her a picture and when he skinned his knee: something like heartache. I wanted to reach out and pass my thumb over her brow, to relax the tension there, but instead I said: "That photo album you made from this summer is so fantastic. You're the historian in this family; without you we'd lose all sense of ourselves."

I leaned over the box then and read the features, and somewhere in my monologue about the virtues of these, I slipped into bed and switched off our lamps and trailed off into the dark. An elm branch blew against the window, a soft tick and scrape. When our eyes adjusted, we would still be able to see little. The elm tree stood just outside the window, and its thick canopy obscured any moonlight. In one month, after the last leaf fall, it would be different, our ceiling a shadow theater of blown branches and passing clouds.

She said, "Adolescence is a tough time, Luther. He sees himself change; he might be worried we won't accept him. It's probably just a test."

"Exactly," I said. Although ordinarily this assurance from her would have relieved me, the abruptness of her return to the subject carried the somehow threatening insight that my gift had not been a digression. That my keyed-up talk of its features had been making my feelings plain all along. Downstairs the dishwasher churned.

"He's growing up," she said.

"Yes."

"Getting ready to leave the nest."

"Right."

She said, "In two years, he probably won't even live here. We'll be all alone."

I thought about this. I had that feeling I sometimes had that she was suddenly speaking in code, leading me gently somewhere I did not want to go.

She said, "What will we talk about all day?"

"What?"

"When he's gone." When I didn't respond, she laughed falsely, to maintain her momentum. "Most people would say something like, 'Our aches and pains.'"

"Really?"

"Or 'Our golf game.'"

"But I hate golfing."

She said, "Or, 'Honey, we don't talk all that much now.'"

"Well, that's ridiculous."

The dishwasher stopped—the strange, long pause before it drained.

She said, "That's what Eleanor said that one time."

"What?"

"That thing after her divorce. You remember."

The talc smell of her lotion came to me, and made me think of her body. I tried to recall. After each phone call, Liz tried to neutralize the subtle poison of her sisters' comments with exaggerated impersonations I knew she loved them too much to mean: a bossy voice, a dullard's drone, the piping of a little girl.

"I don't think I remember."

"You know."

She rubbed her feet together, a whispery sound. I wanted to reach under her T-shirt and lay a hand on her stomach, but I knew she would see this for the advance that it clearly would be and take it as a sign that I was not listening, instead of a sure sign that I was.

Her voice grew infinitesimally softer. "She said she had always thought she and Jim were talking but they really weren't. Not about the things that mattered. She said I might think we're happy, but . . ."

"But what?"

I turned my face towards her to read her face but it was too dark to see anything clearly. Not even her lips when she finally made herself say it aloud: ". . . but maybe I just don't know that I don't really know you."

THAT WEEK I SAW THE FIRST OUTWARD SIGNS THAT MY EVASION was taking its toll. On Saturday afternoon, she came down to the laundry room wearing a yellow satin blouse over a short black skirt I had not seen in years, and when she descended half an hour later to defrost a casserole for Elliot, she was wearing a strapless velvet dress. Before we left, she had changed earrings twice, finally settling on no earrings but a long pendant necklace that drew attention to the dark well between her breasts.

The occasion was a sixtieth birthday party for Don Moraine in the bar at the Capitol Hotel. Earthquake scaffolding still hid the old brick façade, but somehow it retained its grandeur. Management had strung the steel poles with lights and rolled a red carpet down the plank ramp that covered the damaged stairs. Liz had finally settled on a green silk dress with a matching jacket that hid the surprise of bare shoulders, and she moved around the room to each of my colleagues, laying a hand on their forearms. When she was flushed with two vodka tonics and the regard of men, she steered us towards Robert Belsky. He was standing by the buffet table, eating cocktail meatballs directly from the chafing dish. Behind him, his wife held two drinks.

Belsky saw us coming, and he reached out to touch Liz at the small of her back. "How'd you persuade Mr. Big to go slumming tonight? We're on the first floor here. And no view." He speared a meatball with his toothpick and winked at me over Liz's shoulder. "He's such a big shot now, I thought he'd come with a bigger entourage. Lackeys. Fan clubbers."

She laughed lightly and looked over his shoulder. "It's good to see you, Joyce."

Belsky's wife had just taken a sip and had an ice cube in her mouth, but she raised her glass in greeting.

"What about me?" Belsky said. "What am I, chopped liver?"

Liz sidestepped away from his touch now, and her embarrassment for Joyce made her flush. She slipped off her fitted jacket.

"Va-voom!" Belsky said.

Joyce laughed. "No kidding. You look fantastic."

My first year in high school, my father began to comment on other women in front of my mother. She always laughed too, but I can't help but wonder how the memory of it made her feel when she was alone, surgaring her tea or appraising her reflection in the diamond-shaped mirror above her dresser.

Belsky punched me in the shoulder. "How'd a sap like you ever rate a woman like that?"

"I'm a lucky man."

"I guess the nickname can stick then."

"What nickname is that?" Liz said.

"Lucky Luther. I was thinking of changing it now that he's under the microscope."

She said, "You can't be talking about that routine investigation."

"Jury's out on routine, sweetheart."

She rolled her eyes and took a lipstick and mirror from her purse.

He said, "A dam like that one nearly wiped out half of Los Angeles in 1971. It was during an earthquake about the size of the one we had last month."

She applied a fresh layer and pressed her lips together.

He said, "You never know what they might find."

Liz snapped her little bag shut and laughed. "I know exactly what they'll find," she said, and she kissed me full on the mouth.

She pulled back a few inches and looked me in the eye and smoothed the shoulders of my sport coat. Then she licked her thumb and rubbed the trace of her kiss from my lips, and it was this, not the kiss itself, that made me blush.

"You win," Belsky said. "The nickname stands." Joyce tipped back her cup for a last cube of ice, but it clung to the bottom by molecular cohesion. Liz saw this too, and it touched both of us in the same way. We looked at the carpet.

Belsky stabbed another meatball with his toothpick and looked at me, eyebrows raised. "'Course I bet you're counting on a downgrade in a few months."

For a moment, I thought he was referring to my wife. "A downgrade in what?"

"Office views."

I looked at him.

He turned to Liz, as if he were sharing a secret. "Don's is on the southeast corner. Higher, and closer to Krepps, but no view of the dome."

I shook my head.

Belsky leaned towards my wife. "That's what a shoo-in he is," he whispered, loud enough so I could hear it. Joyce had set her empty cup on the table and was stealing a sip of her husband's drink. He cupped a hand to Liz's ear, "He doesn't even have to think of me as competition."

We did not stay long after this. We stood and talked with Don and Lorraine for ten minutes about Maui, where they were about to go for Don's annual vacation, and where I imagined—all right, I'll admit I couldn't help thinking about it—he might make his decision about retirement. Two men carrying a cake aflame with candles appeared from the swinging kitchen door behind a row of potted palms, and they placed it on a table near the four of us. Someone dimmed the lights, and Don's face was lit up by candle fire and affection for his wife, at whom he glanced just before he took a deep breath and blew.

Liz and I shared a piece of cake, standing alone in the corner, and although even after two vodkas she had the judgment to restrain herself from whispers on the subject, she kept cutting looks at Belsky or at Don and then looking at me smugly. She did not really need words. In the two weeks since I'd begun to mislead her, she had been formulating an unwritten list of the differences between Belsky and me. She took us on another neighborhood walk to his house, which she had clearly driven past herself since our last visit, to allow me to see a sloping flagstone driveway that in time would buckle because the contractor had not used edge boards. "You're more careful," she had said in bed that night. And when I told her about his reaction to the new office assignments, she had said, "You're more mature."

Now she set down our plate, and as she led me towards the door we saw Joyce following Belsky towards the buffet. Liz took me through the lobby, out through the big oak doors into the fresh cool air and the view of the capitol, lit at night in a way that always made me feel quiet and respectful. She took my hand, and it came to me with sudden certainty just how she would exaggerate his rivalrous barbs and harmless flirtations. I was surprised by the dread this made me feel.

"Add two more to the list," she said. She was grinning but her eyes flitted from my eyes to my mouth and back again.

"What would those be?"

"Not morbidly competitive."

"And?"

"Better husband," she said.

THREE NIGHTS LATER WE WOKE TO A SOUND OUTSIDE: SOMETHING striking the east wall near my study and Elliot's bedroom. Liz rose quickly and opened a window. I joined her there, our hands touching on the sill. We saw no movement in the dark yard, but a girl's voice drifted up to us, a harsh whisper.

"It's me. Peggy."

Elliot's voice answered. "What?"

"Peggy Lefkowitz. From school."

"What are you doing here?"

"Come down a second."

He didn't answer right away. Crickets pulsed beneath the elm tree. Then he said, "I can't."

"I just want to talk to you."

"You better go," he said.

"Elliot."

"I'm sorry," he said. His window slid shut. I looked at Liz, but she was straining to see something on the lawn. A girl had appeared beneath our window. In the moonlight, I could make out the silver hardware on her leather jacket. She stepped behind our elm tree, and we heard her clothes rustling, and then a liquid pitting. She was urinating on our lawn.

By the time she started to pull up her jeans, Liz was halfway down the stairs. I caught up with her at the kitchen door, and as she threw it open, I worried that in the heat of her indignation, she might provoke her. Although it seems ludicrous now, I thought it was possible that the girl would hit Liz, or knock her down, but it turned out her instincts were a lot better than this. Before Liz had even opened her mouth to confront her, Peggy turned to run.

"Wait!" Liz said.

But she was already running. Liz yelled, "I just want to invite you inside."

Peggy stopped and regarded Liz for the first time. I was always startled anew to see the range of people who were caught short by her beauty. The girl's own hair was short on one side, hanging no further than her earlobe, and long, to her shoulder, on the other. "What do you want?" she said.

"I heard you say you wanted to talk to Elliot."

"So?"

Liz put her hands on her hips in the teasing manner I remembered from her days at the bank. "So why not do it inside where it's not so damp?"

Then, in another of the string of events that fall that should have inured me to surprise, Peggy allowed herself to be turned, and inside, when Liz offered her something to drink, she asked for milk. She sat at our kitchen table waiting. Her silver rings clinked against the side of the glass. She didn't wipe her lip after she sipped, and a rim of white masked her dark lipstick.

"Luther," Liz said—she closed the refrigerator door—"why don't you go up and get Elliot?"

"Oh," I said, and could think of nothing further. She and the girl both looked at me, waiting for me to leave.

In the front hall, I paused, hoping to hear what my wife had to say to her, but the sound was muffled except for a surprising shock of laughter: the girl's. I wiped my T-shirt. "Crazy," I said quietly, just to test the sound of it, and then looked at my hands: palms, then backs. Stingy nail beds and thick knuckles. My father's hands. I heard Liz laugh now, and then Peggy, and then Liz together with her. A little fugue of laughter. Then I looked up the stairs and to my embarrassment saw Elliot there, looking down at me over the banister. I opened my mouth to normalize the scene, but he put his finger to his lips and walked back down the hall to his bedroom.

Briefly, excuses for the eavesdropping he had witnessed occurred to me, and a handful of weird explanations for the word I had muttered, but I was able to keep myself from refining these as I walked up the stairs.

When I entered his room, he was seated on the edge of his bed.

"What's going on?" he said.

On his wall was a calendar with a girl in a swimsuit the color of ripe limes that had not been there the last time I visited. His hands lay open-palmed on his race-car bedspread. It could be disorienting, parenting.

I said, "Your mom was hoping you might come downstairs."

"Is Peggy in there?"

"Yes, she is."

"And Mom is talking to her?"

"Yes."

"Telling her to beat it, I guess."

"I don't think so," I said. His face registered no alarm, and the realization that he may have expected this unnerved me. This evening was going somewhere everyone but me seemed to understand. "I think she's hoping you two might talk before she calls Peggy's mom."

He exhaled sharply, just like his mother. "Does she know Peggy has been on probation three times this year?"

"Probably not."

"Does she know Peggy smokes clove cigarettes?"

"I don't think so, no."

"Does she know Peggy pees in public?"

"She may have surmised that, yes."

He looked at me fully.

I said, "She peed on our lawn after you closed your window."

He laughed briefly at this, with what appeared to be genuine appreciation, but stopped abruptly and a sadness seemed to overtake him. "Her hair is weird too," he said.

"Original, I would have called it."

He touched his glasses, the stalling gesture that in earlier years was the most frequent prelude to revelation. "You still haven't invited me to your office."

"How about Friday?" I said.

For as many as thirty seconds he held still enough for tension to settle on the features of our landscape like strong lighting—how close I'd inadvertently come to him, standing next to his bed; a reddened cuticle around his thumbnail; my hands trembling as I slipped them self-consciously into the pockets of my robe—but whatever he was gathering the courage to say, he thought better of it. He stood and walked past me out of the room.

There was a time when the scenarios presented within my home seemed fairly predictable to me, but following my bald son down the hall at midnight toward a girl in leather who whispered with my wife in the kitchen, I had lost all confidence that I might know how things would unfold. His loose-fitting pajamas preceded me down the stairs, and when I entered, Liz was sitting at the kitchen table. Peggy stood behind her, a pair of scissors in hand. She had cut a good seven inches off the back of Liz's hair, and the yellow strands lay on the tile, splayed like straw.

Peggy raised the scissors slightly, like waving. "Hi, Elliot."

Liz looked up at us, brushing loose hair from her chest and shoulders. "Peggy's giving me a new style. Short in the back and really long bangs. Who has it again?" She turned her head over her shoulder toward Peggy, inquiring.

"Flock of Seagulls," said Elliot.

Peggy grinned, and Liz turned to him.

"Flock of Seagulls," she said.

We watched Peggy finish, and then Liz insisted she and I go outside a moment so she could feel the cool air on her bare neck. When she'd closed the door behind us, she explained that this was the only place where Elliot and Peggy could feel sure we were not eavesdropping, and in the cold damp grass she turned back towards the house. It was dark except for our bedroom light, and of course the light from the kitchen, and we could see the two of them at the table, talking. Elliot's hands stayed on the table, and Peggy's gestured once or twice, but mostly she kept them still as well, both of them moved to shyness it seemed, by the hour, and by Liz's impulsiveness maybe, but most of all by the sudden surprise of their privacy.

"What do you suppose they're talking about?" I said. I could hear the filter on our neighbor's pool cycle on. I was barefoot, and I was cold.

"It doesn't matter," she said.

"You're not curious?"

"Of course I'm curious; I meant it doesn't matter to them. They're making small talk. Whatever it is, it's not what they're thinking."

This made me take her hand.

And in the days that followed, I found myself distracted from Elliot's change by my wife's. I watched the nape of her neck as she inclined her head over a pan of bacon, or leaned over the sink to take a cupped handful of water to rinse her mouth at night. When I met her for lunch one day that week, I did not recognize her. I saw her only as an attractive stranger, and when I realized it was my own wife, I felt a flush of excitement that I let pass before I stepped from the door to join her. As much as I had loved her long hair, at moments both the extremity and the contrast of this cut were thrilling. The night she did it, she had pulled off her T-shirt in our bathroom and stood, head bent over the counter, so I could brush the cuttings from her shoulder blades. She was speculating with relish about the crush Peggy had on our son, and her voice faded in and out as I looked at a chain of small pale freckles along her spine. The next morning she woke me in the midst of an unsettling dream to ask me what I thought of the cut, and I struggled from a still-vivid half-world to tell her part of the truth—that I thought she looked beautiful, that a change was fun. But all the while I was distracted by the memory of a short-haired woman who had stepped from behind a curtain and put her hand to my mouth in my dream. I kept track of a weak intention to interject mention of this as we talked, and thought of it again when Liz peeked out of the shower to ask me for a new bar of soap, but in the end I never did. It would only have frightened her. No woman can imagine how little the male desire for variety actually means in the context of love.

I also hid my enjoyment because I believed the haircut was a symptom of her old self-doubt—a sign that she felt her power to help us was waning. One morning she came to the kitchen wearing a purple halter top the likes of which I hadn't seen since the early days of our marriage, and at the sight of her bare shoulders and the slice of skin at her waist, the boy's blood rush I felt was checked by a twinge of guilt. The next evening, I found two shopping bags of new clothes in her closet, and although she rarely wore makeup at home, when she raised her wineglass to her lips by the stove that night, I saw that she was wearing lipstick. She slept poorly. When I finally thought to ask her if I should invite him to meet me at my office on Friday— maybe take him out for a drink and talk to him man to man—she was so surprised it took a count of ten seconds for her to gather the words to encourage me. Then several moments of silence passed during which I imagine she conjured, as I did, the phantom words and gestures that might make up such a meeting, and at last her breathing slowed, as it had not in weeks.

AT TEN MINUTES TO FIVE, I TURNED MY DESK CHAIR AND LOOKED out my window. Here and there, people walked head-down in trench coats or leaned towards car doors fumbling with keys, and over the next ten minutes, the numbers swelled. From storefronts, from the tree-flocked park paths, people streamed onto the sidewalks. For his report, Elliot was required to include a small section on the times that had produced my father, and all afternoon I had pictured him at work in the library, winding a microfilm reel, his twill cuffs buttoned and his domed reflection haunting the dark screen of the reader. The white clouds were high and the late sun illumined them. The fan palms along L Street panicked in sudden winds and then calmed, and finally I saw him, his pale head passing into the crowd at the corner of Eleventh Street. He was wearing a cobalt windbreaker, zippered up to the neck, and I was seized by the tenderness that had overcome me so many times that month looking at the slight bumps and flat spots, the nicks and blemishes, the faint trace of a green-blue vein running from temple to crown. He must be cold. Even from my distance, I could see people glancing at him, heads turning as they passed and snapping back just short of a stare when the possibility of illness occurred to them.

That afternoon, I'd made several starts at my door to tell Elena about this meeting, wondering if I should warn her about his appearance so she could hide her alarm. In the end, I settled for telling her only to treat him as she would the most senior of my visitors, offering him a drink, and, if circumstances required him to wait, a chair. Circumstances would not, but I hoped the memory of my instructions would put her in a respectful frame of mind that would help her mask her surprise. Instead, she opened the door a hand's width, and her eyes fluttered in the way that they did when I pointed out errors in her work. She brushed her dry red hair aside. "He's here," she said.

Then she took a step backwards, and, as soon as Elliot had slipped into my office, quickly shut the door.

He took off his backpack and set it on the floor. When he straightened, instead of looking at me, he pretended to study the picture he had taken of the bluff that would become the right abutment of North Fork Dam. I had always imagined that at the time he had believed everything in the picture would be in focus; that he had meant just as much to capture me and my laughter in sharp detail as the vast space behind me. I stepped around my desk and took up a position at his side.

"That's one of my favorite photos," I said.

"Why?" He touched his glasses at the hinges, setting them back on his ears. Even in my peripheral vision their silver stems drew attention, they were so stark against his bare skin.

I said, "Because I don't know why you took it."

"I don't either."

"That's okay," I said.

In consideration of this mystery, a stillness came over both of us, and without looking I knew that his jaw had relaxed slightly in the way that it did in the dark of a cinema, or on our reading sofa in the moment before he fell fully asleep. We searched the photo for clues: the sliver of sky to the left of the bluff; the blurry green cloud of sagebrush around my boots. In the lower corner his cap lay where it had blown as he framed the shot.

He said, "I showed you that beetle just before."

"I remember."

"You were out of breath from climbing up the hill."

Neither of us moved. For a moment, I felt we could go home, that there was no closer I could be to my son, that this ease would surely cast its warmth on every small choice he made in the future. But then the vent above us breathed a sudden mouthful of cool air, and my son started, his bare scalp feeling it like a touch.

He adjusted his glasses. "For the record, I don't think Elena likes it either."

"Likes what?"

"My hairstyle."

"I'm not sure I like hers."

He laughed in spite of himself. But he recovered his air of persecution quickly. "I'll grow it back if it's embarrassing you."

"Nonsense. I think it's very bold."

"I know you wish you'd brought me here before I cut it."

"I wish nothing of the sort."

"Then why are we hanging out in your office with the door closed?"

"You just got here," I said. "But by all means, let's go out and meet some of my friends."

There were half-a-dozen engineers closer at hand, but I wanted to begin with someone I was sure would hide his surprise at Elliot's baldness. I'd given it some thought. At a Department picnic one summer, I'd watched Ken Gonzales tie and retie the sash on his daughter's sundress, patiently accepting her counsel on the size of the bow. His door was closed, but when he saw me through the glass, he waved me in.

I said, "I want you to meet my son, Elliot."

Elliot stepped through the door, and Ken's eyes widened slightly, but he stood and extended a hand across his desk. "You go to Del Campo?"

"Yes, sir."

"My son's at Foothill. On the soccer team. You play soccer?"

"No."

He had clearly been hoping for a yes, but he made something of it anyway. "That's good, I guess. I hate to think of you kicking each other in the shins."

I laughed in the polite way that expresses more gratitude than amusement, and Elliot did too. Ken's laughter was halting, as if between intervals he was trying to think of a new topic. I was about to relieve him by telling Elliot I wanted him to meet David Shoots, when I heard Belsky's voice behind us.

"Well, well. And who might this be?"

I turned no more than was necessary to answer his question. "This is my son, Elliot."

Belsky took a step backwards and placed his hands on his hips in a pose of taking stock. It was an obvious prelude to comment on Elliot's appearance, but no sooner had he assumed it than the expression on his face changed. I think the possibility of illness had occurred to him. Still, the impulse to say something mocking had already risen, and he needed to satisfy it. "Albright Junior," he said. "So how does it feel to have your dad named a threat to the people of Sacramento?"

"What?"

"Public Enemy Number One. His big dam's being investigated."

Elliot cut a quick glance in my direction. "Fine."

"Is that on the record or off?" He punched Elliot playfully in the arm, harder than I would have liked.

Ken said, "Those investigations are no big deal. Routine. Red tape."

Elliot said, "Benign distraction."

"Benign distraction!" Belsky slapped his stomach. "A regular chip off the old Albright block!"

I laughed. "My wife calls us the twins."

"I can see why," said Ken.

"Except for the hair." Belsky said this with the wide-eyed self-congratulation that he wore when he made any of his jabs, but immediately it froze there. It's hard to describe, but truly, looking at Elliot recalled some deep store of poster images of young chemotherapy patients, and I think this echo signal of fragility and menace registered even on a radar as weak as Belsky's. But to my surprise, in the awkward silence, Elliot began to laugh. I've thought about it many times since then, and in memory it still seems as it did at that moment: genuine laughter, the most comfort he had shown since his arrival. It relaxed Belsky's brief spasm of sensitivity; he reached out and punched my son in the arm again, and, this time, without hesitation, Elliot punched him back.

"Yes," I said. "He's hipper than I am."

"Right," Ken said, winking at Elliot. "Your dad's a little square."

"We should get away from him sometime then," Belsky said. "Your dad's always turning me down; maybe you'd be up for some fun."

"Sure," he said.

The forced casualness of his tone betrayed so much vulnerability even Belsky was moved by it. He had just been baiting me, but now he glanced at me and then back at Elliot. "Uh, you water-ski?"

"Not much," Elliot said. He had never water-skied in his life.

"I just bought a ski boat for Folsom Lake. I've got a kid about your age; maybe I'll teach you to slalom sometime. If your dad doesn't mind."

Elliot looked at me hopefully.

"Of course not," I said.

I took him down the hall to David's office and then introduced him to a few Senior Engineers, but with each brief encounter he grew more withdrawn, and finally I clapped my hands together and suggested we get a drink at a place where I sometimes bumped into senior officials from our Department—even politicians he'd recognize from the local news. On the short walk past the capitol, I told him about an article I'd read about a woman who had killed a pedestrian not far from there by trying to eat a bowl of cold breakfast flakes while driving herself to work, but his eyes strayed first to a flag luffing high on a rooftop, and next to a crow pecking at a cellophane wrapper, and I couldn't escape the feeling that he was tuning me out completely. At our table, I ordered a scotch and soda and Elliot ordered a root beer, and when the waiter turned his back on us, I felt a ridiculous wave of panic at the loss of his company. In the dim glow, my son's baldness had a different quality. He looked not sick, but old. He took the fingers on one hand with the other and gave each a brief squeeze, index to pinky, and then began the sequence again. I had seen him do this when another teenager asked him about his favorite bands. Liz tried to assure me that his discomfort around kids his own age was natural for an only child. He had access to an environment free of conflict and judgment and competitive hostility. When I heard her describe this, I couldn't help but wonder why anyone would ever choose to leave it, and now I found myself marveling that it was those very guarantees of love and acceptance that seemed to make him suspicious. I felt both an urge to delay our conversation and the need to hurry, and the distance between us made me long for an ambassador's assistance from Liz.

I said, "I brought your mother to this bar on our second date. She ordered a boilermaker."

He looked up at me. I'm not sure I can describe the physical details that make up that rare quality of attention one occasionally invites from others. Maybe his angle of incline towards me increased by a degree. Or his eyes, often focused on mine, opened just a millimeter wider. Something charged entered the air between us that was at once a reward and a threat. "What did you have?" he said.

"A ginger ale."

"Why only a ginger ale?"

"I was driving home later," I said, but it wasn't enough. He waited for me to explain, and suddenly the truth occurred to me. "I wanted to appear responsible."

Even on our second date, it had been clear to me that Liz had been drawn to me by my uneasy caution—that she'd felt empowered by the notion that a certain reserve and numbness to pleasures were hers to cure.

The waiter set down our drinks. Elliot stirred his root beer. The room around us seemed still and dark, other conversations quiet. He said, "Didn't you ever do anything crazy?"

"Like what?"

"I don't know. Just . . . anything. Something kind of wild."

I looked up at the chandelier and pretended to be thinking. It had false candles topped by twenty-five watt bulbs with orange glass to cast a flamelike light. It hadn't been dusted in a long time.

He said, "Like did you ever get in any fights?"

"Your mom and I?"

"No. Fistfights. With kids from school."

I regarded him. If this had been a problem, surely we would have known it by then—seen blood on his clothes, some bruises—but still my pulse quickened. In the dark of the bar, the lower rims of his glasses cast shadows above his cheekbones, making him look tired.

"I never did, no. But I came pretty close. A boy in the class below mine challenged me to a fight."

"What did you do?"

"I considered skipping school that day, and in the end, although I wasn't the type to cut classes, I did. I went to the public library and checked out a book on boxing. It showed men in various stances. I decided the uppercut would serve me well, but at that point I still wasn't sure I would actually go. Finally, I arrived at the fight scene early. I had a vague idea that familiarity with the spot would give me an advantage. Also, that the sooner I got there, the less time I would have to decide not to go. A sort of forced commitment."

Elliot hadn't moved since I started. I took a sip of my scotch.

"What happened?" he said.

"He never showed up."

"He chickened out?"

"I don't think so. He was much bigger than I was. I've always thought it was more likely that he forgot."

He nodded.

I said, "Or double-booked."

He laughed, but in that complicated way he had in front of me now—the ease so quickly checked by self-consciousness. In the after-quiet, I was tempted to ask him outright if he'd been fighting, but through what felt then like a sensible discipline I let the silence stand. He picked up his root beer and took a sip. Then he said, "How come you checked out a book?"

"I wanted to imagine what the fight would be like. And I think I also hoped it would prepare me, but I guess that's a little like training for a marathon by watching one."

"It probably would have helped a little."

"Maybe."

He stirred his drink. "Why didn't you ask someone to teach you?"

"I didn't run with a very rough crowd."

"You could have asked your dad."

I said, "Until just before I went to the school yard to wait, I wasn't even sure I planned to fight."

The period of regular interviews for his paper was over. He had handed in his outline and was writing his rough draft now, but of course his interest had not faded.

"Did you even tell him about it?"

"Who?" I said, although of course I knew what he meant.

"Your dad."

His eyes were still on me. The fact was I didn't tell my father, but it was clear to me that Elliot was searching for a new model of conduct to fit his changing circumstances, and to him this might have suggested that distance between a father and son is normal, when the truth is even now I sometimes wake from dreams in which I have told my own father my secrets: about that dog I watched die; or the way, when he entered rooms, I came to expect disappointment.

I said, "No, but I can't remember why."

After several seconds during which I feared he might press further, his eyes strayed to a group of men laughing across the room, and the charged quality left the table between us. I recognized one of them as a former coworker named Nathan. He had been at the Department before me, and when I arrived, he had taken me under his wing without seeming to notice the chasm of incompatibility in our personalities. He took me out to lunch at a bar called the Pine Cone where people sat at large common tables, and each time, before long, I found myself making jokes with men I had never met about my own small daily frustrations and getting swept away by the surges of clear-hearted ebullience that filled them all when they watched a home run on the tiny bar screen. We never saw each other outside the workday, and I suspect even back then if asked to list them, he might not have thought to count me among his friends, but the weird truth is that that was the closest I think I have ever been to another man. It didn't last long though. Shortly after Belsky arrived, Nathan began asking him along too, and something about Belsky's company—his aggressive humor, or his finger-licking, or his complaints about his wife and children—stripped the lunches of ease and pleasure for me. It wasn't any kind of principled decision on my part, but I found I started joining Nathan less frequently, until, after a while, I never went at all.

I said, "That one in the purple tie used to work with me." I uncrossed my legs and recrossed them. "His name is Nathan Sattler. He was passed up for promotion, and he threw a stapler at the wall."

This was the type of thing I normally would have kept to myself, but it brought Elliot out of his trance. He set the straw in his glass and sat up straight. He said, "Did he deserve the job?"

"I think so. Yes."

"Why didn't he get it?"

"He has a bad temper."

He thought about this. "What happened?"

"He was born that way, I guess."

He smirked. "I mean when he threw the stapler."

"Oh. Nothing right away. Later that year he was offered a transfer to an office down south."

"So what's he doing here?"

"He didn't take it. He quit to start a consulting firm."

Within a year he had earned a strong enough reputation to win a small job that had also been bid by Bechtel. Elliot glanced at the men again. Nathan was turned in such a way that he would not see us, and suddenly the contemplation of his success made me grateful for this. He was gesturing wildly, the way he used to in meetings just before he made a point of surprising insight. There was no mistaking these windmilling motions. In meetings they had made me feel superior, but in my son's company they made me feel self-conscious. I took a sip of my drink. The waiter placed a dish of peanuts on the polished wood table. Elliot asked for another root beer, and when the waiter left, he rotated the ice cubes in his empty glass with his cherry.

"Dad?"

"Yes."

"Can I ask you a question?"

"Of course. You can ask me anything."

He looked up at me now. "Did what that guy at your office said make you uncomfortable?"

"Not at all."

"Not even a little bit?"

I leaned forward in my chair. I set my drink on the quilted paper coaster. The opportunity I had been waiting for had come, and I wanted his full attention. "Elliot, I think you're wonderful. I've always thought that. Whenever you make a new choice for yourself, I respect it."

"Not about my haircut," he said. "About your dam."

It took me several seconds to even imagine what he meant. "Why would it make me uncomfortable?"

"Because they're saying there's something wrong with your design."

"They're saying they have more information now than when I designed it."

"Doesn't it bug you even a little bit?"

"Doesn't what bug me?"

He squeezed his eyes shut and shook his head slightly, as if the very sight of me were hard to accept. When he opened them, he was squinting with disgust. "The suggestion that you could have screwed up, Dad. That with all your training and experience you could have spent six years building something that big and that expensive in a way that threatens the safety of tens of thousands of people."

It was difficult, at times, to keep his vulnerability firmly in mind. It was clear to me even then that he knew enough about science to understand that a determination of structural deficiency based on data unavailable during design did not indicate an error of expertise or attention on the part of an engineer. Yet, for reasons I could not yet fully fathom, he wanted to pretend that he did not. Behind him, Nathan's party rose, laughing, to leave the bar, and at the sharp bark of this, Elliot did not even turn his head. He was focused on me, with that special attention, and then, quite suddenly, on a spot on the table I could not trace.

I said, "If they doubted my competence, Elliot, they wouldn't have given me the geothermal project. They wouldn't have just relocated me to the best view corner in the building."

But his eyes did not rise, and I had the impression that my voice came to him from a great distance. The false flames of the chandelier were a blur above us. Everything in the room seemed faint next to the glow from his inclined head. He stayed this way a long time, until the waiter came back with his root beer. Then he looked up, and I told him I didn't want to make Liz wait with our dinner. He took a few sips as I counted out the bills from my wallet, and then we left the lobby for home.

OUR BEDROOM CLOSET WAS SPLIT DOWN THE CENTER BY A floor-to-ceiling unit of shelves, a feature I had designed to achieve more shelf space without realizing what a strangeness it would introduce into our undressing. We always ended up on either side of this, enjoying a privacy we did not need. When Liz finally asked me how my drink with our son had gone, she was hidden behind these shelves.

I said, "We went to the lobby of the Capitol Hotel. I told him you'd ordered a boilermaker on our first date there. He liked that."

"How on earth do you remember that?"

"You wore a spangled halter top."

She laughed.

"I didn't mention that part."

She laughed again, invisible. I tried to picture her. In her bra and jeans. Or her blouse and underpants. Barefoot. Blinking at the shelves. She had made sloppy joes and milk shakes for dinner, and when we sat down she had initiated a game in which each of us quoted lines from movies and the others tried to guess their sources. Both of them were good at this, their memories filled with the words of fictional people I could not even remember having seen, and my inability to offer any material or identify even one of the lines they repeated was the subject of a lot of joking. His laughter seemed a magic trick, and my mind returned to that moment when Belsky had called attention to his hair, but I forced it away. In the car on the way home from the bar, he had been quiet, and I had taken the opportunity to try to think through how I would share what had passed between us with Liz. Now I heard the wicker of our laundry hamper flex, and she stepped around the shelves: PTA T-shirt and underpants.

"So??" she said.

"So what?"

She rolled her eyes. "What did you talk about?"

"Different things."

"Such as?"

I knew something important hung in the balance, but the thought of telling her how contemptuously he had challenged me filled me with panic. It seemed to me that Elliot's happiness had been her main consolation in our marriage, and each new twist of his behavior was persuading me that the responsibility for his teenage angst was mine.

I shrugged. "Such as what you ordered on our second date. Such as a guy in the bar I used to know."

Her shoulders fell. "Do you feel better at least?"

"About what?" I said, although of course I knew what she meant.

She closed her eyes. Even then, I felt sorry for her. When she opened them, she reached up and took my face in her hands and stood on her toes to kiss me on the forehead. "How was work today then?"

"Good."

"Any pissing from Belsky?"

"I didn't see him much."

"That must have been nice," she said, and she turned away to pick up her jeans. As she stuffed them in the hamper, I wondered if she might be fighting back tears, but she did not let me see her face again until we got into bed. For the first time in our marriage except during a war or a natural disaster, she turned on our bedroom TV, and I watched with her aimlessly—the end of *Fantasy Island,* the eleven o'clock news, Johnny Carson's monologue—stealing looks at her face in the flickering glow until she drifted off to sleep.

After our wedding we had moved her things from her parents' house into my apartment in the bed of my green Ford for a life I saw now as very different from the one she'd wanted. At first, my hesitation to have children had seemed almost to please her—as if my relief at her patience and understanding were their own reward. With every blockade to intimacy, my fears and inhibitions were making of her marriage a more challenging and noble occupation, but her fantasy of tumbling the high walls of my hesitation did not last. I can count the harsh expressions of disappointment she made during our marriage on one hand, and in every case they came during the two years when I stalled and evaded her suggestions that we start a family. I had lain awake many nights worrying silently that I might lose her, until finally it dawned on me that despite all my fear about becoming a father, a child might at least distract her from her discontent. And so he had, but lying beside her now with the Tonight Show Band playing "Johnny's Theme," it struck me suddenly that it was not only Elliot's adolescent judgment I should fear, or his scrutiny, or even his loss, but also how his growing and leaving us alone together would resuscitate Liz's dissatisfaction with me.

This is all I have to explain the choice I made then. When the idea came to me, it seemed a gift—an obvious solution that would be as much of a salvation to her as it was a relief to me—but a more enlightened part of me was just frightened enough of its potential to make me hesitate. I turned the TV off, because it seemed to me the conversation would be easier to have without that flickering glow to illuminate our faces, and when I did, ghost colors swam before my eyes. In the sudden quiet, I could hear the soft click of her tongue that meant deep dreams. My heart was like a bird behind my ribs. I could not make myself touch her.

"Liz," I whispered.

Her breathing was steady.

I said it louder: "Liz."

She gasped and shifted, pulling the sheets. "What?"

"I have something to tell you."

"What?"

Everything seemed so still, suddenly.

She said, "What is it, sweetheart?"

I said, "I think this week you should go to the Crisis Center and sign up to be a counselor."

For a few seconds, she didn't say anything, but it was dark, so I couldn't see her face.

Then she said, "Why?"

"You've wanted to a long time. It's a noble impulse, and I think you'd be good at it."

"Why now, I mean?"

"Why not?"

Even in the dark, I knew the face and posture that went with the sigh she made. She said, "I mean why did you wake me up to tell me?"

Again the crazy beating. I said, "I was just thinking about what you said last week about Elliot leaving home soon. About leaving the nest . . ."

She waited.

"And about what you'll do when he's gone."

"Us," she said.

"What?"

"Not me, us."

I was too confused to even formulate a question.

Her voice was sharp in the dark. "I said, 'What will *we* do when he's gone?' I said, 'What will we *talk about?*'"

"Right. Sure," I said. "Us."

She waited. Not moving. There were no sounds at all in the house.

I was still blunt to the plain truths of my failings as a spouse, but something in the quality of her silence filled me with panic. I groped for words that would make the suggestion seem the tender encouragement I had hoped it could seem. "The point is, I think you enjoy helping people," I began. It wasn't until I'd heard myself say it out loud that it became clear how hurtful my explanation would be: "Volunteering would give you something to do."

4 The Roof

As we crossed the lawn, I found myself falling behind, a fugitive of his scrutiny and a spy. In the two months since our drink at the Capitol Hotel, he had grown his hair back, and it had come in differently than I remembered—darker, and also somehow finer. He opened the driver's-side door, and I walked around the tailgate and marveled at the strange turn of events that placed me here, my son's passenger in my own car. When Belsky had failed, as I knew he would, to follow up on his invitation to take Elliot water-skiing, for my son's sake I had asked him to make it real, and since then Elliot had spent afternoons at their house a dozen times. Belsky's eldest son, Tim, had his license and the keys to a 1974 Ford Pinto. This is how I found myself attempting to teach my son to drive.

In the night, a heavy fog had descended on our valley, and although it was clear now, the windows were still filmed with a fine mist of condensation. From inside the car, we couldn't see out in any direction. As he reached for the rearview mirror, I expected him to notice this, but his adjustment was quick, almost sloppy, and he put the key in the ignition and turned it. Then he laid his hand on the back of my seat as I had taught him to do, looked over his shoulder, and shifted the car into reverse.

Although I was usually able to restrain myself, I turned my head too. Three rivulets of water had drawn lines in the thick film of mist. Through them, I could see the green of our neighbor's front lawn and nothing more. We began to roll backwards, and I felt a pinch of heat beneath my arms.

Elliot braked abruptly and laughed. "Geez, Dad!"

He set the parking brake and got out, leaving his door open. A breeze filled the front seat. He pulled the arm of his sweatshirt over his hand and wiped the windows down with broad strokes, leaving a scalloped border of mist around their edges. When he got back in the car, he was still shaking his head. "Weren't you going to say anything?"

"I wasn't worried."

"I'm thinking, Here we go. I'm going. I'm backing up."

"I knew I was in good hands."

He laughed through his nose and released the brake. This kind of prank had been common since we had begun his driving lessons. He seemed to expect me to doubt his competence, and although he'd made me nervous more than once, I'd controlled the urge to warn him. When we reached the Catholic church parking lot where we had been practicing K-turns, there was a gardening truck directly behind us and a bicycle was making its way down the sidewalk towards the driveway, and Elliot turned into the lot without signaling. I was considering saying something about at least this when he said, "I've got one more question for you."

"What's that?"

He pulled into a spot by the rectory door. A rough draft of his biography paper was due the following week, and the truth is I was looking forward to the lull this might provide. I was glad he was learning to manage a long-term project, and his teacher had done her best to break it up by dividing the work into three six-week phases,

but his questions had not really subsided after he'd finished the outline of his research. In the last two months, I had sometimes wondered if the questions he asked were even for his paper. In fact, if I
am being honest, I sometimes had the temptation to telephone Mrs.
Parks on some pretext to learn whether the assignment had ever truly
been changed to require focus on an ancestor.

He threw an arm over the back of the bench seat, his hands inches
from my shoulder. It might have seemed affectionate, but his eyes
weren't looking at me. They were on the space behind him where any
driving instructor should want them to be.

He backed up slowly. "I need to know about a time when your dad
scared you," he said, and he braked and shifted into drive again.

The parking lot was empty. There was a church service program
stuck to the pavement by rain.

"Your teacher asked you to include this?"

"Yeah." He pulled forward.

"Every student is to include a segment on the frightening behavior of an ancestor?"

"That's right."

He shifted into reverse and backed into the space he'd left along
the hedge.

I said, "How did she phrase it? What exactly did she tell you
to do?"

"She said to make sure we got a full picture of the subject. We
should ask our primary sources about bad behavior as well as good
deeds."

He threw a hand over the seat again. I looked in the side mirror,
waiting for his reversal. When it didn't come, I turned to see that this
time he was in fact looking not at the space behind him, or the
stretch of asphalt ahead, but instead at me. The corners of his mouth
turned up.

I said, "I thought you were doing a K-turn."

"I did it already."

"Another one, I mean."

He coughed into his fist—a fake cough designed to relieve tension: mine. Then he said, "You don't have to answer now if you don't want to."

"No, no. It just seemed a little odd, is all."

"We can talk about it at dinner—"

"Let me just think a minute. . . ."

"Really, Dad. I'd rather have you come up with a good one than make up something lame or evasive on the fly."

And with that, he shifted into drive and carried me back onto the road.

When he was late for dinner that night, I was at first grateful, but after twenty minutes, I sat down at the kitchen table where through parted curtains I had a view of the cul-de-sac. I opened the newspaper. "Drought in Ethiopia." "Artificial Heart Still Pumping." It wasn't the first time in the last month he'd been late, and although this should have made it easier tonight, so far each time was just as difficult as the first. This was something elemental, I was beginning to see, to parenting an older child. Even at a distance of yards, each step away was a fresh shock.

For example, looking back, I am bewildered, even a little embarrassed, by my surprise when, just after Christmas, he had asked if he could move into the attic. The remodel had been his idea, he had worked hard on it, suggested the addition of a bathroom at the last minute, and he was a teenager whose small bedroom shared a wall with his parents' and opened onto a stairwell that carried even the faintest radio noise all the way to the kitchen. "I was thinking . . . ," he had said. "I mean, I already do my homework upstairs, and you and Mom don't really use it." I knew right away what he was going to say—was in fact already feeling stupid for not having anticipated it—and although immediately I saw that I would say yes, a tightness in my chest made me pretend for more than a minute to believe he merely meant he wanted to use some of the attic for storage.

When I finally conceded, I did not feel much, but I had imagined stalling would be possible in the logistics of it—the purchase of a different bed or the installation of a hanging rod in the closet for his shirts. As it turned out, he was happy to live a life split between rooms until these details were resolved. He kept his clothes downstairs and slept on the attic couch until his new bed was delivered, and I felt foolish as I watched the delivery men heft it up the stairs. A new bed was obviously not a necessity, but once I had used the suggestion to delay, I could hardly make this point. There were blinds for the dormer windows, which shone two bright squares on his bed at six A.M.; a low bureau that fit the height of the knee wall; new bedsheets. In the end, the move upstairs cost almost nine hundred dollars. Although on principle this probably should have formed some part of my hesitation, the fact is, it was something much simpler. My stomach felt light at the thought of him moving farther up the stairwells of my house, his footsteps mere taps above our bed and altogether traceless from the kitchen, as if this move were a late stage in the rising-and-vanishing that has been the cartoon representation of all the fears I was granted on the day he was born.

These late arrivals at dinner seemed another. Now they happened once, sometimes twice a week. I glanced at the window again and tried hard not to think of the kind of amused detachment with which he had regarded me during the driving lesson that morning. I read an article about the long preparations for *Challenger*'s maiden flight. Finally, finally, Belsky's old gray Pinto with the rusted fenders and the missing side mirror pulled into the cul-de-sac and jerked to a stop in front of our driveway. Elliot stepped out of the passenger side and laid a hand on the roof, talking. When he slammed the door, the car lurched away, and he walked towards the house across the lawn. He brought cool air in with him, and Liz turned on the flame beneath a frying pan.

"Sorry I'm late," he said.

"That's okay," Liz said. "Did you have fun?"

"Pretty much."

"Did he have any good new Atari games?"

"One, but we didn't really play it."

"What did you do?"

"Sat in the hot tub, mostly."

She cut a look at me and winked. Every week she had a new ex-planation for the hours he spent there: Joyce served junk food; Robert let them tinker with the engine on the beat-up Ford.

The hamburgers hissed as she set them in the pan. "That hot tub must make Tim's a great place to hang out."

"I guess." He pulled a spatula from a pitcher of spoons she kept on the counter and handed it to her. He had grown deft, almost overnight, at evasion. "How was work?"

"Great," she said. "They say I'm almost ready to take calls on my own."

Last month, she had begun training at the Crisis Center, just as I'd asked her to, and at the time I was still proud of myself for the boost it seemed to give her. Twice that month I had overheard her talking on the phone to one of her sisters, describing her trainer, or explaining the principles of "passive assistance," and although she still tried to engage me on the topic of Elliot's visits to Belsky's house, in general my deflections seemed less of a frustration to her. I was considering this, trying to focus with satisfaction on the way I had helped her, when the stack of plates on the counter began to rattle. Little jolts of movement beneath our legs. All three of us grabbed the lip of the counter. I am sure Liz would have stepped towards us to usher us to safety, but it did not last long enough. She turned off the heat beneath the pan, and we followed her into the living room.

Already there was a bright red icon in the upper-right-hand corner of the TV screen: AFTERSHOCK! The newscaster's lipstick was candy pink.

"What may have been an aftershock of the October earthquake . just struck the greater Sacramento area. We don't have details yet, but the flood of calls to our hotline suggests that the people of Sacra-mento are deeply concerned and ready to band together again as they did last fall." Then they ran a montage of clips from their coverage of

the earthquake: again the ten-car accident; again th
ing senselessly from the façade of the capitol buildin

"Oh, man," Elliot said.

Liz laughed. "Should we eat in here?"

And although I suppose I sensed even then that the sp
miliar ease in him would not last, briefly I was overcome by
gratitude for the trick of nature that had triggered it. On sc, ..i, a
broken window on a stagecoach in Old Sacramento. Liz and Elliot
laughed again.

"Yes, let's," I said. "But I think we're going to need some popcorn."

THERE IS SOME IRONY THEN THAT, WHEN I OPENED THE
kitchen door a few evenings later, I smelled sewer gas. My father and
I had encountered something like this only once, on a call to a row
house on Adeline Street. A heavy woman and four children waited on
the stoop beneath dripping icicles, and we could smell it through the
windows, which were open, before we even climbed the stairs.
Steam rose in a column beside her skirt where one of them had vom-
ited in the snow.

Initially, at least, all I felt was fear. Sewer gas is a noxious mixture
of methane, hydrogen sulfide, gasoline vapor, carbon monoxide,
acetylene, ammonia, hydrogen, carbon dioxide, nitrogen, and a little
oxygen. Ventilation is important, but methane, hydrogen, gasoline vapor, and acetylene are explosive in the presence of oxygen. Hydrogen
sulfide and carbon monoxide are poisonous. Hydrogen sulfide is also
corrosive. And standing at the threshold to my kitchen, what bothered me most was that sewer gas has a notoriously varied effect on
people. While some may work a lifetime in poorly ventilated sewers
without trouble, others have died shortly after descending too hastily
into a manhole.

When I reached the front hall, they were both standing there. Liz
had kicked off her shoes, a pair of pumps she sometimes wore to volunteer, her toes a smooth unit beneath her panty hose. A fine run

raveled up her leg from the heel. Elliot's forehead betrayed the barest trace of perspiration in its shine.

Liz said, "I picked up Ellie at the library. We haven't been here long."

I felt a breeze on my forehead, and the sheer underdrapes in the living room sucked out the window and waved like flags.

She said, "We opened all the windows."

Elliot said, "What happened, Dad?"

I made myself smile. "Let's find out," I said.

We started in the powder room, and this time I did the work myself, because I knew I couldn't feign patience if he was slow. He made himself of use. He put a baking pan under the pipe to catch the water that would slop out if the trap was full, and sitting on the threshold with the flashlight he did his best to shine a beam on my work. But I didn't really need it. When I swung the trap free, it was easy to see the pipe was empty. "Eureka," I said, but neither of us could make ourselves smile at this. I swung the pipe back into place and scanned hopefully around the floor of the cabinet for signs of leaking—at the little basket of colored guest soaps and the stack of white hand towels Liz stored there—as I tightened the nut. But there were none. I stood and turned the water on.

Fixture traps started appearing in American homes around the turn of the century; their proper functioning, by this time, is well understood. A little slug of water in a U of pipe will keep gases out of the house, and when a tap is shut off, gravity will make water settle in the U every time. Not much can get in the way of this. In Saudi Arabia or Death Valley, a plumber probably comes across some that evaporate, but even this only when a family leaves for a very long vacation. If a piece of floss runs down a drain and by luck gets beached on the high side of the trap when the water is shut off, it can draw the water slowly across the hump and leave it dry. But this is as unlikely as it sounds, and the evidence is there when you open the trap. A clog or crack can conceivably create a vacuum when you run a fixture somewhere else in the house, and this could suck a trap dry if the conditions are just right.

The primary offender, though, is installation error, and now that my fear of the potential danger had waned, I found it was replaced by a distressing suspicion that the culprit was the vent pipe Elliot had roughed-in in the attic. There was a long horizontal run behind the knee wall. If he hadn't used enough strap hangers to attach it, a plastic pipe might sag enough to collect a slug of rainwater during big storms. As I said, I had checked his work each day, but in my yearning to show respect for him I had often moved too quickly to approval, and I saw how easily I could have overlooked something like this. The work had been reviewed by an inspector as well, but the man the county sent had been an amateur gardener, and he gazed out the new opening at Liz's roses to ask me questions about the composition of our soil. He smelled of cinnamon gum and jiggled his keys in his pockets. His lack of focus had bothered me even then.

It might have saved me some time to suggest this possibility first, but at the thought of implying and investigating an error in Elliot's work, I had difficulty swallowing. We would have to move his bed away from the wall; take down the calendar with the girl in the green swimsuit; cut through the Sheetrock we had raised together with a block and tackle; pull back the insulation he had stapled to the studs. It has since become clear to me that I was guilty of a thick-headed obliviousness to most of Elliot's deepest needs, but at the time I still believed that respect for his privacy and competence were chief among them.

Instead, we spent the next half hour on tests. Elliot jogged down the hall and ran a faucet or flushed a toilet, and when he called to me from the landing, I lowered a screwdriver bit down the drain. Each time it came up glistening. "Still wet," I would say, and wipe it dry with a hand towel. When he came downstairs finally, he was panting.

"That's everything," he said.

"Did you run the tubs?"

"Yes."

"And then did you run the water through the shower heads as a separate test?"

"Yes."

"What about the attic?"

He nodded. This was enough said, for now. I moved quickly to the only other explanation I could think of.

I said, "It must have been simultaneous use, then."

He furrowed his brow.

I said, "You flushing a toilet while Mom was running the dishwasher, for example. If there's a crack or clog in the pipe, a combination of fixtures can siphon a trap too."

He set his glasses back on his ears. "So how will we figure it out?"

"We'll have to do a smoke test."

And before he could ask me what this was, Liz appeared in the hall with a glass of wine. "Dinner's ready," she said.

She was prepared. While we worked, she had closed all the windows, betraying an underestimation of the problem I could not bring myself to correct, and she had brought out the new slide projector and screen, along with four carousels from the history she'd spent the holidays organizing, sorting through paper bags and shoe boxes of old photos, eyeing negatives with a jeweler's loupe, and making long lists for the specialists at Ken's Cameras of the images she'd use to tell our story in slides. As we ate, she clicked through them: the frame of our house tied with balloons, the grandfather clock I had built, Liz pregnant and asleep on the sofa, Elliot's second birthday, a potluck celebrating my first promotion, Yosemite, and finally the three of us at the Grand Canyon, the one that made my heart swell. As each new image flashed up on the screen, she shared little memories, and soon so did we, and by the time we stood up, we were able to clear the table and do dishes and switch off lamps talking about what she had made us see, conjured magically from my gift of cowardice to eclipse the details of the plumbing problem.

But of course, for me, beneath the surface ease, it was always there. As she washed her face, she kept up a steady patter about the slides, but I was focused on the water swirling down the drain. It took only fifteen minutes for her to fall asleep, and as soon as she did,

I got up in the dark and crept downstairs to check. The trap was still full, but I couldn't help worrying about what might happen if either of them rose in the night and flushed a toilet. I tried to console myself that we were not in a densely populated neighborhood, so the concentration of gases in the city line was probably low, but, given the potential danger, this was an irresponsible line of thinking. I went to the keypad by our front door and deactivated our burglar alarm. I slid the powder room window open, stepped out into the hall, and closed the door. Then I went back upstairs and sat down at the desk in my study and looked out over our lawn.

In my twenty years living there, I had heard of only two burglaries in our neighborhood, but this did not really make me feel any better. When I was five, at my mother's insistence, my father had installed iron safety grates on all our windows in Trenton. These were hinged, and could be opened, but we always kept them locked, and as I fell asleep, at first I found them a comfort. I wasn't old enough to know then about the crime in our neighborhood, but what I did know was that before he installed them, my mother would come to check and recheck the latch on my window as soon as she thought I'd fallen asleep, and afterwards she did not. It was the waning of her fear that calmed me. She was not an openly emotional woman—her eyes didn't well up when I painted her a picture, and she didn't yell when I tracked mud on the floor—but the full, violent force of her maternal love could be glimpsed in her irrational obsession with my safety. She wore a pair of nursing gloves in the kitchen when she was sick. She held a hand to her chin when I pumped high on the swings at the Veterans Park playground. And when I went to stay the night at other boys' houses, she called their mothers to ask a list of pointed questions: whether they kept their doors locked at night, whether they heated their house with a woodstove, and whether they kept a gun in the house.

In my earliest memories my father was sympathetic, even delicate with these worries. He did not protest when she insisted on the security grates, although it hurt his sense of aesthetics to install them. He liked to whittle in the evenings—toy soldiers for me, mostly—and although I sat close to him while he worked and pestered him with requests to let me handle the knife, each time, he would slide his eyes towards my mother to read the look she gave him and then tell me it wasn't time.

It may in fact be the first sign of the changes that would come over him later that when I was nine, he sat me down at the kitchen table and gave me my own knife. I looked immediately to my mother when he did this, and although she did not say anything, there was something—a whiteness in her skin tone, or a stillness in her posture maybe—that made me sure he had not discussed this with her. I suppose it is a measure of just how much she trusted and loved him that she didn't object. Her breath caught when I stood on a stool to get a cup from the cupboard, but she said nothing each night when my father took my whittling knife from his dresser and handed it to me over the kitchen table. Even after my second accident, she did not question his choice. Blood seeped out of my thumb in time with my heart, and she made a businesslike bandage of gauze and tape because the precut adhesive variety were more than we could afford. Then she served us some chicken.

Even back then, I recognized the half hour when I whittled with my father as a violation of the natural order of things in our house. All predictability of behavior was suspended, and as much as I loved the knife, and the attention from my father, and the challenge of the whittling, the strangeness of these lapses was painful. My mother's fear had always been a burden to me on the playground, but I found its absence was much more unsettling. I spent most of the time as I worked the knife trying hard to imagine what she was thinking, and I think each cut I suffered can be attributed to the distraction of this. Looking at the grates on my windows as I tried to sleep, I would try to reconcile these contradictions, and I would fall asleep trying to see the world through my mother's eyes.

Now in my study looking out at my cul-de-sac, I think some of the sensitivity I felt to the open window below me was hers. My eyelids grew heavy, but I felt a buzzing at the top of my head and looked out my window at the three-quarter moon. Finally, I went downstairs to the kitchen and took three cans of tomatoes from the cupboard and stacked them outside the closed powder room door. It made me feel better, but seemed somehow embarrassing, and so upstairs I groped quietly for my travel alarm clock in the closet and set it for five o'clock. I slept fitfully, thinking of prowlers, waking to every sound, and trying not to lose heart at the thought that Liz noticed this and pretended that she was still asleep. I tried to remind myself that they had preoccupations of their own. Elliot had been working in his room each afternoon, hunting and pecking out the long rough draft of his paper on my father, and other days driving, I guessed, on back roads with Tim Belsky in a car that engine-work had made seem his own, and Liz had finished her training and begun answering calls at the Crisis Center. At breakfast she filled the air with stories of this—a man who had not left his trailer in a week; a girl with a handful of purple pills—and Elliot flipped through his *Road & Track* so that I could almost imagine they were not thinking about how the house I had built had filled with poisons while they were at home alone.

I forced myself to endure a normal morning at work, but at lunch, I drove to Briggs Plumbing Supply. Through the window glass, I saw Larry's wife sitting behind the counter watching her TV. The show held her so rapt that she did not notice me there, less then seven feet from her, staring. On the counter next to her was a small box of fruit punch and half a cheese danish on a paper plate spotted with oil. When I came through the door, she looked up. "Back for more Drano?" she said.

"I'd like to rent a smoke pump."

She picked up her box of punch and took a sip through its tiny straw. "What for?" she said.

I can still recall the mixture of ire and disorientation she stirred in me. Larry had worn an apron and kept a bottle of glass cleaner behind the counter. I wondered what had drawn him to her.

"Something I'd like to check with a smoke pump," I said.

She smiled a little and shook her head. Then she slid off her stool and disappeared through a narrow doorway into the storeroom.

Next to the cash register lay a strip of paper from a fortune cookie and a gray button on a piece of broken thread. Behind the stool sat a pair of running shoes and socks shaped by recent wear.

When she reappeared she had a box of bombs and a device that looked like a hair dryer. "If you're such a big do-it-yourselfer, you should consider buying one of these," she said.

"Thanks, but I think I'll just rent."

She started ringing it up. "I just helped the last of my three boys pass his licensing exam. The book says on average homeowners who do some of the repairs themselves end up paying for twice as many service calls from licensed plumbers." She paused over the keys and looked at me. "My point is, you could have a lot of work cut out for you that calls for a smoke pump."

"I'll just rent," I said, and handed her my credit card.

She shrugged and then held the card with two hands and examined it. Her fingernails were pink, but the polish was chipped. "Luther Albright, eh?" she said.

I didn't say anything.

She looked up at me. "So what do you do if you're not a plumber?"

She picked up her juice box and took another sip. It was annoying, but it seemed peevish not to answer her question.

I said, "I'm a civil engineer."

She stared at me blankly. She was holding me hostage again, asking me questions instead of ringing me up. I said, "I design dams."

She grinned. She was clearly waiting for me to ask what was funny about this, but for some reason it felt critically important not to. My resistance didn't seem to bother her in the slightest. She said, "You're going to need a lot of Drano for a clog like that." Then she turned and ran the credit card through the template.

When she handed me the slip, she held it down for me with those chipped fingernails. It would again have seemed absurdly testy to pull the slip out from under them and hold it for myself, but that is what I wanted to do. Instead, I signed it quickly and she picked it up to separate the copies. She held one out for me, but not very far, so that I had to reach for it.

"Bye-bye, Luther Albright," she said.

Then she turned back to her TV.

It seemed right to me to ask Elliot to administer the test. Somehow I was already certain the path of this problem would lead us to examining his work in the attic, and I felt any respect for his abilities I could demonstrate along the way would counterbalance this. So it was that I found myself crouched in the grass beside him again, checking for signs of decay in my house.

When he lit the first bomb, the air filled with a singed smell and he set it inside the cleanout. Then he switched on the pump, which was loud, like a hair dryer, and fit the nozzle inside the pipe behind the bomb.

"What next?" he said.

"We have to wait at least ten minutes for the smoke to fill the pipes. If there's a crack, the smoke will work its way into the walls and out into the room around the switch plates and doorjambs."

"And if there's not?"

"We won't see any smoke inside the house."

"Where will it come out?"

"The vent stack. On the roof."

He looked up to indicate his bet. I ignored this.

I said, "I think I'll go inside and have a bite to eat while we wait."

He made no move to join me, and I didn't try to lure him. Alone in the kitchen, I took a mason jar of mixed nuts from the windowsill and sat down at the table facing a wall, hoping to see the smoke that would reveal a freak cause. The summer I worked for my father he had gone to a convention in Atlantic City, and he came back with plumbing mysteries of various kinds. For trap-seal loss, there was the story of a squirrel that had crawled down the vent stack and could not turn around to escape. As he struggled over the next few days, his body position from time to time occluded the passage completely, causing siphoning in one or more fixtures. The problem was not diagnosed until, after several days of struggle, the squirrel died and produced a smell distinct from the sewage stench the trap-seal loss had caused.

Although he must have known from the way I pored over my plumbing manual that I would have been interested in this story, it was days before he got around to telling it. When he first returned from the trip, all he seemed to want to talk about was what the attendees had done with their evening hours. There had been a show, apparently, with dancers who wore very little but sequined body stockings and feathers like exotic birds, and my father had a picture of himself with one of these dancers. My mother laughed when she saw the photo, not in a mean-spirited way, but as if she thought that was what had been intended, and her laughter seemed to make my father angry. "That's good, Lucille," he said. "Most of the wives don't see it that way. They'd be afraid their husbands would run off with dancers." Then he slipped the photo into the frame of a mirror that hung in our living room where it still sat, curling at its free edge, when I went home years later for his funeral.

It was a posed picture, clearly the kind of thing men stand in line to get, and that performers offer grudgingly, checking a clock between shots to see how soon they'll be free to enjoy themselves, but when he'd first shown it to us I was too young to know this, and it seemed a remarkable thing. In my early boyhood, my father had been devoted to my mother. Like Belsky, he had never bothered to hide his appreciation of other women's looks, but it was a clear escalation of this self-indulgence to hint at the possibility of infidelity. And if anything could be more selfish than joking about lust in front of your wife, it would be allowing your adolescent son, who is no doubt wrestling with such urges for the first time himself, to witness this same hint of how destructive they can be.

But I was allowing myself to become distracted. This was happening more often as Elliot typed out his draft, and each time it seemed a weakening of my resolution to keep such stories to myself. I put the jar of nuts back on the windowsill and got up and wandered the house, scanning for plumes of smoke. Basement, front hall, laundry room, up the stairs into our bedroom, our closet, our bath. Warring impulses had kept Liz from transforming Elliot's old bedroom completely. It was tidy, and the drawers had been cleared for guests, but it still had his old bedspread, and a poster of cars through the decades on the wall. I headed upstairs and braced myself for a familiar feeling of dislocation. More and more, his new room in the attic was striking me upon my rare visits as a foreign land. Ticket stubs from an Oakland Raiders game. Soda cans from a drink called Squirt. There was the swimsuit calendar on the wall that I remembered, but now there were dirty dishes that seemed unlike him to leave out, and, even more conspicuous, through the open doorway of the bathroom he had built, hanging over the shower curtain rod, a pair of girl's underpants.

I should say in defense of my insight that I knew right away that he intended I see these, but it seemed to me that the response he was testing for was some expression of distrust, or disrespect, or paternal misunderstanding of the adult he was becoming and the privacy that he felt should be his right. I imagined what my own father would have done, which was to say something crude that at once showed a galling assumption on his part that he understood what I wanted from intimacy with a girl, and that also belittled whatever more complex relationship the presence of her underwear implied; this, or quick outrage at the sneaking around that was only one possible explanation for how they'd made their way into my room. Now, standing in Elliot's bathroom, to my utter surprise I felt the easy rise of these same assumptions and this outrage, and it was partly due to shame at this unexpected kinship with my father that I decided I would not comment on the underpants at all.

The window behind them was wide open, and I knew this was for my benefit as well. When I leaned out to look up the roofline, smoke was streaming out the vent pipe and Elliot sat next to the chimney, eating an apple.

The dormers sit about four feet above the eave and the roof rises at an angle of thirty-five degrees. Unless it's raining, it is not unreasonably treacherous to climb out the window, but somehow it was something it had never occurred to me that he might do. In addition to the distraction of the panties, it may in part have been embarrassment about my nervousness at seeing him in so vulnerable a place that made me act as if there was nothing unusual about his location, but I see now that this was probably a letdown as well. I climbed out after him as if I myself had done it before, keeping a hand on the eave of the dormer as I worked my way up to the ridge and settled next to him on the damp shingles. When I did, Elliot wrapped his napkin around the apple core and crumpled it. He pulled his two hands back just above his right shoulder like a basketball player and held it there a moment. Then he pushed up and cocked his wrist to release it, and it disappeared down the chimney.

It was a strange thing to have done, disrespectful and provocative and too-unimportant-to-be-upset-about all at once, and I decided right away I would say nothing about this either.

Our neighbor was trying to start the mower in his yard. One pull. Two pulls. Three. It was a relief, finally, hearing the motor whine.

"So what do you think?" Elliot said.

It may have been my imagination, but it seemed to me that recently he had asked a lot of questions that could be interpreted in any number of ways: some dice-throw kind of effort to see what I might reveal. Although it was very likely he was talking about the cause of the trap loss, and not the underpants or the apple core, I didn't take this for granted.

"What do *you* think?" I said.

"Design flaw maybe." His tone was innocent, but I had difficulty believing he was not aware of the slight embedded in his guess. I waited a second before responding so I could keep the trace of irritation from my voice.

"Could be. It probably would have caused more than one failure in all these years though."

"What then?"

Immediately, I pictured him working alone in the attic, bare-chested and bobbing to angry music, fitting the vent to the studs behind his wall. I pictured this, and then I told him the story about the squirrel.

He furrowed his brow. "You think there's a squirrel in there?"

"No, no." We rarely saw squirrels in our neighborhood. "I'm just saying weird things can happen."

"So what do you think caused it?"

He was squinting now, his jaw set in an expression of disdainful mock confusion. It would have been easy, and I'm ashamed to admit, sort of satisfying, to wipe the look from his face by pointing out that by far the most likely cause was his own adolescent sloppiness. But in a feat of paternal empathy I would briefly count among my greatest, I said: "A temporary clog."

"But we didn't see anything backing up."

"It may have cleared spontaneously on its own after it siphoned the trap."

"So what are you going to do?"

"Wait and see if it happens again."

"I thought you said it was dangerous."

"It is. It can be. We're going to keep all the windows open until we've diagnosed it."

He regarded me and held my gaze as if to break it—thirty seconds; sixty. Then he laughed through his nose. "You're not even going to ask me about it, are you?"

"About what?" I said.

"The girl's underwear in my bathroom."

I paused. I have since thought of a few better answers to this, like "I trust you," or "You're old enough to make your own choices," but at the time what came to me was, "Not unless you want to talk to me about it, no."

As we spoke, he'd been watching the smoke stream from the vent, and when I said this, he did an amazing thing. With both hands gripping the chimney crown, he stood and then leapt around it in the air.

The fraction of time for which he hovered there, grounded only by his hands, was a long one, and the sound that came out of me was most similar to the bark of a small dog. I scrambled to the chimney and stood to reach out for him, and when he landed on the other side, his bare feet straddling the ridge cap, I was gripping his shoulders with whitened fingers. Our faces were so close that when he began, suddenly, to laugh, his breath was hot against my lips. I pulled him towards me, and he stepped cooperatively around the chimney.

We sat down and looked out over our neighborhood. I had to catch my breath. I raised my arms discreetly to let the breeze cool the damp part of my shirt. On the steaming surface of a swimming pool a neighbor kept hot year-round, the head of a pale bird dog bobbed earnestly after two children on a rubber raft. They called to it as they paddled away, goading it along. It went on this way, the dog paddling after until the children reached a wall at the deep end of the pool and pulled the raft out of the water. The dog scrambled against the wall, and the larger of the two children tugged on its collar until, in some way, their end was met, and they collapsed on the chilly lawn at the patio's edge, grasping their thick towels around them. For a moment, I could not take my eyes from their rest. Something about it. Their bodies would leave sweet imprints in the grass.

"Well," I said finally.

"Should we go inside?" he said.

"I think so."

We turned towards the dormer, and he motioned me to go first. As I crouched to ease myself towards the window, he laughed again and touched my shoulder, and I turned to catch the look on his face.

He smiled at me. "I've never seen you do that before."

"What would that be?" I said.

"Yelp."

THAT NIGHT, LIZ SAT UP IN BED, LOOKING THROUGH ELLIOT'S high school face book and watching the local news. The aftershock had resuscitated all of the most absurd of the producers' ideas: interviews with insurance underwriters, demonstrations of earthquake safety products. I stood beside the bed and looked down at the page of children's faces. Elliot's photograph was slightly blurry, as if he had noticed something off camera at the last moment, his eyes sliding to the right.

She said, "It sounded like he had fun today."

"It did," I said.

He had come home late again that night, this time with grass stains on his shirt from a game of touch football in their yard. Through questions about the rules and how teams had been chosen, she had drawn it out of him quickly: Belsky himself had not played.

She turned a page of the face book, but she glanced at me again, waiting, I suspected, for me to ask about the pictures she was seeking: Peggy maybe, or Tim. In the last month, her manner of interacting with me had changed. She had fewer questions, and although most of the time I believed that this was because she was finding the fulfillment I'd intended for her with more willing patients, a part of me worried that her conversational pauses and lingering gazes were "passive assistance" techniques she'd learned at the Crisis Center. The idea annoyed me, and this feeling towards her was so unfamiliar that each time it surfaced, I tried to dismiss it. But the next time our talk strayed to any topic that had preoccupied me, I found I could not shake the idea that I was the secret object of her eager, clinical pity.

Through the open windows, we heard a crash and clatter: our neighbor hefting a sack of garbage into the metal can by his garage, the sound as clear as if I were holding the lid open for him. He coughed. He inhaled sharply. In his room, through his own open windows, I thought, Elliot could hear this as well.

Liz said, "He really seems to get something out of his time at Tim's house."

She looked at me, and here I was meant, I could see, to ask what she thought that might be. So I did.

She said, "More kids. A hot tub." She smiled. "The unfamiliar spectacle of parents fighting with each other."

And I touched her hair in answer so she would not say more to comfort me.

I stepped into our closet to change for bed. Half of our hanging clothes were left open to the air, but I had enclosed a section at either end in a redwood cabinet lined with cedar to protect them from moths. We kept these cabinets closed, but the hot, dry smell of these panels still escaped them. It was a refreshing, but somehow tiring smell—one I savored when I entered but was always glad to leave. When Liz was pregnant with Elliot, she was sick in the evenings and said the smell of cedar settled her stomach. One day I came home and found her asleep on the carpeted floor, her head between open cabinet doors, and that night I moved the thin mattress from our sleeper sofa into the closet. We slept there every night until her second trimester.

When I came out again, the reporter had turned the news back over to the anchorman, a tall man with dark hair parted whitely. All that week, the last two minutes of news had been devoted to aftershock effects, and today he told the story of a school in Citrus Heights where two acoustical tiles had loosened and dropped from ceiling to desktop. I could picture these tiles: white, formed of mineral fiber, too light to do anything but surprise, but still the solemn description of the incident. The camera panned slowly across the ceiling to the hole where the tiles had been.

"Ha," I said.

"More pseudo-calamity?" she said.

"Yes."

When I slipped into bed, her body did not shift or rise. I was a restless sleeper, and years ago I'd purchased separate twin bed mattresses we bound together with a king-sized sheet to mitigate the disturbance caused by my turning, but lately her stillness when I moved seemed freighted with meaning, a blunt symbol in a simple movie. When we made love now, she was more athletic—a kind of compensation—but she no longer whispered. She was watching the news now, but I saw that while I dressed she had turned the face book to a picture of Tim. He stood somehow closer to the camera than the other students, so that his head was larger than those above and below it on the page.

"There's also the driving," she said suddenly.

"What?"

"Reasons for Elliot hanging out there instead of here." She turned away from the TV screen to face me. "Riding around with Tim like that. Maybe he even lets Ellie drive."

I had thought of this too, of course. It was illegal for a learner's-permit holder to drive without an adult present, but I doubted this would matter to him.

I said, "I think he'll probably take his test next month."

"Do you think he'll be ready?"

"I do."

For my own driver's test, I had taken my father's service van to the DMV. He had not used it in months. My mother was with me, and after I got my license, I drove us along the turnpike all the way to the Lincoln Tunnel. Although the drive took more than an hour, she never once asked me where I was going or suggested we turn home. She was quiet next to me, but this wasn't strange. Instead, I had the impression that she was in fact hoping I would drive farther—that her fate was in my hands. At the same time, I knew that were I to speak aloud the possibility of driving far or missing dinner with him, she would tell me to turn around that instant. Our freedom seemed fragile, predicated on not speaking, and so I did not acknowledge the strangeness of the accumulation of missed exits, or of the growing Manhattan skyline as we went around bends in the turnpike. There was never at any point in the drive any real possibility of leaving, but in our silence, I felt our mutual desire for it, and the unspoken fantasy I was sure we shared was the closest we had ever come to discussing our disappointment. It made my chest light. Only the terror of passing the narrow underwater lanes of the tunnel with all the nervous twitches of a new driver could begin to dispel this. Then the stoplight on Dyer Avenue, the sudden stillness among honking horns and buildings taller than any I had ever seen; it was a splash of cold water for us both. My mother smoothed the lap of her skirt. "The end of the line," she said lightly; she smiled but could not look at me, and for this, it played like an epitaph for what we had just shared; "It's time to go home."

Liz shifted beneath her sheets, and her bare leg touched me. She smelled like soap. With the windows open, sound carried in the air above our yard to his room. It was an inhibition, but sadly it was not the only one.

"Will you want to go with him?" she said.

She meant to his driver's test. Suddenly I did want to, very much, but courtesy had begun to curdle our exchanges. I said, "What about you?"

"Maybe we should both go."

"I'd like that," I said.

She drifted off quickly, but dozens of times that night I woke with a start to the thought of the seven gaping windows on the first floor with a kind of panic I had learned from my mother. Liz did not seem to share this. The few times Elliot had asked to spend nights at other boys' houses, she'd said yes without even knowing where they lived. It was my job at night to close all our windows and set the burglar alarm, and on my rare business trips I would call before bed to find that in my absence she hadn't bothered. I had built my staircase with a precision-routed stringer and a generous bead of construction ad-hesive to keep the treads from squeaking and then added a thick run-ner that muffled the impact of any passage. Through an open first-floor window, I thought, a man could make it into Elliot's bed-room without notice. Under the shield of these night sounds, he could creep into my own room and put a knife to my wife's throat while I slept.

On Monday morning, I called Pacific Security. For a twenty per-cent rush fee, the serviceman who came to measure our windows re-turned just a few days later with a full set of custom screens and interfaced each one with a short flexible cord to a contact on the sills.

I drifted in and out of rooms where he worked, hoping he would finish before my wife and son got home. But he did not hurry. He took a stick of gum from his pocket and explained that the mesh was interlaced with thin wires that would detect cutting. He sat back and wiped his brow with a handkerchief from his back pocket; the sill contacts would detect removal, he said. Liz and Elliot both returned as he reprogrammed the keypad, paging slowly through a manual in our front hall. Then he tested it twice, filling the house with an urgent blaring while I stood behind him, oddly shamed by the noise. After he left, I went into the kitchen, where Liz stood at the sink washing lettuce for a salad, and Elliot sat at the table flipping through a magazine.

I felt the urge to reclaim something.

"There," I said. "Now we can protect ourselves from gas poisoning AND prowlers." When nobody laughed, I said, "We'll just keep the windows open a couple more weeks as a precaution."

Elliot turned a page, but I could tell he was listening. I said, "Then, if it doesn't recur, I think we can safely assume the smell was caused by a temporary clog."

I STILL THINK IT'S ODD THAT I DIDN'T ANTICIPATE WHAT happened next. I was at my desk in my vast new office, trying to make sense of a junior engineer's rambling memo about the pedestal design for Bottlerock, when my telephone rang.

"Luther, hi. It's Sylvia de Silva."

I couldn't place her name, but it sounded vaguely familiar, and I didn't want to insult her: "Yes," I said. "Hello."

"You were the designer for North Fork, right?"

I rarely interacted with anyone outside the engineering group, and at that point, I figured she was an administrator of some sort. Or someone in Accounting. Belsky had just submitted a proposal for budgeting on some new tests. "I managed the design, yes."

"And you're doing the investigation?"

"Robert Belsky's doing most of the work, but I'm supporting it."
There was a small pause. Then: "So, how's it going?"
"Fine."
"No problems?"
I heard a leaf of paper turn on her desk and a distant telephone ringing. Belsky hadn't mentioned a particular person in Accounting, and at that moment I found I couldn't remember the names of anyone in that department at all.
I said, "What sort of problems?"
"Glitches. Surprises of any sort."
"No."
"Really?"
I heard another page turn, and then another telephone. Then a third began ringing in concert with the second: not the soft warble of the incomprehensible new-fangled system we used inside the Department, I finally noticed. There was a slight rustle, and the sounds of the telephones became muffled.
"Sylvia, I'm sorry, we've probably met, but I don't remember."
"Oh, gee, I'm the one who should be sorry," she said. "I thought you'd recognize my name. I'm a reporter for the *Sacramento Bee*."
What I felt first was irritation at not anticipating what immediately seemed to have been an obvious and inevitable development. Quickly, however, my shame was displaced by anger. "You thought I'd recognize your name?"
"Yeah."
"How long have you been reporting on water allocation?"
"I've done several stories."
"Then you must know that there are two spokespeople for the Department of Water Resources, and I'm neither of them."
It is of course in the best interests of a reporter not to register surprise or allow awkwardness to creep into her manner, and she took this in her stride. I thought I heard the pop and pressurized release of a soda can opening. "Hunh. No, I wasn't aware. I just thought people would like to hear your perspective on things."

"You did?"

"Yeah. I thought they'd be curious to know whether you thought it was necessary—whether your dam was sound or needed a little shoring up."

"Have you got a pen?"

"Yeah, sure." It was more difficult, then, for her to mask her excitement. I heard a rustling again, and then a thump. The conversation had taken an early turn that made her believe I'd say nothing of value, and now it had changed. "Go ahead."

I cleared my throat and coughed. "Excuse me, I'm a little congested."

"That's okay."

"My wife thinks it's a cold, but I think it could be a mold allergy."

"That's too bad."

I coughed again. "Well," I said. "Where was I?"

"You wanted me to write something down."

"Oh, right. Are you ready?"

"Yes." Her impatience was gratifying.

"Leonard Berkman and Christine White."

"Okay." There was a pause while she wrote this down. "Who are they?"

I looked out my window at the capitol dome. Then I said, "They're the spokespeople for the Department," and I hung up the phone.

Although it was winter, my new office had so many windows that, by late morning, the room began to overheat. The sun warmed my neck and shirt back and drew odors from the room, and now I was overwhelmed, suddenly, by the smell of banana. Liz sent me to the office each day with a little cooler. She always put a piece of whole fruit inside, which I ate at my desk feeling lucky, but now I bent over my garbage can to find the peel. It was cool and dry, and when I pinched it between my fingers, the vein-work on the inner walls gave and slid and released more of that smell.

The air by Elena's desk was oddly refreshing. The faint scents there were discernible to me in some heightened state of sensitivity:

hair spray and hot pencil erasers. She made a lot of mistakes, and walked around the office with a telltale dusting of the pink-black rubber filings clinging to the lap of her acetate skirts. The air felt cooler, too, and the noise of typewriters and telephones was welcome. I went to the kitchenette, where a secretary I didn't recognize was heating a container of leftovers in the microwave. She was humming "The Girl from Ipanema," and her anonymous company was somehow soothing. I dropped the banana peel in the garbage can and stepped to the window. I rested a hand on the cold steel sill. On the sidewalk below, a mother was attempting to pull a tandem stroller up over the curb. She might have loaded them into it on the sidewalk, or wheeled it along to the corner where the Architectural Barriers Act required the curb to thin and meet the asphalt, but instead, this struggle. Behind me, the microwave pinged, and the secretary stopped her humming abruptly. The door chucked open, and she said "Voilà" and walked out with her lunch.

I went down the hall and popped my head in Belsky's doorway. "I just wanted to warn you about something," I said.

He was eating a doughnut, and he raised his eyebrows in a way that called attention to the connotations of reprimand my opener carried. I saw that I should have led with something else: a question about Tim, or another expression of false gratitude for the hospitality he and Joyce were showing my son. But it was too late for that now.

I said, "A reporter just called me from the *Bee*. She tried to pretend she was someone I knew to get me to talk about the investigation, but I figured it out before I gave her any comment. Her name is Sylvia de Silva."

Standing on my front doorstep to pick up Elliot for water-skiing that first time, he had eyed my house, up and down. Sometimes I thought of this as meaningful, but other times he was just any man on a doorstep. I tried to remind myself that his offer to take Elliot had been a joke.

I said, "I just wanted you to know who she is. You know—in case she calls you."

As I finished my last sentence, he took another bite, and he regarded me while he chewed. When he swallowed, he said, "Thanks."

He crumpled his napkin into a ball and then set his hands above his right shoulder. He flicked his wrist and it sailed past me towards his waste can where it landed on the floor next to another.

"For the warning," he added.

Then he looked out the window at the rooftop garage next door.

My pulse quickened. It was unclear whether he intended that I leave.

Before I could decide, he said: "That blue Celica's been parked in that same spot for a month."

On the other side of the door, his secretary's phone rang. He turned back towards me and smiled slightly, waiting for me to comment, but there was no response to this he could not make light of. He knew this. When it had been just long enough to make my speechlessness clear, he winked and said, "I know, because Krepps gave me the better view of the parking lot."

THE EVENING MIGHT HAVE GONE DIFFERENTLY IF I HAD BEEN A better predictor, at this point, of what my son would do, but in that respect I think it is clear that I had never had much intuition. I had guessed that he would have pointed questions about my story. So on the way home, tapping the brake pedal in traffic, I had rehearsed answers to these. Then, because I wanted to afford it as little importance as possible, I told them in the kitchen. Liz was generally garrulous, I had noticed, when she came home from the Crisis Center: a little flushed and talking fast and quick to laugh. Counting on this, I did not do it as soon as I arrived home, but instead waited until she finished a story of how she had gone to her hairdresser to touch up Peggy's cut and he had not recognized her.

Maybe things went worse because of how entering upon this simple exchange unsettled me. Liz was in the kitchen unwrapping barbecue sandwiches onto our plates. She was only a few sentences into her story, but somehow my small sense of being a bystander in my own kitchen was magnified by the memory of my disorientation the night of her haircut, and the way the quality of Elliot's attention made me imagine that he and Liz had talked about Peggy since then, maybe even about that underwear, and that if I was right about this Liz had not even tried to share her knowledge with me. I set my briefcase down and took off my suit coat in a weak attempt both to busy myself and to bridge the gap between us, and Liz, in a gesture of courtesy that was at once kind and surprisingly sad, turned a little to include me.

"He was giving me directions to a place called Counter Culture Cuts when I said, 'Danny, it's me, Liz,' and he almost poked his customer in the cheek with his scissors he was so surprised. He asked all the other stylists over to look at me, and then he told me he could shape it into a soft Dorothy-Hamill-kind-of-thing."

Elliot snorted, and she laughed with him.

She said, "He was flipping through a magazine to show me pictures before I could explain that I liked it. I said, 'You're like a small-town barber with your don't-worry-we-can-fix-its. I just want you to touch it up. I actually want to keep this same cut.'"

Elliot laughed again, but his eyes shifted towards me, and in hindsight it is sweet I suppose, that his sense of my outsider status made him uncomfortable. But to dispel the awkwardness of this, I said, "Something funny happened to me today too. A reporter called to try to get me to say something interesting about the investigation for an earthquake scare piece. It was like something from a spy movie. She tried to pretend to be somebody I knew."

Liz's eyes grew wide for less than a second. This was worse. Elliot picked a slice of sweet pickle from his plate and popped it in his mouth. Through the open window, we heard an airplane pass overhead. I picked up my plate. "I didn't fall for it, of course."

Liz said, "What did you tell her?"

"I told her to get her pen ready, and then I gave her the names of the spokespeople."

"I love it," she said.

We set our plates on the kitchen table. It was damp out, and this made it feel colder than it was. Liz was wearing two sweaters. I slid the window halfway shut, and, as I sat down to eat, I imagined Elliot was ticking through his options. *Did it make you angry? Why didn't you tell her what you thought?* He watched Liz lift her fork and then he cut a piece of brisket and put it in his mouth. Just as I was marveling that he was not saying anything to heighten my discomfort, he said, "So, did you ever think of an answer?"

"Sure, but the point is she's supposed to talk to the spokespeople."

"No," he said. "Not about that. For that last question for my report."

"What question?" Liz said.

I said, "A time when my father scared me."

I still have not sorted out how much of what he did that year was natural, and how much of it was calculated to unseat me with surprise. He took another bite of brisket and watched me as he chewed.

In the last few days, the truth was I had thought a number of times about his question, and what kept coming to me was the night my father came home and announced that he had been fired.

"Well, they're foolish," my mother had said. She slipped on her oven mitts. "They don't know what they're losing."

My father had always been prone to quick irritation, and at first the rise in his voice when he spoke next didn't really strike me as strange. "I got fired because I messed up, Lucille."

She dismissed the idea with a mitted hand.

He said, "I mouthed off like I always do. I've got a big mouth, and it finally got me into trouble."

"You're one of his best plumbers."

"His best plumbers don't tell off his customers."

She pulled the pot roast from the oven, and when she set it on the stove, he turned her with both hands and took her oven mitts off. He held on to her hands, but low, close to the wrists, and in his eyes there was something beseeching. "How come everything I do gets the same reaction from you? How about if I socked a customer in the nose? How about if I threatened my boss? How about if I ran over Luther with my van?" Their faces were close, and she looked as confused as I was by this flash of desperation, something altogether different than his anger. "I lost my job, Lucille."

"I know."

"So what are you going to do now I don't get paid every Friday?"

"Serve less pot roast," she said.

"Serve less pot roast." A muscle twitched in his jaw. "What'll you feed Luther if I don't get a job?"

"You will. You're ten times the brain of anyone you've worked with. You should start your own outfit."

"It takes time to drum up clients. Especially if you're a jerk."

"So?"

"So what'll you put on the table till then?"

She smiled. "Eggs, potatoes, and apples."

Somehow instead of appreciating her faith and good humor, he received this easy specificity like a slap. He let her hands fall. If his frustration was hurtful to her, she chose not to show it. She smiled again and kissed him on the forehead. She was taller than him, and prone to gestures, I see now, that made him feel it.

Of course, it was only in hindsight that I was able to recognize this conversation as the catalyst that it was. It seemed to me that there had always been an underlying self-hatred in my father, latent in his temper and his slavery to impulse, which at first drew him to a long-suffering love like my mother's but was ultimately bound to question it. Sitting at my dinner table with my wife and son, I suppose it is telling that after the initial fear this analysis always stirred in me, I felt the silent rise of a pulse-pounding outrage: not at the weakness behind my father's insecurity, but at his selfish failure to hide it—the first step along a slippery slope that would give him license to test her over and over with ever-greater assaults on her love. Elliot might be doing the same to me, I admitted—I did understand that—but, unlike my father, he deserved not my anger but my patience. He was only a child, and besides, with one lapse in the attic I had given him reason to doubt the honesty of my emotions.

Across the table, he was watching me. I picked up my napkin and made a business of wiping my lips.

"No," I said finally. "I didn't think of anything."

THE NEXT MORNING, I WOKE FIRST, OF COURSE. OUR BEDROOM smelled of damp grass and my nose was cold, and so my first thought was not of the newspaper, but of the sewer gas. But it didn't take long to remember. I put on a sweatshirt and went outside.

Ms. de Silva got front-page placement, and the headline was worse than I'd imagined: "Earthquake Risk: Dam Failure Could Flood Sacramento." The *Bee* is a decent paper, but they fall prey to the same temptations other papers do. They printed a bar graph showing the size of earthquakes in California over the last one hundred years. The November earthquake was a 6.8. The El Centro earthquake of 1940, which had killed nine people and caused six million dollars in damage, had been a 7.1. The 1906, which was the most famous earthquake in history and may have killed as many as three thousand, was an 8.3. And to the right of these, a bar showing a 7.8 earthquake labeled, "Magnitude that would rupture North Fork Dam, flooding most of Sacramento County." The editors made no effort to point out that an earthquake with a magnitude of 7.8 is actually ten times larger than a 6.8, or that the epicenter would have to be within twenty-five miles of the dam to have this ominous effect, almost inconceivable given the fault patterns in the area. More irritating still was a box to the left of the article titled, "What You Can Do to Protect Your Family," and a list, including purchasing flood insurance, stocking up on emergency supplies, and writing to your local legislators urging more stringent safety requirements. Of course, Ms. de Silva fanned these flames with quotes from uninformed people. Mothers and fathers said, "Terrifying" and "How do things like this get approved?" The mayor, who has virtually no influence over state politics or interactions with the Department of Water Resources but was facing stiff reelection competition said, "I will take any measure to protect the safety of the citizens of Sacramento."

As I read, I kept bracing myself. I imagined Belsky would have offered to talk to her only as an unnamed employee—a quote implying serious danger or embarrassment to the Department—but the only comment from within our division was from Leonard Berkman, and Ms. de Silva twisted it to her purposes: "In the face of scrutiny, criticism, and fear," she wrote, "the DWR would comment only in vague terms through a professional spokesperson who said: 'A very likely outcome of the investigation is greater confidence that North Fork is one of the safest dams in the country.' In the meantime, the citizens of Sacramento will have to hope that the aftershocks are over."

Liz snorted at the amateur melodrama and tabloid partiality of this line, as I'd hoped she would, and kissed me on the crown of my head as she read it over my shoulder, but Elliot merely set it down when he finished, and it was somehow more disturbing to me that instead of challenging me with a question he merely returned to reading *Road & Track*. At the time I attributed my anxiety to a worry that he was biding his time for a surprise attack of some kind, but the feeling I had was more hollow than that. It's as if briefly some stunted part of me understood that the testing he'd been doing was at least a sign of interest, or a sign that he had higher expectations for me, and that this resignation, or indifference, or both, while less obviously hostile, was a lesser kind of love.

The reactions from my coworkers were more gratifying. On my desk that morning was a white-frosted Danish like the ones I often saw Elena eating with a knife and fork at her desk. Leonard stopped me in the men's room to laugh about the way Sylvia de Silva had called him for comment from a pay phone at an A&P at five-thirty and told him there was no time to research his answers. When I went to the lobby to buy a can of soda, I returned to find a stainless steel spaghetti strainer on my chair with a note attached in Belsky's cramped hand: "Safety of Dams asked me to collect any early models you might have constructed of North Fork. I hear there's one that looks something like this," a typical dig, but one laced with some empathy nonetheless. At noon, Ken Gonzales stopped by my office to ask me out to lunch. I told him I planned to eat at my desk, and he rapped twice on my doorjamb and said he hoped I wasn't letting the article get to me.

When lunchtime came, though, I went not to the deli downstairs, but instead to a store on Sunrise Boulevard whose sequined aquamarine marquee had burned itself into my memory in the sharp five o'clock afterlight of thousands of commutes home. I wish I could describe or even remember the exact quality of the feeling that overcame me when I did such things. It was not a strong drive or a panic or even a despair. It was a blankness, a kind of hollow nothing that must have been conjured through force of some will but over time had become like a reflex. Sometimes a generalized sadness or a quick flare of self-loathing would rise, but it never lasted very long. The salesman descended on me at the door with an assault of questions and a gambler's hand of glossy brochures, but the truth was any model would do, as long as it could be delivered that afternoon.

By then Liz had had long experience with my surprise purchases, and even as distracted as she was those days, I suppose there was a strong enough plea implicit in the pattern to get her attention. She tried to give me what I wanted. That evening, although it was only sixty degrees, she met me in the driveway wearing a sarong from a trip to Mexico over her sky-blue tank suit. She had set up dinner at our garden table and a boom box playing Spanish music on the brown, new-smelling vinyl cover of the hot tub. She sashayed to me and bumped her hip against mine.

"How long have you been planning this?" she said.

I shrugged and smiled.

"Fifteen jets!" she said. "He can invite half his class from school."

She threw a shawl over her shoulders against the chill and served sangria to all three of us and did not raise her eyebrows when Elliot poured himself more. I had several topics in reserve, but she did not let the subject stray from our new acquisition. She floated half-a-dozen ideas for parties around the hot tub, and Elliot entertained these gracefully, with a kind of eye rolling and smiling that from a teenager reveals a grudging affection.

Over slices of pound cake, finally, I shared my coworkers' reactions to the article with my wife and son. Liz lifted the lid for a dip in the hot tub, but of course the water inside was still very cold, and to salvage some of the spirit she'd intended, she led us across the lawn and slipped off her shoes to stand ankle-deep on the top step of our pool. She goaded me along with easy questions and lighthearted comments, and abandoned her plate to eat the slice of cake from her hand. Elliot was quiet. He sat on the copingstones with his feet next to Liz's in the water and passed pieces of cake between his lips at those moments when he might have been expected to weigh in with a comment of his own, leaving Liz to construct a lean-to of comfort without the support of his ease and humor. The sun kept setting, until the pool was dark above their feet, their ankles disappearing beneath the glassy surface, and I wished I had set the underwater light on a timer that matched the earlier nightfall of the new season, a task I had somehow let slip, despite my vigilance.

5 The Book

IN FEBRUARY OF THAT YEAR, THE WEATHER CHANGED. THE RAINS subsided. The fog burned off and temperatures reached a record eighty degrees. At first people were wary, but in the second week of this, some removed the covers from their swimming pools. Drugstores displayed sunscreen near the cash registers, picnic blankets dotted Capitol Park, and, one afternoon, my wife knocked at my office door in a yellow sundress with a Thermos full of lemonade and a sack of sandwiches from the barbecue restaurant. She pulled one of my guest chairs around to my side of the desk, reached into the bag, and handed me a warm, damp bundle of waxed paper. "Happy heat wave!" she said, and she kissed me on the cheek.

Although I have come to think this was just an uncomplicated romantic gesture—a reaction to the same foretaste of loss I myself was feeling—at the time, I was instantly suspicious. Ms. de Silva's article, of course, had not been the last mention in the paper about my dam. The following day there had been an impassioned editorial, and from this, two camps had quickly emerged: those who felt it was a large waste of money to consider structural modifications, and those who feared the dam would fail and wash away our city during the next tremor. Sometimes Liz read these articles and letters aloud at breakfast with a mocking tone, but with her new daytime hours she was often in too much of a hurry to mention them at all, and it is at least some sign of feeling on my part that I was conflicted about this. Occasionally I registered it as a loss (although more out of nostalgia than out of an understanding that something important was changing). But more frequently I vacillated between relief at the waning of her sympathetic scrutiny and worry that the silence was merely some kind of passive-aggressive technique she had devised in the dead time between calls at the Crisis Center.

I think I knew even then that there was something destructive about my suspicion, and I tried to dispel it as I chewed, but each time I focused my attention successfully on what she was saying— about the tenderness of the brisket, or the jets in the new hot tub, or a profile she'd read on Sally Ride—a wave of bitter astonishment invaded my thoughts. *How did we get here?* I was struggling with this when Belsky waved at us through the hall window. He opened the door and held up a can of Sprite. "Well, well. Lookee here. I had intended this for my partner in crime, but I'd much rather give it to a lady," he said. "Nice haircut, by the way. A whole new you."

"Oh," she said. "Well. Thanks." She touched herself at the nape, but looked at the carpet. She was always a little uncomfortable when other men flirted with her in front of me, but her discomfort when Belsky did it seemed to be growing stronger. I tried to assure myself that this was because she shared my dislike of him, and not because she felt it would be a blow to my ego to see that a man who had built rapport so easily with our son could do so with her as well.

He popped a can open and handed it to her. He licked a drop of Sprite from his finger and leaned on the edge of my desk, facing her. "Your son is a great kid."

"He really enjoys Tim."

"Polite, personable, great laugh."

"It's sweet of you and Joyce to host him so often."

"All that and a great mother too." He shook his head. Then he turned a little to look at me. "I just came by to get any notes on tests you didn't submit to the files."

"You asked me for those last week."

"Did I?" he said, scratching his head.

"Three times, in fact." I laughed to diffuse the irritation I felt. "Once in a memo, once in the middle of a staff meeting, and once in line at the cafeteria toaster. I gave you everything I have."

"You only did fifteen core samples?"

"That's right."

"Come on." He looked at Liz. "Does that sound right to you? Fifteen core samples. I think he's hiding something."

I said, "I think you stopped by to see my wife."

Both of them looked at me. Belsky raised his eyebrows, but he was caught short, I think, by the truth of it. Liz's eyes moved minutely around my face, for clues.

I picked up the Sprite he had given Liz and sipped it. I had been too harsh, I thought. He was just a coarse man, and he meant me no harm. The interest he had taken in my son was at my request, and for whatever reason even seemed to be good for him. I said, "I can sympathize with the impulse, but I'd like her all to myself."

"I don't blame you," he said, and stood up. "But we're having a party Saturday—a barbecue if the weather holds. Maybe you could share her then—bring Elliot and join us."

Liz did not wait for me to hesitate on this.

"We'd love to," she said.

As he walked out, Elena poked her head in to remind me that I had a meeting, and by lingering in the room to pull files as Liz gathered her things, she robbed me of any chance to joke with my wife about what had just happened. I expected her to mention Belsky's visit as soon as we were alone in the bedroom that night, and when she didn't, a dread began to build inside me. I waited to see what she would do, and listened with wonder as she talked about the strange heat wave, and the way it was bringing out buds on the China plum, keeping up the conversation when it flagged, and all the while leaving the topic glinting in the corner of the bedroom untouched.

It is ironic that Howard chose the following morning to visit my office unannounced. He laid a trembling hand on my guest chair and raised his eyebrows, his request for an invitation to sit. He was an engineer who had been promoted into a position that was almost entirely interpersonal in nature, and, over the years, he had adapted himself to it as best he could. He always began impromptu encounters with a series of social questions that through tireless repetition in the halls and elevators had formed the unlikely foundation of his popularity. In the context of his power, his awkwardness was somehow endearing.

Predictably, he picked up the photograph on my desk. "Beautiful family," he said, as if looking at it for the first time.

"Thank you."

He set the picture down. "How's Liz?"

"Great," I said. "She's working at the Crisis Center now."

"Crisis Center, eh?" His eyes strayed to his notepad. He looked up again. "And that house of yours?"

"Terrific."

"Built it from scratch yourself, didn't you?"

"I did."

"Impressive."

"Thanks."

He looked at his paper again. "Well, Luther. You've probably heard Don's retiring."

"Yes. I'm sorry for the Department, but happy for him. I'm sure Lorraine will like seeing more of him."

He smiled, but a muscle twitched at the corner of his mouth. My response had interrupted his rhythm. He glanced at his notepad and pressed on. "And I just want you to know that the way this investigation is going had a lot to do with our decision on filling his post."

He sat back in his chair, relieved to have finally set the meeting on its irrevocable course. The air conditioner ticked on, and I felt a pulse in my stomach, like a tiny hand tapping. I cocked my head slightly to encourage elaboration, but he said nothing. I said, "I'm not sure I understand."

He trilled his shaking fingers on the plastic chair arm, smiling slightly, hopeful that I meant this rhetorically—that he would not have to begin again. "Sure you do."

"I'm afraid not."

"Come on, Luther." He was looking at his notepad, eager to move forward to his next point.

I said, "But so many have been investigated."

"None like yours."

The pulse in my stomach quickened. I said, "If you're going to start letting the press dictate your promotions, I don't think you'll be happy with the results."

I took a Kleenex from the box on my desk and wiped my forehead. There was no use now trying to conceal my agitation. I did not look at him directly, but I could tell he was holding very still. When I looked up, he looked down at his notes to afford me an awkward privacy.

"Excuse me," I said.

"Well, no, that's—"

"I didn't mean to lose my temper."

"Oh, well . . ."

He picked up my photograph, lost in his routine, and then set it down clattering on my desktop. He ran a palm across his pant leg. "You're not tracking me here, Luther. That's the thing." He skimmed his pant leg again and then settled his hands on the chair arms. "You've impressed us with the way you're taking the investigation. Most of the guys lose their cool at least once anyway, and then Robert is no picnic to work with. Plus all that business in the papers."

I must have looked confused, because at this point he laughed. He said, "We'd like you to take Don's post."

Although my failures of intuition that month were numerous, in a

way the next one strikes me as the most pathetic. I was incredibly excited, as if there was some kind of magic in my news. I bought a bottle of champagne on the way home in anticipation of the ease it
would rekindle among us, but in the end the moment of telling my
wife and son about my promotion was not all that different from the
one three weeks earlier when I had told them about the call from the
reporter, with forced exclamations of pride from Liz and a silence
from Elliot that could have expressed either indifference or judgment. And although the evening before she had neatly avoided it,
that night in bed Liz introduced the topic of Belsky's party with an
analytical relish that showed me she had been thinking about it all
along. She wanted to know if I'd seen Robert since Krepps talked to
me about my promotion, and I told her I had not. Robert and Joyce
would probably feel a little threatened, she said, and she recommended we try to ease this as best we could. Especially in light of
their difficult marriage because things like this can add to the strain.
"We could bring up how nice their house is," she suggested. "I'll bet
the fact that they can afford such an expensive house is a big point
of pride with a guy like him. Talking about it might make them feel
less awkward." I conceded that this was true, but as she talked, I
could not shake the idea that her work at the Crisis Center had made
her cagey enough to architect an entire conversation about how to
ease Belsky's competitive feelings simply in order to assuage my own.

Although of course I agreed with her, already my thoughts were
turning to the party with an eagerness that in retrospect seems foolish. It had been over two months now since he had taken Elliot
water-skiing, and since then Elliot's attachment to his family had
grown until he spent almost as many waking hours underneath their
roof as he did under ours.

Liz said, "And if he's insensitive to Joyce, we have to build her
up somehow. Maybe he does it out of feelings of inadequacy," and
again I felt that rise of suspicion. I pictured a pale-fingered social
worker reading to a class of volunteers from a textbook, Liz nodding,
taking notes.

THAT MY SON WAS QUIET IN THE CAR ON THE WAY TO THE barbecue should not have seemed a rebuke in the context of the recent changes, but as we glided along the wide sapling-lined streets of the Sunrise Villas, I felt my palms begin to sweat on the wheel. When Elliot was eight, the parents of boys at his school had entered a sort of birthday party arms race. He went to events at which he rode in a real fire engine, swam with dolphins, and bounced in someone's backyard in an inflatable room the size of a one-car garage. He came back from each glassy-eyed with sugar and an awe for the fathers of these boys that had me worrying about his own birthday party seven months in advance. At a certain point, without really examining the implications of what I was doing, I began to interview purveyors of entertainment. I met with a juggler who worked a heavy measure of realistic self-injury gags into his routine, a falconer with trained birds of prey he taught children to call to their mitted arms with scraps of raw beef, and finally a magician. Each time, I took them to our yard where Liz couldn't hear us because I was vaguely embarrassed by the overseriousness of my project, and near the trunk of our elm tree, I asked them to tell me about their routines. The juggler and the falconer both gave me a businesslike description of services, breaking their programs down into increments of time, and specifying exactly how each of the children would get to participate. But the magician simply told me he'd bring equipment for all thirty of his most popular tricks and do ten he chose based on the vague measure of "audience response." I asked him what he meant.

"After the first trick for any group," he said, "you can see in their eyes what they want more of. Do they want the pure surprise of a rabbit from a hat, or to have their cynicism snuffed by helping with a card trick they thought they could figure, or to feel a scary mix of empathy and brutality bubble up while they watch a friend trust me with knives?" He sipped his 7-Up. He was wearing a cable-knit sweater, but he had a handlebar mustache that helped me to picture it. He said, "I've been doing this for twenty years, and I'll tell you there's still nothing like it."

"Like what?" I said.

"The joy of surprising them with what they want."

When the boys were cross-legged in the grass, he had appeared, not from the kitchen door, but from the limb of a tree above them. He was wearing a cape with a collar that stood up, which I would have guessed would strike a lame note with boys that age, but there was something about the shock of his descent from the tree that earned their respect before he had even done any magic. They were alternately slack-jawed and laughing the kind of wide-eyed, gasping laugh that signals amusement not at the humor of a performer but at the improbability of the feelings he has managed to stir inside them. When the show was over, he asked if they had any questions, and, as I'm sure he predicted, the first was about the methods behind a certain trick. He nodded gravely and asked them to come close, and they stumbled over one another for position.

He took out his deck of cards and fanned them out, faceup. "I start with them spread like this, see? Then I turn the fan over, like this, to show you their backs, and when I flip them over again, that's where the gimmick comes in," he said. He paused here, and by doing so, allowed me to feel the tension he'd produced. The boys' eyes did not stray from the cards or his hands. When he flipped them back, finally, all of the cards were blank. "Shucks," he said, "I guess I'll have to show you another time," and what I saw on every boy's face was not irritation but a kind of relief. The magician closed the deck, smiling.

For almost a month after the party, Elliot had sat at tables with a deck of cards. He checked out a book at the library. He spent his allowance on a kit that came with a set of metal rings and a wand, and he wore its dark cape. I was no longer envious of the fathers who had planned his friends' parties, but something worse had replaced it. One night Liz found me by the living room window thumbing through the book of tricks he'd left on the coffee table. She kissed me on the cheek. "He thrilled him, I won't argue you on that, but try to keep it in perspective," she said. "It's infatuation. Nobody can develop real love for a man in a cape. Not even a boy."

Belsky's house looked different finished, and in the light of day. Although I'll admit I'd been curious, I had resisted the small temptation to drive by after Belsky told me they'd moved in. I suspected Liz herself had given in to the urge, but still she commented on how nice it looked as if she were seeing it for the first time. It was apparent now, in the way that it had not been to me in the dark, that this was one of the largest of the lots, more private from the neighbors and with a better vantage of the golf course and the lake on the ninth hole, and that the window above the door was taller than two stories—more like twenty-five feet.

"We just go around back," Elliot said.

"We should at least ring the doorbell," I said.

But he had already started across the lawn. By the time we rounded the south wall behind him, he had stripped off his shirt and shoes and was moving through the crowd. A brawny man running to fat threw a football to a group of boys. A girl in a bikini pushed a baby on an old metal swing set. A dozen children bobbed up and down in the massive swimming pool. Elliot ran toward it. "Fish out of water!" he yelled, and grabbed his knees to his chest as he sailed out over its middle. Then another boy, whom I thought I recognized from the face book as Tim, jumped on his head and crushed him under the surface. They came up laughing. A girl pierced the surface and spat a stream of pool water in Elliot's face. He filled his mouth to return fire, and only when she raised her hands—a-glint with silver rings— to defend herself, did I recognize her as Peggy. I was so stunned by the whole scene, I didn't notice Joyce sidling up beside us.

"Well, hello," she said. She waved in the direction of the smoking barbecue. "Bob, they're here!"

He waved a spatula to disperse the smoke. "Hey! I thought you'd be hobnobbing with a senator or something."

"Congratulations," Joyce said, and she kissed me on the cheek.

He stuck a finger in the sauce and tasted it. "Needs more of the fancy mustard."

"We're out of fancy," Joyce said. "We only have yellow."

"What would your dad think?"

"He wouldn't think anything."

He turned to me. "Joyce's dad is a kingpin."

"That makes him sound like mafia, Bob." She looked at me. "He was a nylon manufacturer."

"The nylon mafia."

She rolled her eyes.

He said, "This house was a twentieth-anniversary present, if you can believe it."

"How generous," Liz said.

"No kidding. He wasn't even embarrassed when she married me."

"Stop it," Joyce said. "He wasn't embarrassed at all."

"He said, 'At least you didn't pick a deadbeat dad.' "

"That is absolutely not what he said, Bob. He said, 'You picked a good father for my grandchildren, Joyce. It took me fifty years to figure out that nylon wasn't important. I'm glad he doesn't care about striking it rich.' Those were his exact words. He wishes he were more like you." She tilted her chin up with pride.

"Of course he does," he said. "He can't do this, for instance," and he put his hand up under his T-shirt. He pumped his free arm and made a flatulent sound you could have heard from the street. From all points in the yard, this triggered a familiar braying laughter that could only have been his children. Two ran at him from either side and leaped at his back, and somehow he caught them both around the waist so that he held them like footballs. He started spinning in place, and his children bucked and laughed under his arms and screamed "Stop! Stop!" When he finally did, one of them threw up on his apron and started to cry.

"Damn it, Joyce!" he said.

"What did I do!?" She picked up the boy and stroked his hair.

"Stevie threw up again!"

"I see that!"

"What are you letting him play and eat barbecue for, for Christ's sake?"

"He's not sick, you spun him on a stomachful of hot dogs."

"He throws up holding perfectly still all the time."

"Don't be an asshole," she said. She pressed Stevie to her chest and strode toward the house. Robert took off his apron and held it up for me to see. "Jesus," he said. He crossed the lawn and went in a sliding-glass door as she passed through French doors at the opposite end of the sprawling house. Although we were suddenly alone, for a moment neither Liz nor I said anything. Behind us there were splashing sounds from the pool; the slap of a caught football; shrieks of children—an unfamiliar two or three, and then our son's. We kept our eyes on the doors Robert and Joyce had passed through. At some point Liz made herself say, "Wow," and I responded with, "Yeah," but it was not clear from this what exactly had surprised us, and although I suspect she had intended, as I did, to adopt a tone of superior amusement, the truth was that somehow, despite the fact that we had clearly just witnessed a domestic dispute, my predominant feeling was one of inadequacy.

Robert returned first, wearing a white lace-trimmed apron and carrying a tall glass of scotch. He held it up to us, smiling, and took a sip. "Time to get some more of these babies on the fire," he said, and he took the tinfoil off a platter of raw hamburger patties. As he set them on the grill, they sizzled fiercely.

When Joyce came back, she was wearing a UC Davis sweatshirt and Stevie was wearing a pair of He-Man pajamas. She winked at us and stood next to her husband in a cloud of barbecue smoke. Stevie stared at me from behind his sucked thumb until I looked at the grass.

Robert said, "I'm ignoring you."

Joyce grinned and said, "Good, I'm ignoring you too."

Stevie pointed at the grill and said, "That one's not getting any fire, Daddy."

"Thanks, Chief." He moved a patty toward the center. "How do you feel?"

"Okay."

Now Joyce leaned to kiss Robert and noticed his apron. She reared back. "Well, don't you look sweet!"

"Mine had Steve's puke on it."

"I have to get a picture." She set Stevie down, and he ran off toward a sandpile, stopping midway across the lawn to put his hands on his hips in a muscular stance and admire the lay of his pajamas. Then he kept on running. Joyce took an Instamatic from the pocket of her sweatshirt and held it with her finger over the viewfinder in one hand and her drink in the other.

"Curtsey for me," she said.

Robert held one corner of the apron out between pinched fingers and did a deep plié.

"Wait," she said, "I can't see the frilly bottom." She backed up a step and he curtsied again.

"Wait, wait," she said.

"Christ, Joyce."

Then she backed up another step and fell into the swimming pool. The splash was huge. When the water cleared, we could see Joyce's drink hand above the surface. Her head bobbed up and she drew the camera out of the water and set it on the side of the pool, laughing.

Robert cupped his hands around his mouth like a megaphone. " 'Least you saved your drink!"

She set her drink on the poolside and hooked an elbow over the copingstones. Her thick sweatshirt was dark with water, and she could not stop laughing. Here and there on the lawn people clapped and shouted catcalls. Little children in pajamas jumped up and down at the sight. Elliot stood dripping on the side of the pool between Peggy and Tim, his face wide-eyed and smiling in unself-conscious delight such as I had not seen grace him in over a year. Liz stepped to my side and watched with me as Robert leaned over, his heavy waist peeking out from under his T-shirt, and took both of his wife's hands. He hoisted her out, and somehow I knew before he did it that when he got her up on the patio, he would hug her soaking body against his own.

EVERY YEAR, SACRAMENTO IS BESET BY RAINSTORMS. PARKING lots become reflecting pools, and people cross downtown streets in the center of blocks to avoid gutter puddles deep enough to flood their pant cuffs. Without an umbrella, a rush to a waiting car will soak one's suit jacket through to the skin. The rivers overflow and eat away at their own banks, so that when people go to sell their properties years later, they're surprised by the loss of acreage they have suffered.

The last two weeks of the February of 1983 were particulary wet ones. Just a few days after the Belskys' barbecue, the record heat broke with a heavy rain that woke me. It had flooded the windowsills and pooled along the baseboards, and I moved from room to room to swab it with towels as they slept. In the moonlight, the house held still for me, spellbound for my baffled, outsider's eyes—the living room with the remnants of a game of Yahtzee between Liz and Elliot, my own bedroom where my wife lay smiling sadly through a dream, and up, up, up, above me, my attic where my son lay snoring, one long, strange, man's calf exposed atop his sheets. I took the wet towels to the washing machine and sat down at the table in our dark kitchen. I poured myself a tall glass of milk. I ate three dried apricots and a Saltine. It had been three weeks, I told myself. The trap problem had not recurred, and I had seen no other signs of trouble in our pipes or vents. And one by one, I stole back to each room to close all of our windows.

When I woke up the next morning, I was glad I had done so. It was still raining, and by lunch, three counties near San Francisco had flooded. Our papers covered the damage with vivid photographs—families paddling down their streets in canoes, and dogs standing on the roofs of their houses awaiting rescue—and by journalistic magic, these rekindled the dying embers of the story about my dam. It was illogical; no one had suggested heavy rain could cause my dam to fail. But the images of people displaced from their homes filled people with fear, and it doesn't take much to fan such flames. A picture of water running along the spillway at North Fork (which, of course, is precisely what a spillway is designed for) appeared on the front page of the newspaper with a caption that read "Rainwater overflow at North Fork Dam, still under investigation for risk of failure." A local radio-talk-show host parked himself by a guardrail one day and measured the depth of puddles along the right abutment. Two days later, a raving cautionary editorial titled "Noah's Ark" spanned two pages at the end of the A section of the *Sacramento Bee*. By the end of the week, protesters had assembled on the capitol steps with rain slickers and canoe paddles to dramatize the imminent danger posed by my dam. That night, I brought home a sausage and mushroom pizza, but Liz had left a note on the kitchen counter. Elliot was spending the night at Tim's, and she was taking Rita out after work to cheer her up, and my surprise that in the last two months she had become a confidante to a coworker whose name I didn't even recognize somehow made eating the pizza alone in front of the protest coverage even more depressing.

Many of the roofs in Sacramento are flat and prone to leaking, and the bulk of the real damage in our county that month could be blamed on this alone. My office building suffered some. A leak in the roof allowed rain to seep through the ceiling. It wasn't a large leak, just a dripping in the hall, but it ultimately soaked a fire detector, shorting it out and deploying the sprinkler system on the northern half of the fourteenth floor.

This forced a temporary move for me and six other engineers. Howard insisted on my having a corner office, and he found a vacant one for me on the southwest corner of the second floor. The eastern wing of that floor housed the cafeteria, and from the elevators, I could smell corned beef, French fries, sugar. In the hallway outside my office hung a photograph of the capitol building. The picture was so old that the paper had yellowed, and the skeletal remains of a spider were trapped behind the glass in one corner of the frame. The office itself was spacious but low-ceilinged, and the view lacked grandeur. Even the prospect of I-5 was obstructed by a telephone pole.

Howard assured me it would take less than a month to perform the necessary repairs to Fourteenth East; so I didn't give much attention to such things. The office didn't have a filing cabinet, but I didn't request one. When the thermostat worked poorly, instead of contacting Building Services, I brought an oscillating fan from home. And although Facilities had ignored my instructions and delivered my photographs to me there, I did not unpack and hang them. The boxes of files and frames against the wall gave the space a storage-closet look, but this didn't really bother me. In fact, I didn't give the state of the office much thought at all until one afternoon when I had been there almost two weeks Elliot appeared in my doorway.

"It took me a long time to find you," he said.

"They didn't change my location on the directory because the move is only temporary." Suddenly I saw how my not having mentioned it to him might make it seem like cause for shame. I searched for a description that did not sound defensive. "They're repairing some water damage upstairs."

He set his backpack on the floor. He looked for my guest chair, and it was under a stack of papers. On top of these was an editorial about the upcoming decision on modifications to my dam. The author was against modifications, but mostly because they were so expensive. We should accept the risk, he felt, even though he seemed to suggest the risk was huge. I stood to move it aside, but Elliot got to it before I did. He sat down, and the oscillating fan passed over him, making his shirt billow. I had been taking all my meetings in a seventh-floor conference room; I hadn't noticed how awkwardly placed it was for company. His eyes slid sidewards to anticipate the next passage of the fan. "I was headed to the library to meet Tim," he said, pointing over his shoulder. "I thought I'd stop by and bring you a root beer."

"Thanks," I said, a brief hope flaring inside me, but I quickly told myself it was unlikely that it was as social an impulse as this. I wondered if Belsky had told him about my new office—suggested he drop in and surprise me. I felt a sort of dreadful certainty that my son would use both the shock of his visit and the vague denigration of our surroundings to set me off balance in preparation for whatever he had come to say.

He took two bottles from his backpack and set one sweating on my steel desktop. He twisted the cap from his own and took a pull. His eyes flitted around the office.

"I wanted to improve one last thing in my report before I hand it in," he said.

"What's that?"

His paper was due the next day, and although in the last two weeks I had counted half-a-dozen times when he might have done so easily, he had not repeated his question about a time when my father had scared me.

"The section about how he died. I only know a little about it, and it seems like I should sort of describe it."

"It was an aneurysm."

"Right." He took another sip. "But did he, um, fall down somewhere? I mean, was he at work, or at home?"

"He died in bed."

"So Grandma found him in the morning?"

He had taken to calling them Grandma and Grandpa. When he first began this project, he had referred to them as my mother and father. "Your mom; your dad." Both things made me sad.

"I'm not sure when she found him actually. I was at college. I flew home when she called me."

"Oh."

I had been in Pasadena two years and home to visit only twice, both times at Christmas. Although in some ways, the husk-light relations with strangers in a sunny place had been exactly the opiate I had intended, I have never quite forgiven myself for this.

His bottle dripped condensation on the editorial, and he wiped it, but the newsprint had already absorbed it, and a dark welt rose over the type. He set his bottle on the spot. "That must have been sad," he said. "I mean, was it? Going home for that?"

"Yes," I said. It was obvious to me that he wanted me to elaborate, but these were not things I wanted him to picture, and I was anxious in a grim way to rush the conversation—to learn why he'd really come.

He took a sip and glanced at my bottle, which sat unopened next to the telephone. Finally, he said, "Can I ask you a question?"

My pulse quickened. "Of course. You can ask me anything."

He held up the newspaper. "Do you ever feel like writing a rebuttal?"

"No."

"How come?"

"Because the allegations are stupid."

"You could tell people that."

"It would be defensive. It would give them more credit than they deserve."

"It might make you feel better."

"But that's the point, Elliot. That is exactly the point. I don't feel bad. I don't feel bad in any way."

Condensation dripped from his root beer to his pant leg. A stridency had entered my tone that undermined my argument. I felt the need to diffuse this, and also to regain my footing for the assault to come, but I had trouble thinking of anything to say. Before I could even try, he said, "I better get going."

"All right," I said, surprised. I had expected tougher.

He said, "I'll just head to the library."

"Okay."

"Unless you have time to look at something," he said, laying a hand on his backpack. "I mean, I brought something I thought you'd like to see."

At this my pulse raced. I felt a hunted conviction, a certainty that he was finally drawing his sword. Wild guesses flashed through my

mind—nude pictures, drug paraphernalia, his report on my father—
but I cut my thoughts short. I did not want to pause long enough to
allow him to complete his move.

"Oh, Elliot," I said. "I really wish I could, but today I can't."

"That's okay."

"I have a meeting."

He put both hands up, and he blushed more deeply than I'd ever
seen. "No big deal," he said.

I felt the rise of a new kind of panic. Curiosity made me brave. I
said, "Maybe another time . . ."

He shrugged.

I said, "You could bring back whatever it was you wanted to
show me."

He was still blushing.

I said, "What is it anyway?"

"Just a book."

"A book?"

"Yeah." He could not make himself look at me.

"What book?" I said.

He unzipped his backpack then and drew out a book with a torn
dust jacket and a faded bar code from the public library. He held it
still in his lap for a few seconds, considering, and then flipped it over
shyly to let me see the cover: an old photo of two men in gym shorts
and 1950s crew cuts standing face-to-face behind the protection of
upraised gloves. I read the title: *The Sportsman's Guide to Boxing.*

"Oh, Elliot," I said.

"I thought maybe it was like the one you checked out in high
school before that fight."

"It is," I said.

He made a show of studying the cover.

I said, "It might even be the same one."

He slid it on my desk next to my unopened root beer.

I said, "Maybe we can look at it together later."

"Sure," he said, not unkindly. He zipped up his backpack. "Or you
can look at it without me," he said.

It's interesting how strong a role timing plays in history. So near to his leave-taking was the next knock on my door that I was certain he had returned. But when I called out to come in, Belsky appeared, one hand holding a bologna and lettuce sandwich and his tie tucked ridiculously into his shirt pocket. Mustard crusted one corner of his mouth.

"Oops. Got lost on the way to the ice machine."

I forced a smile.

He held up a manila folder. "I'm here to take your fingerprints."

I waited.

"We're going to have to incarcerate you for the drowning deaths of a thousand citizens."

"What can I do for you?" I said.

"I'm here for those extra pictures of North Fork."

"I filed everything I had."

"There's one I've seen in your office though." He glanced around. "A framed one, I think."

He had difficulty describing it, as if he had not paid very much attention during his visits to my office—as if he did not even remember that I myself was in the photograph. As he stumbled about, referring to one of the right abutment, or the left one maybe, or of the whole canyon, yes the whole canyon, I remained silent. When he sputtered out, I told him I was afraid he'd have to be more specific.

"Come on, Albright. You've had it on your wall for six years."

"I'm not sure what you're talking about."

"It's probably in that box right there."

"You must be mistaken."

At this point, my telephone rang. Belsky held up a finger, as if to stop me from answering, and it was specifically this that made me take the call. The voice was immediately familiar, although this time she took a more respectful approach. "Mr. Albright, it's Sylvia de Silva. From the *Bee*."

I have thought many times about how things might have turned out differently had the circumstances preceding that moment been altered in any way. Had I remained in my prior office and the picture still been hanging; had Belsky come by without that sandwich that somehow highlighted all I disliked about him; even had I not requested that he close the door behind him. That might have been enough. I would have paused long enough to rise and close it myself. Instead, when it clicked in its frame and I saw his body pass down the hall, I uncovered the mouthpiece on the receiver. "I'm not the spokesperson for the agency. I said so before."

"I know," she said. "I've already called Leonard Berkman, and I can leave you alone, I just, you know, things have changed a little. I thought you might have something to say."

As she said this, her voice grew fainter, as if she had drawn her face away from the receiver to look through some papers or take a sip from a cup. I learned later that she had been writing for the *Sacramento Bee* for many years at this point. She had probably become so accustomed to asking such questions and receiving refusals to comment like my last one that she had placed this call to me with no more agitation than she did a call to verify the spelling of a name. I pictured Elliot searching the shelves of the public library for something that could touch me. I pictured Belsky getting out of the elevator on the fourteenth floor, within earshot of his phone. It was late afternoon, and the aluminum louvers on my blinds were warm to the touch when I parted them. Below me on the highway, traffic was clotting near the J Street exit. A yellow dog lay in the far left lane, and the cars slowed and swerved to avoid it.

I said: "The dam is sound."

She coughed and drew the mouthpiece closer to her face. "Then why is it being investigated?"

"Slow year for Safety of Dams."

"How do you mean?"

"The rest of us are busy. Applying for funding. They don't want to get cut."

I heard a page turn. "Ooh," she said quietly, as if to herself. Then: "What else?"

"I think that's enough."

"Wait, wait. What do you think about the remediation proposal?"

"I think we can all agree that it's a big waste of taxpayer dollars to reengineer a dam constructed on the same principles the Romans used to build structures that have been standing for almost two millennia," I said. I felt a dryness in my throat. I hung up the phone.

I stood then and took a pair of scissors to the box leaning against my window. The truth is I had opened it and retaped it several times since I had moved there two weeks ago: twice on Monday mornings when I puzzled over what made Elliot spend so much of the weekend at Belsky's; but more often in response to a feeling I cannot describe except to say it passed over me like the sudden silence in a hotel room when the stranger next door turns off his TV. Such things can take my breath away. They bring with them such quick sorrow.

Withdrawing the photo from its box had a different effect on me every time. The details of the photo itself, of course, were always the same: the crest of the high right abutment wall. Cap; gravel; sky. My own clear pleasure. Usually this last made me grateful, but today more than anything it was a kind of taunt. My hair was windblown, and I was wearing that expression of unguarded delight unique to men whose sons have not yet begun to doubt them.

WHEN ELLIOT WAS TWO YEARS OLD, I LINED THE BASEMENT WITH shelves. I built them from red oak, and sometimes Liz brought him down to play with a small box of tools at the foot of the stairs. It slowed me down. I would ready myself to sand a shelf and notice him hammering at the hand rail four steps from the bottom, his little heel overhanging the riser. I would set the board against the wall and cross the room to show him the pin on the hinge to the mechanical closet door; it needed banging. Then just when I had set myself up again for sanding, I would notice a can of varnish with a loose lid and stop to move it out of his reach. Work took three times as long and was fraught with an awareness of his mortality that made my stomach light. But his presence was a sort of food to me. Every ten minutes I redirected his heart-swelling focus to new tasks whose importance I inflated just to see the seriousness that came over his face. He cut his eyes to my hands and changed his grip on the tools to match mine. He accented my work with reasons to encircle his small torso with my fingers and move him bodily—that tiny rib cage and protuberant belly; his smell of soap and crushed apples; the soft hairs on the back of his neck. That is what I remember: those sudden swells of physical restlessness that parental love fills one with—*maybe if I tickle him, or toss him in the air, or take his head in my hands, or press him close to my heart . . .*

The shelves took three months to build, and when I was done he watched me line them with banker's boxes and hang a pen holder on the wall. Already, he had drawn pictures—a circle; a series of lines; the tiny hatch marks that were letters to him at that age—and this is where I planned to keep them. Over the years, other things went into the boxes too: photographs, awards, class projects, pieces of family history—and when I got home from work the day I spoke to Sylvia de Silva, I went downstairs to find one.

It was mixed in with my coursework from a mechanical engineering class because I did not want them to find it. I am not sure why anymore. It was a brown paper accordion file full of mementos of the successes my mother was always celebrating: a one-dollar bill from my father's first customer; a picture of my father installing a pipe on a Tudor house in Hopewell; the schematic from the plumbing system he designed for a small hotel; the invoice he never sent an elderly woman in Hoboken; a program from the 1949 Plumbing-Heating-Cooling Contractors Convention that listed my father's speech, "The Mysteries of Drain-Waste-Venting Systems."

I put them back in the accordion file. Upstairs, I found the door to the attic closed. I knocked, and instead of calling out, he padded across the room and opened it.

"I'm sorry for interrupting," I said.

He was looking at my hands. "What's that?"

"Something I thought might help you with your report."

"What is it?"

"A folder of things my mom kept of my father's."

His report was due tomorrow; the offer, coming now, might reasonably have made him angry, but he looked behind him and opened the door wider. He gestured toward his spare bed—moved up at Liz's urging for friends he would never bring home—and so that is where I set it. Then he looked through them quietly, one leg bent on the bedspread and the other foot flat on the floor while I stood beside him, too chastened by his private manner at his door to really feel welcome. He turned them over one by one.

"Where did you find it?"

"It was downstairs. Mixed in with my college notebooks somehow."

He examined the invoice long enough to constitute a question.

"He did that work for free," I said. "My mother was proud of him."

He looked up at me. His pupils moved around in tiny abrupt increments, just like his mother's: my mouth; my eyes; my hands. He ran a hand over his dark new hair. "Do you want a chair?"

"That's okay."

"Or you could sit on the bed, too. There's room."

"I'm all right."

"There's room."

"Okay," I said, and remembered, as I settled there, how soft his old mattress was. It had been a long time, I guess, since he had invited me to sit.

"What about this?" He held up the dollar bill.

"From his first solo job," I said.

"What was it?"

"A clogged toilet."

"Were you there?"

"Yes. Sort of. I was in the car outside. My mom wanted us to watch."

He pushed at his glasses. He was looking at the photograph from the 1954 science fair my father had not attended. At first glance it looks like a crowd shot, all of the people are so small, but far in the background I am standing in front of my display explaining the workings of my centrifugal pump to a man with black-rimmed glasses. It was an odd thing to store among the work things that had made my mother proud, but as I looked closer, I realized that the hat and coat on the woman in the corner next to my station were my mother's. My father must have taken the shot.

Elliot held it up to me.

"It's from one of my science fairs," I said. "That's me back there."

"Who took it?"

"He did."

The fair was in Passaic, a ninety-minute drive in each direction. When my mother and I got home afterwards he had been sitting in his chair next to the Austrian clock. He had a deck of cards laid out that made it appear he had done nothing with his day. There were dishes in the sink from both breakfast and lunch—a half-eaten ham sandwich; a hard-boiled egg—meals he could not possibly have eaten. "Sorry," he had said, regarding my mother coolly. "I got distracted."

Elliot held the photo close to his face, studying it. Although I only saw my mother cry twice in my life, both times it had been from the sort of joy only relief from sorrow can bring, and there was no question in my mind that she had done so when she discovered this picture. When it began to seem Elliot might never stop studying it, I said, "I looked through the boxing book after you left."

"Oh yeah?" he said, but he was still holding the picture.

I said, "It's got some of my best moves in it."

He forced a smile.

I said, "Maybe I could teach you a few."

"Yeah." He set the picture on top of the file. "Sure." His stomach growled then, loudly, and he glanced at his watch. I had a sudden image of him arriving home alone, trying the kitchen door before remembering he had to use his key, and I thought about the way he and Liz had stood in the kitchen together last month, discussing his favorite bands. I wondered if he knew her absence was my fault, and because I could not apologize for this without inviting questions about a lot of things, instead I said, "I thought about what you suggested."

"About what?"

"About writing a rebuttal."

It was still light out, but he had already changed into his pajamas, the same cotton button-front-and-pants style he had been wearing since he was eight. I don't know what made him decide to change early some evenings, but it always made me uneasy, sometimes tongue-tied, at once recalling a thousand nights of bath time and stories and making me aware of their passing, his size and his Adam's apple making a costume of those clothes. He drew his foot from the floor up onto the bed and gripped it, waiting. My ears felt hot.

I said, "What I meant this afternoon is really true. I mean, I still mean what I said—that I think it would give them more credence than they're due—but I respect your opinion, and I thought about it more. I think there are a lot of people who don't know what to think one way or the other—not the reporters or the people who write those editorials, but the people who don't have an opinion in the first place and then read the paper."

I became aware from his gaze that my hands were troubling the elastic band on the accordion file. I laid them on the bedspread. "That reporter called again after you left, and I told her what I thought."

"You did?"

"I gave her a comment."

"What did you say?"

"I said I thought the investigations were mostly a way of justifying funding for a part of the Department that didn't have a lot of work to do."

"You said that?"

"Yes."

He laid a hand on the scrap file. His forehead was a little damp from where his hair had rested. He had taken an evening shower, probably because he had done push-ups in his room. Liz used to wash his hair with something that smelled like daisies to me, and I remembered that now, his slicked back hair, wet feet slapping on the hard wood; he had made a game of being dried. Part of me wanted to tell him the other things I had said, but I felt the need to be careful, and I knew these things would appear in the paper anyway.

He said, "How did you say it?"

He held my father's dollar bill in his hands.

I said, "What do you mean?"

"Like what kind of words did you use?"

"I don't remember exactly."

"Was it an accusation, the way you said it?"

"I guess we'll see in the paper."

He folded the dollar bill. Once; twice; again—a tight little roll of green.

He said, "Isn't it bad for your department, what you said?"

Of course it was, and although it's obvious to me now that he was in fact desperate to hear that I had finally given my anger sway over principle, I myself was too ashamed of this to do anything but mislead him. "Public sentiment will affect the decision about structural modifications," I said. "There's a lot of money at stake. That's important too."

He looked up at me. "That's what you were thinking when you talked to her?"

It was the first time, I think, I ever lied to him about my own character. "Yes," I said.

Elliot followed me down the stairs then. He stumbled once to keep from overtaking me, and I noticed that one of his knees popped loudly in its socket every time he stepped down. We moved together like this, silently aware of each other, into the kitchen, and made a quick dinner of scrambled eggs and bacon, which we ate in front of the TV news. In a hospital in Utah, Barney Clarke had died after one hundred and twelve days of life with the world's first successfully implanted artificial heart. Elliot went upstairs to his typewriter to finish off his report on my father, and although a number of times I tried to force myself to stop listening, I did not hear the last keystroke until an hour after Liz got home and slid quietly into bed beside me in the dark.

It isn't necessary to recount what the article said. It quoted me exactly, and because the *Sacramento Bee* is not one of the country's largest papers, it didn't make as much of this as it might have with more reporters to research my allegations, but it made enough of it to appear damaging to my department. Elliot was quiet at breakfast, his report sitting next to his napkin ring in its blue cover where I imagine he had hoped it would demand attention.

When Liz read my quotation, she looked up at me with more interest than she had shown since she started work at the Crisis Center but, to my surprise, showed no suspicion that what I'd done was anything but carefully considered.

She smiled. "Did you really say this?" she said.

"Something like that."

"What made you decide to do it?"

"It just seemed right," I said.

She nodded as if this confirmed her expectation and looked down again to finish the article. I was at first relieved, but there was a fear I didn't quite understand already beginning to haunt me. The man she had known before I sent her away was a man who suppressed all impulse. By now she was too distant from me to guess that my self-control had finally been plundered by my sorrows.

Elliot said, "Did you tell your boss, Dad?"

"No," I said. "It was too late for him to do anything. He'd just have worried until he read the article."

"Won't he be mad?"

Liz said, "Your father's their best engineer."

"Yes," I said. "He'll be mad."

"What do you think he'll do?"

"Give the nice office to someone else next time," I said, and I laughed. I had given it a great deal of thought in the car on the way home, and here is what I imagined: a nervous and stern reminder about politics, and next, the subtle but distinct beginning of Belsky's ascension—better office assignments, invitations from Howard, and, some years from now, a leapfrogging promotion to Branch Chief when Howard retired.

A timer buzzed, and Liz rose from her chair without finishing the article to take a cookie sheet of frozen doughnuts from the oven. She checked her watch and set about rearranging a stack of volunteer training manuals in her briefcase. She spread them between the compartments and transferred a thick binder to the outside pocket. Then she checked her watch again and clipped across the tile floor in her pumps to take three champagne flutes from an upper cupboard. She transferred our orange juice from their tumblers and toasted my integrity and bravery, as if she believed my speaking to de Silva were the considered act of conscience I had tried to make it seem. Elliot smiled and passed a hand over his mouth—a tick left over from the weeks before he began shaving—and stood in the driveway at Liz's command to see me off to work. Looking at them in my rearview mirror, I thought of myself in the service van with my mother outside my father's first solo job, and I inhaled a bit of doughnut and had to pull over four blocks from my house to collect myself. Tears had welled up, partly from the quick shock of choking that always makes me briefly imagine and accept death, but mostly, I still think, from the unsettling parallels of that memory.

At the office, I was afraid to leave my car. When I finally did, I stood at the lobby store looking at ballpoint pens and watching the crowd gather by the elevator until I remembered that I had been relocated to the second floor. I slipped to the stairwell door and walked up. The hallway was empty and smelled of cafeteria grease. I closed my door and waited. To pass the time, I drew my blinds and looked out the window. Traffic was bunching and spreading in its odd patterns. A helicopter passed low to report, and then banked off to the left.

The first knock on my door was not Belsky, but Howard. I asked him in, and when I sat down, he made a decision to stand. He held his pad in one hand, but it bore no notes, and he did not pick up my picture frame. He closed my door and said, "What were you thinking?"

I was not used to his being direct, and it took me a few seconds to answer. "I wasn't. It was a mistake."

"You're damn right it was."

I was suddenly amazed that I had not thought more about what I should say.

I said it again: "It was a mistake."

He wiped his hand across his brow. There was a sip straw peeking out of his shirt pocket. "I can't believe it was you. I thought it would be Belsky who would do it. I've been by his office six times to remind him not to, he's such a hothead."

"I'm sorry."

"That doesn't help me."

"I know."

"You see what I have to do, don't you?"

Suddenly I did. "I don't think that's necessary. People will know better."

"No they won't."

Now he picked up my picture. I tried to think of alternatives I might suggest, but I couldn't come up with any.

He said, "I'll give you a choice, but it has to be bad enough to send the message," he said.

"I've never done anything like it. You could say you took that into account."

"People won't remember your history; they'll just remember that nothing happened to you when you shot your mouth off and said what everyone wishes they could say."

"I could write something to the paper. A clarification."

"Back-page stuff," he said. He looked at the photograph of me with my family in front of the house I had built. "Damn it," he said. He took the sip straw out of his pocket but didn't put it in his mouth. "So what part of the state would you pick if you had to?"

"I wouldn't."

"Come on."

"Sacramento."

"I'm giving you a choice."

"It doesn't matter; I won't take it."

"Fresno then," he said, and by lunchtime I was loading packed boxes into my car. Office workers were eating their lunches from paper sacks in Capitol Park. When I got home, the house was quiet. I ate some crackers from a plastic sleeve and drank a glass of milk. Then I went to the basement and took out my toolbox. Liz had been complaining that a safety feature on her hair dryer was making it shut off after increasingly short intervals of use. I didn't think it would be difficult to fix this, and I wanted to be busy when they got home. I was standing at the kitchen counter removing the pink plastic casing from the handle when I heard the car pull into the driveway. Elliot opened the door, and Liz came in behind him.

When she saw me, she looked at the watch she had bought for work so she could track the length of her calls. "They did something crazy, didn't they?"

"As a matter of fact, they did."

"Ridiculous!"

"Dad got fired?"

"Not fired," I said.

"Sacrificed," said my wife.

I fit a tiny screwdriver bit into a hole on the hair dryer nozzle. "They offered me a transfer to Fresno."

"And?" Liz said.

"I resigned."

She set her briefcase on the counter. "Good for you," she said, but she did not look at me. She was tucking the folders of volunteer training handouts back inside the zippered flap.

"Did you yell at them, Dad?"

Liz looked up. "Of course he didn't."

"But they took his job."

"From your father? They didn't take a thing!"

"They didn't?"

"Does he look upset to you?"

"No."

"Ask him if he's upset."

"Are you, Dad?"

I made myself smile. "Of course not."

"What did I tell you?" she said, and she touched the shaved nape of her neck.

6 The Lie

Elliot's question stayed with me even after he had handed in his finished report and giving him an answer could not help him. Most often I would think about it at night as I tried to fall asleep, which became increasingly difficult for me. My unemployment itself did not cause much stress—I expected finding a job to be easy, and in fact I had received my first offer just a week after my resignation—but nevertheless, I found myself operating on fewer and fewer hours of sleep. Sometimes I would rise and eat a snack in the slats of moonlight cast by our shutters on the kitchen table. Sometimes I would go to the basement. And sometimes I lay in bed next to Liz pretending to be asleep so that she wouldn't know my anxiety was mounting. When I woke, I kept my eyes closed and my arms at my sides. I might tick through my calendar of appointments for the week. There was a lot to juggle. Consulting engineering was a growing field that decade, and as a candidate I was sought after. I recall a few days when I had two breakfasts, and one when I had two lunches. I ordered a salad to keep my appetite for the second seating.

But more often than not, what I did was turn over answers to El-liot's question in my mind: the strange catalogue of moments with my father when I remembered being afraid. One night, a week after my resignation, I woke hot and perspiring. I should have risen to open the windows or turn on the air-conditioning, but by then, for reasons I can no longer fully reconstruct, I had decided letting Liz know I was awake would be dangerous to me. Instead, I gently peeled back the bedspread and let my perspiration evaporate through the top sheet. As I waited for this to bring me some relief, listening to the sound of Liz's tongue searching her mouth and the thick shade scrap-ing the window casings, I thought about the first time my father came home two hours late. He came through the kitchen door and set a paper bag on the table.

"Sorry I'm late," he said.

"That's all right," my mother said. Although I had witnessed her weeping a few times when she thought she was alone, she always managed to give my father what she thought he needed. "Dinner's still warm."

"I was doing a little shopping." He did not look at me. I was sitting on a stool near the kitchen sink. My mother drew a ham out of the oven and set the pan on the counter.

He said, "Guess what I bought?"

"I don't know," she said.

"I didn't say tell, I said guess."

"A new torque wrench?"

"Nope," he said. "Something just for fun."

Her back was still to him, and now he pulled the bag towards him on the table. He had landed his first customer over a year before, and now his independent practice was thriving, just as my mother had predicted. But instead of allowing her faith or his success to make him happy, he had let his suspicion of the indifference at the core of my mother's devotion consume him. Although I suppose he still loved us, as that science fair photo suggests, his morbid quest to ex-pose her dispassion was apparently worth the price of hiding this. He made promises just so he could break them; he brought home that picture of himself with the dancer; and now, when my mother turned from the stove, he put his hand in a paper bag and drew out a pistol.

"For target practice," he said. "I thought Luther and I could drive out to Walpack and shoot cans. How does that sound to you, Luther?"

I glanced at my mother. Her eyes were fixed on it. I was stunned and frightened, but it's clear to me now that this was less because of any danger the gun itself posed than the betrayal of my mother it represented.

"Okay," I said. I almost added, *If it's okay with Mom,* but these words seemed somehow pregnant with significance and complication—as dangerous as the gun itself seemed to be—and I couldn't bring myself to articulate something explosive that I didn't understand. In retrospect of course it is clear that this would have been the first time I'd called attention to the fact that there was a side to be taken, and this acknowledgment of conflict was something I shied from, maybe because he seemed to relish it, or because my mother, whom I loved, avoided it, or maybe, I have sometimes wondered, because it is just something of which I am constitutionally incapable, and always will be.

Remembering this, I lay awake for two hours without turning, and when I sat down to breakfast the next morning, I couldn't meet Elliot's eye. Although I still believed in the importance of my intentions, sometimes when he looked at me the chasm of omission in my comments for his biography made me feel secretive and shameful. I buttered my toast looking at the newspaper and he read his *Road & Track.* The humidity that had built in the night was just beginning to break in the form of light rain on our closed windows, and that sound, that faint spatter, was like a derisive whispering behind me. I blushed and took a sip of my coffee.

That night I woke again at one, this time to the sound of hard rain that would turn briefly to hail. I had turned the air-conditioning on, and now under the covers I was cold and wide awake. The realization that the temperature last night was no excuse for my inability to sleep only increased my agitation. I tried again to lull myself with logistics: how long it would take me to drive between appointments tomorrow; which of them would involve street parking, and which of them garages. But soon my thoughts strayed again to the question of my father. Elliot's driver's licensing exam was in less than a week, and I remembered how for two weeks before my own test, every night when my mother began setting our filled plates on the table, my father would take his keys to his service van from a nail on the wall and tell her it was time for my lesson. But when we got in the car, I sat a long time awaiting instruction, and invariably my father would at last put a hand on my shoulder and suggest he drive. We traded seats in the darkened street, and he took us five miles along Route 1 and then drove back on a surface road with miles of stoplights, his face changing color, red to green, at the intersections.

At the end of one of these episodes, he dropped me off on the curb. "I'm going to go out for a while," he said.

It had to be almost nine o'clock.

He said, "Tell your mom I don't know when I'll be back and sorry about dinner." He had not turned off the engine. He meant this. But he was still thinking. "Tell her I just went for a beer or a drive."

I sat in the car beside him with the engine idling and tried to imagine what had changed my father. It had been months since he'd purchased that gun, and he still had not taken me to Walpack to shoot cans. Maybe he was in some kind of trouble. "Yes, sir," I said. It was something he had taught me to say, but lately it seemed to irritate him. I walked up the porch steps and into the house.

When he started doing this every night, I began to grow certain he was mixed up in bad business, and worries about our welfare began to keep me awake. I'm not sure if it was these, or a sharp desire to take something from him that made me creep into his closet one day and slip the gun into the waistband of my pants, but that is what I did, relishing the rebellion, this small secret betrayal, even as I longed to find him in the kind of trouble from which he could be

saved. That night when he dropped me off at the curb after our lesson, I got on my bicycle to follow him. I didn't know how far I would
get. He might get on the turnpike, or notice me and stop to yell, but
I didn't think about either thing. My heart beat fast, not from the
prospect of being caught, but from anticipation of the danger I was
now hoping I would encounter. He drove through our neighborhood,
past all the row houses, and onto Route 1. I briefly lost sight of him,
but the traffic lights were poorly synchronized, and this gave me a
chance. I was sweating under my wool coat. The hammer on the pistol chafed against my stomach. I caught him two lights later as he
turned into a parking lot shared by a Sweet Dreams Diner, a Pink
Lady Show Bar, and a movie theater that was playing *White Christmas*. As my father got out of his van, I stayed on the corner behind a
lamppost, as if its cover would shield me should he turn. I wondered
which of these places harbored the crooks who were harassing my father. I bet on the show bar, but instead he walked toward the movie
theater. He even bought a ticket. Then he disappeared through its
double doors.

I had not thought through my plan. Now that the wind was not
on me from riding, I was so hot inside my coat that sweat streamed
down my forehead. I crossed the parking lot and left my bike behind
a Dumpster in the alley. I dug change out of my pocket, bought a
ticket, and went inside. To the right of the men's bathroom was
a flight of stairs that led up to the projection booth where I imagined
thugs might be settling a score with my father. But under the weak
pressure of a stare from the man at the popcorn counter, I faltered
and pushed through the swinging doors into the theater. It was
almost empty, and so in the front row it was easy to detect my father's head.

I followed him five more nights that month, and each time he
went to the movies, twice more to *White Christmas*. When I watched
him spoon soup to his mouth in our kitchen, or sat by my mother as
she glued the handle on a broken teacup, I thought about what I
knew. When I listened to their footsteps through the wall at night, I

thought about it. In the last year, she had developed a secret of her own, a pack of cigarettes she took from under her mattress only in the mornings, a habit so benign it only merited hiding because it was a by-product of her pain. Although I expected the senselessness of my father's actions to damage her further, when I heard him tell her he had something to apologize for, I felt relief.

I sat up on my bed. She was chopping something on the cutting board, and she stopped.

"Set that knife down," he said. "Why don't you sit at the table here."

She set down the knife. A chair scraped the floor. In all my life, I don't think she denied him anything. "What is it?"

"I been coming home late a lot to go for a beer."

"I know."

"It's been making things tough for you with getting meals on the table."

"It's not so bad."

"The thing is, I haven't been going for a beer."

In the silence that fell, I could hear something sizzling on the stove.

He said, "I'm not going to do it anymore, and it's over, but the thing is, I've been seeing a lady."

More sizzling.

He said, "The truth is, I've been seeing her a couple months now. I don't blame you for being angry."

There was a charred smell then. The sound of chair legs and a pan being set at the back of the stove. "I forgive you," she said.

"You what?"

"I forgive you," she said.

I was still thinking about this on Saturday morning when we drove to the DMV. We arrived half an hour before it opened with dough-nuts and coffee. We were not the only ones. On the pebbled-concrete sidewalk, several teenagers sat at the feet of their parents and flipped through driver's manuals to avoid making conversation. It struck me that Elliot had never been one of these children, but in the weeks since my resignation, with me at least, he had become one. It was only three months until summer vacation, and I consoled myself by thinking about how a remodeling project might rekindle some of the lost ease with him that Liz still seemed to enjoy. I remember distinctly that by this point on our outings together I often had the strange sensation that I was watching someone else's wife and son, as if their time together in my presence, even when they were just reading side by side in silence, was charged with an intimacy that no longer included me.

Liz opened a box of doughnut holes and held it out towards him.

"No thanks," he said; "I ate like ten in the car." He looked down at his magazine, something he'd been buying lately called *Auto Craft*. He was reading an article titled "Restore Your Own." He had always been the kind of student who tested easily, and the fact that he had not even brought a copy of the driver's manual was a measure of his calm.

Liz herself paged through one. "Did you read the stuff about licensing requirements? I can't believe you get tested on it, but it looks like you can. As if anyone needs to know what kind of certification you need if you're sixteen and you're visiting from out of state. As if this information actually helps you drive a car safely."

Without looking up, Elliot said, "A California license or a Nonresident Minor Certificate."

Liz beamed. "That's it exactly." Then she flipped to a new page.

I opened the newspaper and read an article about a new sweetener that had been approved by the FDA. As nine o'clock approached, the line began to lengthen quickly: an overweight father and son; a girl in a McDonald's uniform; a man in scrubs; a willowy woman with an embroidery hoop and a bag of orange yarn. At two minutes to nine, a man appeared behind the glass doors with a ring of keys and looked down at his wristwatch. He waited for two minutes to pass and then unlocked the door. Now we all shuffled through it, and Elliot took a numbered paper ticket from a dispenser on the wall. Liz found us three chairs and sat down with the manual.

She said, "Another sample question is, 'You just sold your vehicle.

You must notify the DMV within how many days?' How can that be important? They're obviously just checking to make sure people read the manual." Her eyes slid toward Elliot.

"Ten," he said.

"Right again." She shook her head proudly.

When they called his number, he went up and took a test booklet to a shelf along the wall. Liz closed her manual to watch. He leaned on his elbows as he answered, and his back was to us: loose jeans and sneakers. It took him five minutes to complete, and he walked it back up to the desk. After they checked it, a man in chinos and loafers walked out from behind the counter and led Elliot out the door for his behind-the-wheel.

Liz looked down at the manual again briefly, but this was really too awkward a thing to do now that his written test was over. She shut it and laid it on her lap. The tension that built now when we were alone together was still sort of a shock to me, but I have come to believe there is a kind of natural arithmetic to intimacy—that lack of context between two people will grow exponentially because it makes new data so awkward to exchange. In the last week, I'd been offered two more jobs, but somehow I still hadn't told her, not because the offers themselves were secret in any way, but because my feelings about them were tied to too many things I hadn't shared.

One was a firm that designed tailings dams—the dams that hold back waste left over from mining or distilling done by industrial clients. Their offices were in a new building downtown, and their desks were made of mahogany. Such is the nature of a business with a marketing department. As I waited for my interview, I sat on a thickly upholstered chair and drank coffee from a cup with a saucer. The job description involved site investigation, and they had clients in Mali and São Bento, Brazil. It would no doubt pay well, and the change in the technical aspects of the work might have appealed to me—I knew nothing about designing for toxic reservoirs—but as I neared the end of my interview, I found I was already rehearsing the lines of my refusal. The engineer who interviewed me seemed competent, but as I answered his questions, I could not shake an image of myself sitting across a Formica-topped table from him, unfolding a sandwich wrapped in deli paper. In my mind, the deli was filled with noise, the cashier calling out orders, other customers talking, but our table was clouded over with a silence that amplified the noise of our bags and wrappers. By the end of the interview, I was certain I had impressed him, and took his call the next day for granted, but when it came, I felt no excitement. He asked for an answer within two weeks, and I knew immediately both that I would wait a full two weeks to call him, and that when I did, I would say no.

Sacramento Municipal Utility District offered me a job as a Civil Engineering Supervisor to manage not only the design of dams, but also all the concrete vaults and bridges in their system. I'd been screened first by a Human Resources Counselor in shiny support hose and a blouse that tied at the neck who called me Mr. Albright and didn't look up from the list of questions on her clipboard more than twice during our interview. It didn't pay quite as well as the other, but it involved no travel and the hours would allow me more time at home. These were the items I had added to the list in a small notebook at the kitchen table that night as I ate leftover lasagna and listened to the evening news. Elliot was at Tim's, and Liz was working. It was a very good offer, really. From a technical standpoint, it would involve some new challenges. I added this to the list. The engineer I'd met with had seemed friendly, but now I could no longer remember his name. When I called him the next morning, I had to look it up on his business card. Frank. I asked for printed information on their medical plan to stall for time.

What I found myself looking forward to, somehow, was a meeting with Nathan Sattler, the colleague of mine who had left the Department after he threw the stapler at the conference room wall. He had called me just after my resignation to say he had read the paper and ask if I'd like to talk. He was about to leave town for a dam site in Egypt, but he had suggested we meet when he got back, for some reason at the corner of Thirteenth and L in Capitol Park. I had

always thought of myself as very different from Nathan, even felt superior about it back in the days when I sat at the long table at the
Pine Cone and watched him throw peanut shells at the screen with
Belsky when the umpire made a bad call. But now, as I looked at a
long list of interviews with people whose names I had to track on a
spreadsheet, the comfort of the shared circumstances of our exits
from the Department and the idiosyncrasy of a meeting in the park
and the memory of the ease I had once felt at his invitations were like
pieces of driftwood in a vast ocean. I looked forward to the interview
with unreasonable excitement.

Sitting next to Liz at the DMV, this is what I was thinking about,
but instead of saying so, I leaned forward to watch the Chrysler with
its STUDENT DRIVER placard pull out of the lot.

"Well," I said. "I think he'll do okay."

"Me too," she said.

She picked a thread from the hem of her skirt and broke it neatly.
When she opened her manual again, it was more than I could take.

"I got another offer yesterday," I made myself say. "From the power
company."

She smiled pleasantly. "Are you interested?"

"Somewhat."

"But . . . ?"

"But I'm going to wait to answer them until I've talked to one
more person."

"Who's that?"

"Nathan Sattler. He worked in Design with me before he left to
start his company."

She nodded and ran a hand over the seam of her skirt again, looking for more loose threads. The truth is there had been many times
in our marriage when I had chafed under her attention, but now that
it had waned, it seemed a clear step in the wrong direction. She nodded as she listened now, something she had never needed to do to indicate her listening—a sort of cover. She turned a page of the driver's
guide. Since we had made the appointment for the test, she had

twice mentioned the possibility that we might see more of Elliot once he didn't have to rely on Tim for rides. I wondered if she was nervous, but felt asking might somehow insult her. She was staring at a diagram of a car turning left onto a one-way street. I kept waiting for her to turn the page but she didn't. Her hand rose to her face, and she touched her lips lightly.

Finally I said, "He should be back soon."

"Who?" She blushed when she said this. I still wonder sometimes what she had been thinking.

"Elliot," I said. "From his test."

Color blossomed along her collarbone, and she looked down into her lap again. "Yes," she said. "Soon." And as the flush subsided, she reached into my lap and took my hand.

A moment later, our son came through the door, and he followed the man in chinos to the back where a woman took his picture with a flash from a giant camera. He waited in a chair along the wall until she called his name. Only then did he look for us, and when he saw me, I remember that he smiled. It's memories like this of him that still hold the most mystery for me. It's not so difficult to imagine what he was thinking when he sat down at the kitchen table with his head newly shaven, or when he jumped into the air above our roof. But when he seemed pleased to find my face in a room full of strangers. It's things like this I keep going over. I would like them to be as they felt to me then—pure—but I find I can't help but wonder whether the surprises he unleashed on me that year were just impulses that fired suddenly, or careful plans he held in mind even as he made the simple gestures that gave me hope. When he reached our row of chairs, he handed me his license, still warm from the laminator.

NATHAN APPROACHED IN SWEATPANTS AND RUNNING SNEAKERS, grasped me by the shoulder to turn me, and kept walking, bringing me along with him.

"Thanks for meeting me like this," he said. He was out of breath.

"No problem."

"It's good to see you."

"You too."

He was holding a small set of hand weights. He pumped his arms as we passed the rose garden. "They did that operation with the balloon on me, and when my family picked me up at the hospital and took me out to dinner, I ordered a cheeseburger, and my daughter said, 'Don't you care about us at all?' She actually said that. I promised her I'd exercise every day no matter what. I sent her a picture from Egypt last week of me trudging across the sand in running shorts and sneakers."

A squirrel darted in front of us, but he didn't seem to notice.

"Thing is, I'm not sure she appreciated the effort. When I got home, she scowled when I buttered my potato. I said, 'I'm working on it, baby, I'm trying, didn't you get my picture? That was a *sand dune* I was jogging over. In *Egypt*. Egypt is *hot*.'" The bridge of his nose was red and peeling.

I tried to formulate a response to this, but one by one rejected words of sympathy, humor, and commiseration. People with briefcases hurried past us. When we reached the corner of Fifteenth and N, Nathan pivoted and pumped back towards the center of the park. Finally I said, "How'd the job go?"

"Fantastic. I'll have to go out again next month, but the construction engineers aren't idiots, which was a relief to find out."

"That's good."

"That's unheard of."

I laughed.

He said, "So tell me how it happened."

"Krepps came in the day the article ran and offered me a transfer."

He stopped and put his hand weights on his hips. "The same day?"

"Yeah."

"You're joking."

"No."

"Where to?"

"Fresno."

"Ha!" He started walking again. "What exactly did you say?"

"I said I'd rather look for other work."

"I mean to the reporter."

"I told them I thought the investigation of North Fork was a waste of money."

"Ha!"

"Well, I regret it. It was impulsive, which isn't like me. I wouldn't do it again, regardless of the outcome."

"Then if they call back, give them my number."

I laughed.

"I'll give them a sound bite."

I laughed again.

"You know I'm not joking."

He turned abruptly toward the fountain, and I had to jog a little to catch up.

He said, "So come to work with us, why don't you? We're looking for a fifth, and we haven't found anyone we like around here. My chief engineer is talking to a guy from L.A."

"Really?"

He looked down at his watch and put two fingers to his neck. "Yes. Really. Come to our place tomorrow, and I'll show you around." He glanced up and smiled. "But this time bring some French fries with you."

When I stepped into his office the next day, I felt immediately at ease. It was on the second story of a strip mall in Roseville. Although most consulting firms try to impress their prospects with nice offices, most of Nathan's first clients had been overseas, and as they built up a reputation they discovered its appearance didn't really matter even to those who saw it. The desks were steel with brown Formica tops and all of the office views were the same, of the parking lot and a hardware store, a dry cleaner, and a veterinary clinic in a similar building on the other side of the road. As we talked, people walked dogs and cats and a cage full of hamster tubing in and out of the clinic door. The receptionist showed me wallet-sized school portraits of her daughter and son. Although I had worn a suit, Nathan laughed about this and tugged off my coat, and it turned out to be less an interview than a sales pitch. Each of his partners came into Nathan's office to meet me and ask if I had questions, and when they left, Nathan showed me pictures of the dams they'd worked on and handed me a letter in which he described an offer that was not materially better than the others I'd fielded in a financial sense, but made me feel a surge of relief. He told me to think about it, and in order not to seem desperate, I told him I would, although already I was imagining calling those other people and telling them I'd decided to take another job.

When I got home, that is what I did. I'd already refused one of them, and now I called the others, and when I couldn't get through to the engineers who had made the offers, I spoke to the HR Directors instead. I thought there was a chance I would get a callback from one of them that afternoon with words of persuasion. When I didn't, instead of feeling insulted, I felt only more certain of my choice. That night Liz worked late, and Elliot spent the night at Tim's again, and for once neither thing gave me that feeling I'd suffered so often lately that I can now recognize as equal parts worry and shame. I opened a bottle of red wine and poured some into a glass full of ice cubes. I squeezed an orange into it, and crushed a wedge of apple and dropped this in too. Then I took it out on the porch and sat down in a chair next to the hot tub. Summer would come soon enough, and I let the memory of past afternoons and weekend days working beside my son quell my worry that I would lose him. As for Liz, with her working more at the Crisis Center, it struck me that the shortest distance back to intimacy might be to ask to visit her there and meet some of her coworkers. For the first time in weeks, I made plans about this instead of the plumbing problem or my job search. After visiting her work, I might take her to lunch and bring with me a poem I'd written on a napkin at a coffee shop just before I proposed. It would strike a tone. Stars began to show, and I realized I had been so lost in these hopeful thoughts that I'd forgotten to take a sip of my drink. I raised my glass and when it tasted nothing like Liz's sangria, instead of disappointment, I felt a clean gratitude for my wife that made me laugh alone in my yard.

The following day, Liz was working the day shift, and Elliot told me he was headed to the library after school with Tim. Before he left, I asked him if he'd join us for dinner, and then I bought three T-bone steaks and set the table with cloth napkins. We sat down in the dining room, and Liz asked what the occasion was, and I paused a second to try to temper my excitement before I said it wasn't an occasion really, I'd just been offered an intriguing job.

"It's just four engineers," I said, "but they've been around seven years, and even in their first six months, they managed to land a job that had also been bid by Bechtel."

"Wow," Liz said. Her cheeks were pink, and she was leaning toward me over the table. "What's the company called?"

"Interflow. I think I mentioned it to you. I used to work with the principal, Nathan Sattler."

"Oh, right," she said.

"The guy Bob called for you?" Elliot said.

He was buttering a roll.

"What?" I said.

He said, "Bob told me he called somebody to tell them about you losing your job."

"He didn't lose his job, Ellie," Liz said. "He quit."

Elliot's eyes were on the buttering job he was doing: lots of butter. "He said it was a guy you guys used to work with." He set his knife down. "He said he went on and on telling this guy about what a good job you'd do."

"How nice of him," I said.

Elliot took a bite of his roll. Liz picked up her wineglass. Although I tried to head off the image, immediately I pictured it: the smile on Belsky's face when the idea occurred to him; the studied casualness as he mentioned it to Elliot at his dining room table under an enormous chandelier purchased by his father-in-law.

I said, "Anyway, like I said, they're a great company, and I really liked all the partners there."

Liz took a sip of her wine.

I said, "But I do have one hesitation about working there."

"What's that?" Elliot said.

"It would mean a lot of travel. A lot of their consulting is out of state. Some overseas. I need to think that through."

Liz refilled her wine then and asked Elliot a question about a funny noise Rita's car was making, and I have to say that the tone of the evening had changed so abruptly that when I noticed the smell, for a split second I thought it might be something my mind had supplied as a kind of metaphor. But it quickly grew too strong to ignore. I know just when they noticed it because Liz's eyes fell to her wineglass, and Elliot, normally too focused on his food to pay much attention to us anymore, began watching me intently. I understood immediately that they would wait for me to say something about it, and to avoid the sting of their courtesy I stood up suddenly from my chair. Liz was in the middle of a sentence, but I slid the window open and headed to the basement for my toolbox.

THE FOLLOWING NIGHT, NATHAN TOOK ME TO DINNER AT A restaurant in the Hyatt hotel. His nose was still pink from the Middle Eastern sun. He ordered a bottle of wine from a vineyard in Sonoma I had toured with Liz the year before Elliot was born. Our waiter wore a suit and took our order by memory with his hands neatly folded behind his back. When he turned away, Nathan smiled.

"So, when can I tell the guys the good news?"

"I've thought about it a lot, really agonized about this, and I've decided I'm not the right man for your job."

"You're kidding."

"I'm afraid I'm not."

"What happened?"

I had rehearsed my answer in front of the bathroom mirror as I tied my tie. "I'll probably regret it because I respect you and your team so much, but I'm sure about this. I don't think a job involving travel is the right choice for my family."

He squinted. "It's not that much really. Half of the jobs are in state."

"I think any amount would be too much for us right now."

He stared at me. So much of consulting work relies on sales, and so few good engineers possess the necessary skills, that in retrospect the smoothness of his response alone should have been enough to make me try to change gears right there at the table. He let the silence last, thirty seconds, maybe sixty—much longer than was comfortable. Then he said, "Well," and smiled, not unkindly. "I think we could make it work for you, but I know when to give up. You give me a call if you ever change your mind." He was no doubt aware that relenting under such circumstances amounted to conservation of energy if I was really sure, and persuasion if I was not. "Here endeth the business dinner," he said. "Now tell me about your son."

And so I did. For the rest of the evening, we talked about our children. He had a twelve-year-old daughter who had been mortified this past fall when he suggested that he escort her and a friend while they went trick-or-treating. In years past, he had worn a costume himself, and his fun-loving company had been a source of pride to her, but this year she was embarrassed at the thought that he would be seen by her friends. For his part, Nathan felt it had grown too dangerous for girls to trick-or-treat alone. Last year in his neighborhood, high school boys had set fire to a pile of leaves and driven a car into a tree. A man in a San Francisco suburb had handed out marijuana brownies at his door. This was the world we now lived in. Nathan's compromise had been to follow his daughter at a half-block's distance, ducking behind bushes when other kids passed, and although he laughed when he told the story, as if it were a scene from a comedy we were both watching, I imagined her embarrassment had been both a surprise and a discouragement to him, and the thought of him swallowing his own feelings to protect his daughter's was again almost enough to make me change my mind and accept his offer.

But I did not. I told him a few stories of my own, even one that I claimed was about Elliot's adolescent struggle for independence, but was actually about my own. I had been invited to a party, and when my mother brought it up at dinner, my father had told me I couldn't go. Although our house was only one floor, I was up until two A.M. staring at my window trying to work up the courage to unlatch the security grate and defy him. I did not even want to go to the party, but I had the sense that challenging him would become important, although the next morning when he asked for seconds just as my mother was serving herself her own first helping of eggs, it did not yet occur to me what I might have been practicing for. In the story to Nathan, I found that the made-up symptoms of my own anxiety in bed wondering if Elliot might escape did not differ materially from the symptoms I had felt lying in bed trying to work up the courage to disobey my father. It was a strange thing to have done, but I laughed with Nathan when he signed the credit card slip and suggested that for all I knew Elliot had gone to the party after all. As we stepped out onto the sidewalk into a damp blanket of night that was almost warm, I waited for a last entreaty from him to take a job at his firm, and as he pulled his car key from his pocket, I felt a bolt of loss.

Driving home that night, I thought again about the magician from the birthday party. I had recalled the story during dinner, but I didn't share it because I had a vague feeling that even in Nathan's world, where the social currency of choice was self-mockery, this particular anecdote would reflect poorly on me. The truth was, as it turned out, Elliot's party had not been my only encounter with him. Two years later, I had seen an ad for magic lessons on the bulletin board next to the men's room at the Pine Cone. That morning I'd found a pregnancy test in the garbage in our bathroom. Liz and I had agreed to stop trying to have another child almost three years before, and finding the test had stunned me in a way I worked hard not to explore.

All morning I would catch myself looking out my window, or my fingers pausing above my keyboard, or my coffee going cold in its cup, and at lunch instead of going to the deli, I went alone to the scene of my brief ease among men.

It was probably a bad pick, the bar so urgently begged conversation between its patrons. I ate my sandwich quickly, and when a man sat down next to me while I waited for the return of my credit card, I got up to go to the bathroom. That's when I saw the ad for the Magic School. Elliot had long since stopped dressing in his cape and practicing with his cards, but I still occasionally took out the book that had come with the kit myself, and later that week, I found myself sitting on a folding chair in a room full of men waiting for the appearance of our teacher. When he stepped not from behind the curtain but from a chair in our midst, I recognized him, and I felt an inexplicable panic, as if a secret failure of mine were being exposed. He asked first how people had found out about the class, and when one man said he'd seen a flyer pinned to the bulletin board next to the dancers' profiles at Shipley's, I think I was the only one who didn't laugh. Next he asked people why they wanted to learn magic, and when the most common answer proved to be so they could do tricks for their own children, instead of making me feel better about the company I was keeping, somehow it made me feel worse. He taught us a trick called the Vanishing Knot, guaranteed to surprise, and over the next few weeks, I practiced it at odd moments alone until the smoothness of the effect made my heart skip. The hesitation came when I looked for an opportunity to show it to Elliot and felt only embarrassment at the thought of revealing my ambition. After a week of this, I resolved to let my interest in magic go, but there was a sense of missed opportunity competing for my obedience.

Driving home from my dinner with Nathan, I felt it again, and try as I might to resurrect the feeling of reassurance Liz had once conjured in me, I found I could not even re-create the substance of her argument. Magicians were unlovable? But I knew she would have admitted the joy they gave was real. Something dismissive about his costume? But her comment had struck me as more meaningful than this. It's only recently that I was able to recall her line about the cape with any precision. It was the magician's reliance on mystery to trigger happiness that she'd meant to dismiss. No matter how real Elliot's pleasure at such tricks, or how pure-hearted the magician's joy at stirring this feeling, real love couldn't grow from a bond that relied so heavily on omission.

I wish I'd been capable of this kind of insight then. It might have helped me head off a lot of things. For our father-son time that Sunday, Elliot had asked me to meet him in the living room. When I found him, he was sitting on the sofa, his elbows on his knees and a book on engine design in his lap. I stepped next to him, and he looked up at me.

"Hi," he said.

"Hello."

He rubbed the knees of his jeans. He had the look he often had in early childhood when he wanted permission to do something dangerous, or when he had broken something obviously fragile. He felt this too, and he looked down at his book again for strength. Then he pulled something out from underneath it: a blue folder with a plastic spine. He handed it to me.

"What's this?" I said, although of course I knew what it was.

"It's my report on Grandpa."

I was holding it in two hands, like a serving tray or a hymnal. I should open it, I thought. Instead I said, "Oh."

He waited, and I saw that there was bravery and resolve in this pause. I could hear the clock I had built ticking.

"Terrific," I said finally. "I look forward to reading it."

He laughed, a short burst. Then he waited. Then he laughed again.

"What's funny?" I said.

"I finished it three weeks ago, and you still haven't asked to see it."

"You didn't offer."

"Since when do I have to offer?"

It was a good question. Instead of acknowledging this, I said, "You interviewed me a dozen times, and it's about my father. Of course I'm interested."

"Then why didn't you ask?"

"When you didn't offer, I decided you must not be ready."

"Ready for what?"

His head was jutting forward and his eyes were squinting—a posture meant to signify equal parts disdain and legitimate confusion.

I held up his report. "Well, really, thanks. I look forward to reading it when we get back."

"We're not going anywhere."

"What do you mean?"

"This is it. This is what I set aside time for. Now you've got some time to read it."

He stood and rolled up his magazine.

I said, "I can always find time later this week. Let's go see a movie or get pizza or something."

"I made other plans already."

"Oh."

"I'm going to the A's game. Opening day."

"Okay."

As he stepped past me, he looked as if he wanted to make some affectionate gesture, but he had obviously resolved not to. This was supposed to be a statement of sorts, I saw. When he reached the door, though, he could not help himself. "See you later," he said, and although the front door is huge and swings so freely that to close it softly requires conscious effort, when he shut it behind him, it made almost no sound.

I walked to the open window, and saw that Tim's beat-up gray Pinto was already in the cul-de-sac waiting. As Elliot approached, the driver's-side door opened, and Robert stepped out to offer Elliot the wheel. He was wearing a green cap with the A's gold letter embroidered on the front, and a gaudy sateen windbreaker even though it was already seventy degrees. He clapped Elliot on the back as he rounded the door, and I could see Elliot's head turn towards the house. That he wanted to be sure I had not seen this filled me with more envy than the gesture alone ever could have. Belsky opened the rear door to slide into the back, and seconds later, they were gone.

I walked to the couch and sat down. The report cover itself had nothing on it, which somehow added to the suspense. I imagined opening it and finding something alarming. Something like, "My grandfather, Arthur Lincoln Albright, was not the kind of man most people would consider remarkable. He was a plumber in New Jersey, and he died unemployed of a heart attack at the age of forty-three. But I knew he was an interesting man because my father would never talk to me about him. Now I know why. . . ."

Instead, there was a typewritten cover sheet that read, "Arthur Lincoln Albright, 1915–1958." Below it was a copy of the photograph I had given him of my father standing in front of his house, his shoulders square and his hands folded neatly behind his back. Below this, in red ink, it read "C+: Not enough interview material to meet project guidelines. Neatly organized. Good typing."

I did read the report, but the truth was that the teacher's comments contained the full message he had wanted to pass along to me. It read not unlike a lean encyclopedia entry, plumped up with facts about his hometown and the plumbing trade and a brief biography of my mother that sounded so generic that it mentioned her eye color, something I am ashamed to say he must have gleaned from the driver's license in the first file of things I gave to him: birth certificates, a wedding license, a copy of their mortgage and the title to my father's van. It was exactly the kind of thing I had hoped to allow him to write, although I had imagined that the feeling such abridgment would yield was one of relief.

Later that day, the telephone rang, and he told me without any hint of question in his voice that he was spending the night at Tim's, and the following afternoon, when Liz was called in on short notice to work, I picked him up at school. He slipped in the passenger's-side door and opened his magazine in his lap.

"Would you like to drive?" I said.

"No thanks."

"How was the game?"

"Good," he said, but he did not look up from the page. On it was a picture of a crash dummy striking a windshield with his forehead. He said, "You're not taking that job with that guy Bob called, are you." It was more of a statement than a question.

"It's too much travel, I think. I'm worried about spending less time with you and Mom."

A small nod. He was still looking at his magazine. He brought it closer a moment to indicate his change in focus, but I could tell somehow from his posture that he was only pretending to read. I put the car in gear and pulled away from the curb and thought about what I might say. On the drive to his school, I had tried to prepare for a conversation about his report, but each time I came up with an opening it began with an apology I felt afraid to explain. He held his gaze on the magazine all the way to Sunrise Boulevard before turning the page. He paused here too, but it was only the masthead and an ad for motor oil. The car felt hot. I cracked the window for air, and it riffled the pages of his report on the seat beside me. He looked up at me then, but I could not turn my eyes from the road. I could have glanced at him, but I felt it would cement the strangeness my silence had forced, and so instead I checked my right mirror and changed lanes. The move was abrupt and required me to cut off another driver in a way that was almost aggressive. I knew he would notice this, it was so unlike me, but there was no explaining it away. At last, in the stranger's voice with which puberty had left him, he addressed me. "Dad?"

"Yes?"

"Can I ask you a question?"

"Of course. You can ask me anything." With my peripheral vision I saw his eyes scanning my profile. Neon signs passed behind him. I said, "But you might want to wait until after the surprise."

"The surprise?" he said.

The words had simply risen up in me. My heart pounded. "Yes," I said. Then I winked at him and turned right into a Toyota auto dealership.

He was hesitant at first, but I told myself that this was only natural. In the end, he picked a sporty coupe with a sunroof, and we test drove it together on the softening tar of the access road he had traveled so many times in Tim Belsky's Ford. The dealer reached forward between the bucket seats from the tiny rear bench to turn a blast of cool air on our faces and demonstrate the stereo. It was an instinct for diffusing all strains of tension that is the distinguishing talent of even the coarsest salesman, and within an hour Elliot had chosen the car in a color and trim line they had on the lot. We drove across the lot in separate cars, he in front and me behind him, and as he approached the boulevard, his right turn light began to blink. It was then that the anxiety I might have felt but did not in the salesman's office finally seized me. All the way home, Elliot drove as carefully as an elderly man, coasting to stop signs and watching for signs of me in his mirror.

7 The Stand-Up

WHEN I ARRIVED IN THE ATTIC WITH THE SAW, ELLIOT HAD already prepared the area. He had slid his bed towards the stairs and taken down the swimsuit calendar. He had pulled back the rug. On the bare white wall, he had measured and traced a level rectangle with a razor knife. At the sight of me, he kneeled, and I handed him the saw, thinking that letting him do the work himself would take the sting out of the sloppiness we were about to expose. Then he turned to the wall and forced the sharp tip into the Sheetrock.

It is hard to describe the feeling I had as I crouched next to him watching him cut into the wall. Sometimes I wonder how much of the scene has been revised by hindsight, but there's good evidence that even before I knew what would happen, I was nervous. I remember I'd worn a dark T-shirt, because I knew the tension would make me sweat. Since that day last summer, it seemed he was urging me to tell him I thought there was something wrong with him, to show some disapproval of the person he was becoming, and now in some way the plumbing had once again caused me to do just that. When

I'd suggested that an oversight in our work—I'd been careful to call it ours—in the attic might have caused the problem, he had simply nodded and asked what kind of saw we should use to cut into the wall. I'd considered telling him stories of things I had overlooked building the house, pointing out how errors were inevitable even in the work of the most careful craftsmen, but it seemed to me that this kind of obviously scripted comfort would only make more of his mistake. In the end, out of what I will admit was mostly cowardice, I'd decided to wait to see how he reacted to the evidence of his own heedlessness. But the waiting—wondering what I would say, and what he would do, and suspecting that whatever I would say would annoy him as he made his slow careful cut—each stroke of the saw making a sound like ripping cardboard, almost ten full minutes of this—I think this was some of the greatest stress I had ever felt as a parent. Squatting next to him, the sloping ceiling close above our heads, I was getting hot and light-headed and my quadriceps were shaking. I stood and took a step back to the open air beneath the peaked roof. When he set the saw down and wiggled the long strip of Sheetrock free, my heart was racing.

"It looks perfect," he said.

What I felt first was a little bolt of fear at the sophistication of this. He was making it more awkward on purpose, I thought, forcing me not only to point out his mistakes but also his inability to detect them. I forced a casualness into my tone. "Let me take a look."

When I squatted next to him though, I quickly saw that he was right. The plastic vent arm was well supported all the way down, every strap hanger attached at perfect perpendicularity to the pipe, all the screw heads flush. At the sight of this, I might have felt a moment of relief at not having to shame him, but suddenly the snow of wallboard dust and the misplaced furniture and the ragged hole in the wall were deeply embarrassing. I tried for a tone of clinical interest, almost enthusiasm: "Interesting. Well, the most likely thing then is the temporary clog."

He hesitated. "More than once?"

"Sure," I said. "There could be something insoluble in the waste pipe that keeps catching things temporarily as they go down."

"Like what?"

"A hair clip or the cap to a bottle of shaving cream. Hair or food could catch on it briefly to plug the drain and then work its way loose with enough water flow."

When he nodded at this, I knew he had moved to pity for me. I braced myself for his kindness.

"So how do we get at it?" he said.

We would snake the pipes through every fixture drain and clean-out in the house with a seventy-five-foot power snake. We would begin at the top and work our way down. We would miss nothing. I could tell by the way he looked at the floor just when the length of my description began to betray my uncertainty, and I cut myself off. I suggested a trip to Briggs the following afternoon, and again he hesitated. Then he set his glasses back on his ears and said he'd drive straight from school and meet me.

Larry's wife didn't seem to notice me when I came in, and, given the circumstances of my visit, I was grateful. She was watching an early incarnation of those shows that specialize in getting real people to discuss their personal problems in front of an audience. A woman was describing her husband's lack of sympathy about her depression since the last of her children got married. The man tried to interject, but the woman's voice grew louder and more tremulous, and he no doubt saw the futility of trying to defend his sensitivity by interrupting her on national television. The thought of them eating dinner at home that night after the taping, each silently mystified by the greater distance they felt, made me sad.

I moved to a bin full of neoprene sleeves and focused my attention on the question of a summer project that might be exciting enough to win Elliot's attention. As much as I had been hanging my hopes on this as a path back to intimacy with him, it had of course occurred to me that after all that had happened he might not want to spend the bulk of his summer on a project with me. Somehow I reasoned that if I chose carefully, I could pick something that appealed to him in terms of challenge and objective, but still allowed him enough time during the mornings and early afternoons to spend time with his friends. I thought of setting the hot tub into the deck, but the truth was he had never brought anyone home to use it as I'd hoped he would, and although the work would involve some tricky problems, it didn't seem the end result would be enough of a change to be rewarding. I tried to think of improvements to his attic room that he might appreciate, but all I could come up with was wall-to-wall carpeting, which would take a week at most and would require him to move temporarily back into his old room on the second floor. My best idea so far had been an addition to the garage—a new bay where he could park his car in the winter. It would be an interesting project, including some demolition and a lot of framing, but the scale of the job seemed likely to cut into his time at Belsky's, and I felt a sad certainty that this would be a greater loss to him than the time he shared with me. I was thinking about this, staring at a bin full of screw clamps, when Larry's wife said, "Did you hear that one?"

I looked around; I was surprised that she had even noticed me.

I said, "I was sort of absorbed."

"She really chewed him out that time." She was looking at me over the top of an aisle. "Need help finding something there?"

"No, thanks."

"You seem to be stuck."

"Not at all."

"No man's an island."

I said, "Actually, I'm waiting for my son."

"He's meeting you here?"

"Yes."

"Okay, but no fighting this time."

She meant this to be funny to me, and I smiled to be polite, but the truth was the comment annoyed me. Back in January, when I returned the smoke pump, I had brought Elliot with me. Although I was still putting it off, at that point it was pretty clear that I would have to suggest his own error might be at fault, and I wanted to undercut the insult of this by treating him as an equal partner in the diagnosis. I had shown him the vent increasers, which can be used to widen a vent opening in climates colder than ours. In the winter, the narrow mouth of the stack can fill with ice or snow, and this too can siphon a trap. He was quiet as I talked, and in the end, I may have spent as much as fifteen minutes delving into the physics of venting. When I had gone to the counter to return the pump, Elliot wandered over to a display stocked with flanges, and Larry's wife leaned towards me. "I've got four of my own at home, and sometimes they give me the same treatment."

"Excuse me?"

"The silent treatment. They think it's so much torture." She laughed and shook her head. "Trick is not to fight it. Just take the quiet as a secret blessing."

I didn't point out that a little silence in a teenager hardly constituted hostility because it occurred to me that Larry's death had probably brought a lot of both things into her home. But to be honest, it seemed likely to me that her confrontational style had created plenty of tension in their family even before he was gone. I doubted a person like her would see it this way, though. Not for the first time that year, I thought of that time my father called me to his room to talk to me about the centrifugal pump. Mice had infested the house, but he had not set traps, and their urine scented the hallways. I found him sitting at his bedroom window looking out into the yard, his finger holding a place in a book he had taken from my mother. Outside, the abandoned components lay on a towel in the yellowed grass.

"You finish that pump," he said.

"Excuse me?"

"The pump you started. You've been letting it rust to make some kind of statement, I guess."

"Sir?"

"It's a good plan you had. Follow through with it, damn it."

The room was dim with light from the one bulb that had not burned out months ago.

He said, "Your mom spent a lot of time driving you around town finding those parts."

"I know."

"Some of them cost money."

"Yes, sir."

"You think you can do whatever you please? You think you're not responsible to anybody? You think you can't make people angry and disappointed just the same as you make them proud?"

"No, sir."

" 'No, sir,' " he mimicked my voice and shook his head. "Finish that pump by Friday."

I stared at him.

"Bet you think you're pretty unlucky."

I tried to think of an answer to this.

He said, "To have a nasty, lazy, son of a bitch like me for a dad?"

"No, sir."

I saw my father flinch in the dim light.

We passed a moment in the dark saying nothing, and finally it occurred to me that we were so far apart in this conversation that each of us would be better off alone. As I turned to leave he said, "Your mother, she'd just pick up the rusty parts one day while you were at school and haul them to the dump. She'd be making you soft-boiled eggs next day and sugaring your tea, but me, I'll take the belt to your ass and not stand to look at you for weeks." He closed my mother's book. "I'm the one that loves you."

I was going over this memory a second time when Larry's wife spoke to me again. She had stepped from behind the counter and was refilling a bin of washers at the end of the aisle.

"Excuse me?" I said.

"Your boy. Looks like he stood you up."

"That's unlikely."

"That's the next step. That's it after the silent treatment."

"I seriously doubt he'd—"

"The stand-up."

"Nonsense." I was unsuccessful this time in keeping any of the irritation from my voice, but to my surprise, at the clear sign of it she simply smiled and winked at me. Her hair was a little damp I noticed now, and I could smell chlorine. I was trying to think of something to say that would cut her short and make my disdain for her clear, but instead I pictured her gripping the edge of a swimming pool, her skin sheeting water. Sometimes I watched my thoughts like a man in a theater. They seemed separate from me. Not mine. I looked down at the globe valves. I didn't really think Elliot would keep me waiting like that intentionally, but when it occurred to me how long I'd been there, lost in my thoughts, I was first startled; then, afraid.

I said, "I need to rent a power snake."

And she said, "What's the problem?"

Suddenly, she was more than I could bear. "Please. I just . . ." I think I must have put my hands in the air, a kind of plea or surrender. I am not sure what I did. I said, "Can I use your phone?"

"Sure you can," she said. Her voice was softer now. She went in back for the snake while I called, but after six rings, the answering machine picked up and at the sound of Liz's recorded voice my throat swelled.

When Larry's wife saw me hang up, she said, "Hey, listen, I'm sure he's fine."

I handed her a credit card.

She said, "I used to worry too, but being late never once meant an accident. It was always just to get a rise out of me."

I made a business of arranging things in my wallet. Bills from biggest to smallest. I saw that picture from the Grand Canyon, and this time I did not take it out.

She was saying, "And if you want, one of my kids or Larry's brother could help you out with that clog. I could do it myself after closing. I could even close early if you want."

"I'm fine. Really. Thank you," I said.

"Okay." She cocked her head and shook it once, ever so slightly. "Good luck, Luther Albright."

The traffic on the highway was thick, and it took me fifteen minutes to reach my exit. While he had always been a responsible boy, during our lessons together, I'd detected the seeds of a clear tendency to challenge other drivers on the road. I was aware of the unlikelihood of a newly licensed teenage driver with his own car choosing to ride his bike, but that's nevertheless the absurd kind of thing I found myself hoping for. In the first weeks of ownership, I reminded myself, he actually drove it very little. One night, I woke and went downstairs for a glass of seltzer and saw him standing barefoot in the driveway in his pajamas, just staring. As I turned onto Alameda, I seized on the possibility that Tim had given him a ride, but this seemed unlikely too. Elliot's car, of course, was much nicer than Tim's.

When I pulled into the cul-de-sac, his yellow coupe was there. I opened the front door to the sound of bass music playing above me, and although his taste in music had evolved into something only Liz seemed to understand, I felt a quick lightness beneath my breastbone at the sound. I was as excited to see him as if he'd been away for weeks. Although I wasn't a young man, I took the stairs two at a time. When I crested the second flight, I found him lying on the sofa in his attic bedroom, eating a peach, his hand glistening with juice. He looked up at me from his magazine, eyebrows raised, and I thought of my father holding that hand of cards after my science fair, the sink full of dishes. A rivulet of juice ran into Elliot's sleeve, and I understood with certainty that Larry's wife had been right. My son had left me waiting intentionally.

"Hello," I said.

"Hi."

"I think your mom left casseroles in the freezer for us."

He blinked.

I said, "I like the ham and bean, but I think there's also tuna noodle, if you prefer."

"What?"

"Ham and bean then," I said, and I turned and went down the stairs.

In the pantry, I opened the standing freezer. Inside was a stack of casseroles in blue-lidded Tupperware containers each prepared by Liz when her hours at the Crisis Center first began to increase. Standing there looking at them, I was struck at once by the tenderness of these preparations and the premonition of detachment that allowed her to make them, and again I felt that rise of suspicion that was my stunted heart's mistranslation of a sense of loss. The purchase of Elliot's car had secretly terrified me, but she had not even really seemed surprised, and I couldn't help but wonder if before she had begun quietly moving her emotional life to the annex I'd chosen for her, she would have been able to accept a sign of my desperation so serenely. I popped the lids to examine their contents. Frost covered them like a pelt. I parted the hoary filaments on the surface of each one with the edge of its lid, but this revealed almost nothing. Shapes merged. One looked pinker than the others. A tomato sauce probably, but suddenly I couldn't remember which of her casseroles even contained tomatoes. I picked up the phone and was confronted by the stark fact that she had been working there for three months and I had never tried to call her. I took out the phone book and saw that they had paid extra to have their listing printed in bold-faced type. When I dialed, they answered on the first ring.

"Crisis line. My name is Heather. What's yours?"

I hadn't thought this through. "Um," I said.

She let a silence fall, and I imagined how this might encourage another kind of man to share his troubles.

I said, "I need to talk to Liz."

She paused for a second. Then she said, "Okay. Sit tight."

She put me on hold without sound. I felt a pinch of heat beneath my arms.

Liz came on the line. "Rudy?" she said.

"No, it's me."

"Luther?"

"Who's Rudy?"

"One of our frequent callers," she said. "What's wrong?"

I looked down at the casseroles. "That woman, Heather, shouldn't be giving her name out."

"It's not her real name."

"Oh." I thought about this. "What's your fake name?"

"Sarah."

"Sarah."

In one container, I saw what was probably a potato; a gray trace of a sausage. A breeze through the open windows raised the hair on my arms.

She said, "Luther, what's going on? You've never called me here before."

"I just thought I'd check to see what you'd like for dinner."

"Dinner?"

"I know you won't be home in time to eat with us, but you might be hungry when you get back."

She didn't seem to know what to say to this.

I said, "I like the ham and bean."

"Okay."

"Is there ham and bean in the freezer?"

"I think so."

"How can I tell?"

"Smell for mustard."

"Mustard."

Above me, I heard the thrum of water filling our son's bathtub, and right away I braced myself. These days any plumbing sounds would wake me from a deep sleep, as did breezes and outdoor noises, all of them taunts.

"Luther," Liz said, "are you sure you're okay?"

"Sure I am."

"Where's Elliot?"

"Upstairs." I leaned over the counter and inhaled, and the scent came to me, sharp and clear. "Oh, here it is. Thank you. See you tonight."

I served it in front of the television, because lately this seemed to be what he wanted. Remote controls were new then, and when I had purchased our first I had surrendered it without argument to Elliot's restless command. Now he settled in an armchair with his plate balanced on his knees and flipped through the channels: Pat Sajak clapping for the passage of dollars on his giant wheel, a woman soaking her fingers in dish soap, a map of Sacramento County troubled by paper clouds. He paused on what appeared to be the scene of a dinner party in a banquet hall. White streamers hung from the ceiling, and above a dance floor sparkled a giant mirrored ball. When a man in a bright white uniform and cap approached a table of elderly couples, I recognized it as *The Love Boat,* and to my surprise, Elliot set the remote on the side table and picked up his fork.

I had seen the show probably half-a-dozen times, and from this it had not been difficult to glean that the formula involved the problems of three different couples aboard a cruise ship. It seemed to me that at the age of fifteen, with a new girlfriend, and after the awkwardness about the underwear in his bathroom, he was fairly likely to be uncomfortable watching a show about romance with me—particularly one in which the sex lives of characters was a frequent topic. But no sooner had I completed this thought than it came to me that it was my own discomfort he would be trying to stir. So I braced myself, and, as absurd as I knew they would be, I settled in to focus on the plots.

The first appeared to be about the fiancée of a powerful congressman who was worried that a nude photo she had taken long ago for an erotic magazine would jeopardize her husband's political career. The second was about a divorced couple—a chef and a waitress—who by coincidence were hired at the same time by the cruise line and wind up trapped together in the ship's meat locker. And the third was about a newlywed couple who are prevented by dislocated backs, sunburn, and poison ivy from consummating their wedding vows. I guessed early on that it would be at some point during their disastrously painful attempts to have sex that he would try to set some kind of conversational trap for me, but he was silent throughout each of these, and in the end, it was the divorced couple's plot that drew his only comment.

During their entrapment in the freezer, they had gone through several stages. First they had tried to busy themselves with escape, interrupting their debates about method with an awkward exchange of news about their lives since the divorce. After the commercial break, they shifted their attention to trying to keep warm. As they ran through options for raising their body temperature, it seemed obvious where this plot was going, but ripe as this inevitable climax might be with opportunities to make me feel awkward in his company, it was at some point during one of the less suggestive conversations that Elliot shook his head and laughed through his nose.

I could sense his eyes sliding in my direction. I tried to guess what he was fishing for, but at the time, it eluded me completely.

"People are so fake," he said finally.

On-screen, the man was removing his shoes and socks. The woman was sitting on a cardboard box with her arms pulled inside the body of her tuxedo shirt telling him about a movie star who had come into her restaurant.

Elliot said, "They always pretend the opposite of what they're really feeling."

The chef pulled his socks over his hands and clapped them together with satisfaction. The waitress kept on with her story: how the actor asked for her phone number; how he invited her to a five-course dinner on his yacht.

Elliot made the noise again. "They never say what they mean. They're so fake."

When I felt his eyes settle on me, I nodded, because my agreement seemed important to him, but I felt somehow afraid to engage him with words. Although up until this point he had stolen occasional glances at me, his concentration seemed to deepen during the next scenes. The temptation to simply leave him there absorbed and

do the vaguely humiliating snaking job alone was strong, but I suspected he would detect the shame behind this impulse. So instead I
waited impatiently for the credits to roll and then clapped my hands
and suggested we head upstairs.

Although before he moved into the attic he'd kept his bathroom
neat, recently there had been a change. He still put his toothbrush
and comb in his medicine cabinet after use, but he didn't wipe the
countertop around the washbasin as he once did. Water pooled
there, and in the late afternoon, a faint outline of mineral deposits
and the residue of soap marked their outer boundaries. The lower
half of his mirror was flecked with toothpaste, and, in the sink basin,
short hairs rimmed the drain like iron filings. We kneeled together on
his bath mat, and dampness left there by his morning shower bled
through the knees of my work pants. I worried that as the same happened to him he would be embarrassed by this. Our elbows touched,
and he moved away from me to give me space, one knee on the tile.
For a second, I thought I might tell him he wasn't crowding me. Instead, I said nothing. I was feeding the tip of the snake down the tub
drain when he said, "I'm sorry I didn't meet you."

"That's all right."

"It was irresponsible."

"It wasn't so bad; I like hanging out at Briggs."

When he didn't say more, I flipped the switch on the snake, and
he stared at me as it hummed loudly between us. Then he did a
funny thing. He took off his glasses. I didn't think he could see me
clearly when he did this, but my own vision has always been good.
It's difficult for me to know what my son saw.

I waited.

He looked up at the ceiling, and I noted, as I often had in the
year since he entered high school, that his throat was no longer a
boy's throat. He swallowed hard, and his Adam's apple moved inside
him, large.

Although he was only a foot from me, the snake was so loud I had
to raise my voice a little. I said, "You're trying to tell me something."

He laughed, in shock I think. "Yeah." But then he said nothing.

I said, "This whole thing is a little unsettling."

He nodded. The snake was turning freely inside the pipe, but I couldn't bring myself to turn it off.

I said, "It is for me too. It's frustrating not to know exactly what the problem is."

In absence of his glasses, I could see that the skin under his eyes was dark, and I had a father's yearning to set him at ease. Having given voice to something awkward, I thought maybe a change of subject might be the best tactic, but I had trouble thinking of anything uncomplicated to discuss. I sifted through a few options, and finally, I'm embarrassed to say that what came out under pressure was this:

"The FDA approved a new sweetener."

He looked at me.

"They're calling it Nutrasweet."

"Dad," he said, "I'm thinking about getting a part-time job this summer."

I tried to steady my voice. "Why?"

He closed his eyes and rubbed them with his thumb and middle finger as if they were sore, but I could see that he was trying to remove traces of moisture. I'd been employed without interruption for twenty-two years, and I'd had three high-paying job offers in the four weeks since my resignation. I had thirty thousand dollars in the bank, and another hundred and fifty in a conservative bond portfolio that a less responsible man would have long since been seduced into selling for fast-moving stocks. We lived in one of the nicest suburbs in Sacramento. We had three new cars. There had been no signs, ever, anywhere in his childhood of financial instability, but, in spite of all of this, somehow in the context of my apparent failures—the plumbing, my job loss, my parenting—I wondered if my son had also begun to doubt our security. I said, "Not for money, surely."

The fingers stopped on his lids. For a matter of seconds he was perfectly still. Then he put his glasses back on and looked me in the eye. "Yes. It's the money."

"Nonsense," I said.

"Well, I was kind of short on cash this month."

"Of course you were. You're getting older. You go out with friends; you have a car. But you can have whatever you need."

He looked at me. The snake was still turning.

I said, "How much do you need?"

"A hundred dollars."

"No problem," I said, and I turned to switch off the snake.

Treating every drain in the house took a little over two hours, and left each bathroom smelling faintly of sewage. Although I tried to let it go, as we worked, I kept tallying the changed features of his private life—different clothes, more meals out, movies and sporting events, extra gas for longer drives than I'd been imagining—and my failure to anticipate the increase in his needs seemed just one more measure of the distance between us. We pulled up some hair, a few orange peels, and once heard a cracking noise that left a few fragments of bright red plastic on the tip of the snake. I made as much of this as I could, ignoring the smell, and when we were finished, tried to undercut the sense of failure stirred by the conversation about money and the strong feeling that nothing conclusive had been learned or solved by declaring it safe to close the windows. We started together in the living room and then split up, and he was already upstairs before I saw that the task would lead us naturally to our bedrooms without saying good night.

I got ready for bed, but instead of trying to sleep, for the first time in weeks, I waited up for Liz to return from the swing shift. I still believed in most ways I had been a good husband. Certainly, she had never complained. Or she only complained, in the midst of our infrequent arguments, about little things: that I was inflexible; that I was too tidy; and once, that I was repressed, although when I pushed her on this point, she would not explain what she meant. While that one always bothered me, I used to try to convince myself that it is one of the things someone says in the heat of argument that is based less on reality than a desire to upset.

We were in the car; Liz was driving, and we were talking about the miscarriages. She had just had a third, and when she forgot to signal at the traffic light, I reached over and did it for her. It's true that it was not important from a safety standpoint to signal there, but I'd been generally worried about her level of distraction as she talked, and was pleased in some unexamined, reflexive way to be able to do something to supplement her attention to the cause of getting us home. I just reached over and did it.

"Are you even listening to me!?"

"I've heard everything you've said."

She looked over both shoulders, too quickly to take anything in. "There's no one around to even see that signal! We're alone on the road, and I just told you something amazing; something I've spent almost six years trying to find out, and you're thinking about traffic law."

"I'm not. It was a reflex. I heard everything you said. If people couldn't listen and think about driving at the same time, talking in cars would be illegal."

"There! See! You're still thinking about traffic law!"

"I'm just proving my point."

"Then what did I say?"

"You said, 'Forget about the disappointment, maybe I wasn't even meant to be a mother.' "

And she burst into tears. There were no cars behind us; so we just sat there at the traffic light. This is what she had said verbatim, and I guessed it must have stung to hear it again. I reached over and took her shoulders in my arms and pulled her towards me. I will admit I was tempted to put the car in park before I did it, I did have that thought, but of course I resisted. It was true there was almost no traffic on the road, and I was frantic to calm her. "I'm so sorry, sweetheart."

I had meant for the situation, for the fact that we were having so much trouble having a child, but she took it as apology: "It's the way you say things sometimes. How can you just repeat something that awful like it's something you read out of the newspaper?"

The possibility that she was sobbing so hard not about the miscarriages, but about me, came as a shock. I pulled back. "You asked me what you said. You asked me."

"Oh you are so repressed," she said, and she sat back and put her hands on the wheel.

"What?"

She turned left onto Sunrise Boulevard.

I said, "We were talking about the miscarriages."

"Babies."

"Okay, babies."

Her jaw was set.

I said, "What do you mean?" Neon signs made colors on her face. I said, "That could have been an example of insensitivity, or anal retentiveness, but not repression."

She did not respond. But later that night, when I asked again, she reached over a hand in the dark and put it to my cheek without even having to grope, and this gesture would almost have been enough on its own, but she also said, "I take it back." It made me feel better, until the next morning when brushing my teeth alone in the bathroom I realized with a sudden, evidenceless conviction only people who have been married a few years can feel, that she had done this not because she felt her words had been unfair, but because she felt their truth was more than I could take.

The next week, I went with her to a lab in an office tower near the Hyatt. I was holding her hand, and I tried to measure my slight steps to match the pace of the conveyor belt as it eased her body into a big white doughnut. When the doctor found us in the waiting room later and asked us to come to his office, my pulse leapt. Liz's palm was sweating, but I did not let go. She had three small fibroids, he said, and we had a number of options. Liz interrupted to ask to see the picture on the sheet of acetate he was holding on his crossed knees.

When he handed it to her, she held it halfway between us so I could see, but I had a number of questions for the doctor. I ticked resolutely through them: frequency of recurrence after surgery, likelihood of reproductive success, surgical risks and percentage of fibroids that become cancerous. It seemed to me surgery was a good idea, and I turned to her and said so, and she looked up from the shiny sheets then with much the same look she had worn in the car when I flicked the turn signal.

I was thinking about this, sitting up in bed with an open magazine I had not even glanced through, when I finally heard her footfall on the stairs. One twenty-six. My heart quickened when I saw her.

"You're still up," she said.

"Yes."

Her cheeks were flushed and her eyes bright. She opened her pocket book and took out a roll of butterscotch Lifesavers. "Want one?"

"No, thank you."

She peeled back a bit of the waxed paper and foil and put one in her mouth. It was a small thing, but I had never seen her take Lifesavers from her purse before. She did not even really eat candy.

"So," I said. "How was your day?"

She looked at her pocketbook. "Oh, gosh. Same old, same old."

I didn't know what she meant, and the realization that in all her descriptions of work I had never noticed a common thread was disconcerting. "The same kind of callers?"

"Mhm."

"Like what?"

"Let's see. A woman who said the only time she feels like a whole person is when she's alone in the bathroom. Her husband's a urologist, and he thinks she has a bladder infection. That's why he thinks she goes so often." She opened and shut her purse again. "Another caller was a man who said whenever he looks in the mirror he sees this very small version of himself. Sometimes when he gets to work he sits in his car for as much as twenty minutes with the engine idling."

The image of her holding the receiver to her cheek and listening to these strangers' fears filled me with something I could not name. I said, "That's a good thing you're doing."

She shrugged.

"Really."

A hand rose to her neck. "Thanks."

"It's very kind."

She took her earrings off—one, and then the other—and palmed them.

I said, "Do you enjoy it at all—listening to those people's problems?"

"It feels like the right thing to do."

"I mean for your own sake."

"Not really," she said. She took her necklace off with two hands, like a yoke. She was still wearing her clothes, her shoes; her pocketbook lay on the bedspread; but somehow this removal made her look naked. Maybe it was the way she held herself—shyly—as she never did when she took off her robe to step into the shower or surprised me by pulling back the bedsheet to expose her own bareness, but as she often did when I asked her to remove the towel she had pressed to her body or lingered by the door of the closet to watch her undress. Her eyes fluttered from me. "I mean, of course not. No."

I wondered for the first time if she might shower before coming to bed, and when she did not, a sickening, double-agent's kind of courage came to me. She slipped between the sheets, and I pulled her towards me beneath them to check for another man's smell. Her muscles tensed, at first, in surprise, but then she buried her face in my neck, and the soft sweep of her nose and lips against the skin there brought first relief, and then panic, and then shame. All three of them stayed. She sat me up and removed my shirt. In my excitement closing the windows, I had done a teenager's job on the shades, and now the barest trace of moonlight through the new elm leaves graced her arms and cheek before she laid us down again. In a weird act of will, I made myself imagine how her control might excite another man. But then I lost track of all of these feelings until afterwards when exhaustion came and laid a heavy blanket on my thoughts and limbs that only the most persistent kind of anxiety can invade. *Sarah,* it said. *Sarah.*

I drifted off, but woke an hour later sharing a pillow with my wife, and somehow her hair against my lips, and the smell of butterscotch from her open mouth filled me with a mixture of sadness and panic that sent my heart racing. I had only felt this feeling a handful of times in my adult life, but long ago I had found a way of dispelling it. Our basement was a space of which I was particularly proud, and part of what made this exercise so helpful was that I had to pass through a room I had made so well. Most basements lack sufficient headroom to allow for the installation of a drop ceiling and a plywood subfloor, but my basement is very deep. I ran all the water supply lines through joists behind the Sheetrock and hid the enormous soil pipe by boxing it in with boards stained and joined to make it appear almost indistinguishable from a wooden ceiling beam. And although most basements are damp and cold, by doing the job myself, I was able to ensure good weatherproofing. In particular, I chose to seal the exterior wall of the foundation rather than the interior one, which is more reliable for two reasons. Hydrostatic pressure, exerting force towards the center of the house as it does, tends to push against the surface of, and therefore tighten, exterior sealers, while pushing against the base of, and therefore loosen, those applied to the interior wall. Maybe even more important, exterior sealants prevent moisture from penetrating even the outer layer of the wall, thus providing several additional inches of security. As a general rule, history has taught us to protect a structure as far from the locus of vulnerability as possible.

When I got to the bottom of the stairs that night, I stood there, as I often did, and visualized the pipes and wires running behind the pure white walls. When I opened the mechanical closet door, the light came on automatically, and there was just enough room for me to step in on either side of the machines. Mounted on the wall was a hand vacuum. Once a month, I went there to remove dust and dirt from the closet floor. I tightened the pipe fittings and the packing nuts on the centrifugal pump to keep it from losing its prime. I cleaned the air shutter on the hot-water heater to assure the proper supply of air to burner and pilot light. I polished the contacts on the furnace thermostat with fine sandpaper to remove dirt.

But that night, I did none of these things. It was not what I'd come for. The space behind the furnace was barely wide enough to take my hand, but it was easy to find my way. High in the wall was a hole, four inches by four, that I cut before I installed the furnace. I reached in and pulled out the biscuit tin, and as I removed the lid, the furnace ticked and sighed into motion. Though it was unlikely, I always worried that one of them had found it—run fingers along its checkered grip and drawn wrongheaded conclusions about a life I had kept secret from them. But at the time I didn't really believe I had a secret life. I thought I was merely protecting them. Guns are dangerous, and moreover, it wasn't even mine.

I took it out of the tin, surprised, as I always was, by how heavy it seemed to me. It was a Colt Service Model Ace .22 with a ten-round detachable magazine. One day, I had crept into my parents' bedroom and copied the serial number into my notebook because I thought knowing its provenance might help me understand my father. It did not, but it did tell me he had probably spent too much, even in 1953. Production on the model had stopped after the war, and the scarcity was just beginning to inflate the price of them. I might have sold it easily years ago, just to rid myself of the worry that Elliot might find it and come to some harm. But by throwing all of the bullets away, I was able to convince myself it was safe enough to keep it. Although the warmest emotion I harbor for my father is pity, the truth is, this was one thing of his I really wanted to own. Superstitious as it was, for me, over the years, his pistol had become a sort of talisman. At those few times in my life when, lying in bed next to my sleeping wife, I had felt the beginnings of genuine fear or sadness building inside me, I had gone down to the basement and removed the gun from the hole. There in the dark, I held it in two hands with my back against the furnace room door, and at the precise moment when my breathing slowed and my pulse became itself again, I put the pistol back where it belonged, unloaded and hidden in my basement wall. In this way the gun was a reminder. It was a reminder of how deeply I differed from the kind of man who would burden his family with knowledge of his petty needs and sorrows.

As I said, Liz's schedule now at the Crisis Center included forty hours a week. They'd lost another volunteer, she'd said, and she felt bad for her coordinator, as well as for the callers. When she said this, she looked at me squarely. Our marriage had given me no opportunity to learn what she might look like were she to lie to me. I'd seen her do so once to someone else, a store clerk just after we were married. She had purchased a pair of shorts with LOVE embroidered across the backside, and the zipper broke the next day when she stooped to pick up a flat of strawberry plants at the nursery. When she tried to return them, he said he could only accept the return of unworn merchandise, and without blinking she said it had broken when she tried them on for her husband. In the parking lot, she filled the space in which we might have talked about it with a rant about a mother she'd seen yanking her son's arm in the aisles, and although I knew why she had lied, in fact, respected her motives, it was several hours before the smoothness with which she had done so lost its hold on my imagination.

The Crisis Center was in downtown Sacramento, and on my way to two separate appointments, I might have stopped by to say hello. On the first of these, I left home early and parked so that I'd have to pass its door. I looked for her car, and when I didn't see it, I began to circle the block to find it, but as I passed by a children's shoe store and saw a woman inside kneeling on the floor to squeeze the sides of her son's sneakers, I was overcome by such deep shame I turned in place and hurried on to my meeting. A week later when an interview again took me to her part of town during her shift, I left home with the plan of dropping in with barbecue, and when I reached the door it was not guilt this time but sadness that stopped me. This was my wife. I ate my sandwich alone in César Chávez Park and set hers on a bench beside me before leaving, opening the flaps of waxed paper wide for the birds.

In the end, I learned her secret not through spying, but instead by accident. An early proposal for a very expensive and unnecessary modification to my dam had been voted down, but in the newspaper days later there was an anonymous editorial that suggested this was a mistake we would all live or die to regret. The letter was crazy, and mentioned apocalypse, but one or two lines made it clear that this person had at least some knowledge of structural engineering, and although I've come to feel certain the author was a stranger to me, at the time I couldn't help but wonder if it had been written by Belsky.

It might be a measure of how much things had changed that when I read it at breakfast that morning I didn't snap the paper with exaggerated flourish and read the crazy diatribe aloud. Instead, I felt a little flare of panic, not that the editorial would influence their opinion about my work in any way, but at the thought that this kind of humor and casual talk on topics related to my career were somehow now beyond us. I turned to the front of the section to monopolize it throughout the meal.

When we finished breakfast, I set it on top of the others. I didn't really care if they read it, just if they read it with me around. But in the next days, I found myself preoccupied with curiosity about whether Liz too had seen it and felt at a loss about how to handle the joking it warranted. The question took on an importance in my mind that I can scarcely explain except to say that it's been my experience that generalized anxiety feeds best on smaller objects.

I don't know what made me think I might be able to tell, looking at the discarded newspaper, whether she had read it. The garage was cold, and my breath hovered in white puffs and disappeared as I leaned over the plastic bin. I felt a bolt of irritation when I lifted the lid. We'd had chicken the night before, and the carcass sat loosely wrapped in a piece of newspaper, covered in its own jelly. Liz always emptied the garbage neatly. Even a single item, such as a ham bone, was wrapped in plastic and tied off before deposit into the can because ever since her first pregnancy she'd had a sensitive nose. It hadn't even been his job to empty the garbage last night—it had been an act of unsolicited courtesy on his part—but still I felt annoyed, picturing his untied sneaker tapping the gas pedal, two fingers resting on the wheel as he drifted into the left lane.

I set the carcass aside and began drawing out white plastic bags, neatly fastened by Liz with yellow plastic cable ties. The newspapers slid between them, and it had been cold enough the night before that the chicken smell was not rotten but fresh. It made my stomach growl, and my irritation flared again. Tuesday Sports. Monday Front Page. Tuesday Business. Saturday Home. Some had been discarded inside out after reading, and this made it more difficult to find what I was looking for. Bright, slippery coupons for car washes, hair color, honey-baked ham. It had been in the Friday Metro section, I thought. But before I found it, something else caught my eye. Liz's red ink on a page of Classifieds.

I stood up straight and set them on the hood of my car, but immediately I knew that this was her secret. What struck me first was the variety of the things she had circled: Assistant Bookkeeper, Clothing Sales, Librarian, Pet Sales, Prep Cook, Teaching Assistant, Tutor. Some of them had check marks next to phone numbers—the job as a prep cook at a restaurant near the capitol; the clothing sales position and a teaching assistant's job at a preschool in Carmichael. What was disturbing about it was not that she had looked for a job, but that she had kept it to herself—whether because the distance between us made it difficult to explain, or because she thought her motives for doing so might hurt me.

I separated the sheet from its section and folded it small. My drive had weakened somewhat, but I continued searching until I found the editorial. The section had been folded open to this page, and there was a small dribble of tea alongside it that told me that indeed she had read it. I tore it free of the paper and folded this too, as small as the want ads, and returned the garbage to its can. Then I headed back to the house.

Bad moments that year were plentiful, and so it might seem fruitless to try to select front-runners from among them, but coming as it did at the end of a line of so many, and bearing the weight of all their discouragement, I think it is possible that the most dispiriting of all was opening my front door just then and smelling sewer gas. It was not really a comfort to me that neither of them was home, and I will be honest and say it took a great deal of self-control just then not to open the windows by shattering them. But of course I didn't. I moved through the house sliding them open in casings I'd sanded with three grades of paper. Then I took a ball of twine from the kitchen drawer and lowered one end down the powder room drain. When it came up dry, I let the faucet run a few seconds to fill it and stepped outside.

Even through three years of selfish testing, my father had maintained his house in Trenton with uncommon pride and obsessive care, but in the frozen spring of my junior year he began its destruction with something small. He let the faucet leak. At first, I thought he didn't notice, and I was afraid of shaming him by pointing it out. Maybe my mother was also. We ate our meals listening to it dripping in the background until there was a second sign. He let a pinpoint of rust in the tub basin spread like a sore in the enamel. A lightbulb burned out and stayed burned out. Once, my mother tried to change it, but when my father saw her, he said, "I'll do that, Lucille. I've been busy, but I'm not incompetent." Our house grew darker. The Austrian clock wound down. Keeping time, too, was my father's job, and my mother did not even attempt to do it for him. Finally, when his service van broke down that summer, he did not repair it. He began idling around the house.

It's hard now to explain exactly why I didn't move to fix anything myself, except that as he began to betray us, my mother's model of love was all I had. The more oppressive our passivity grew, the more I longed simply to leave, and this is probably why I chose a college so far away. It was the anticipation of this escape that allowed me finally to feel critical of her. I remember one night she and I were in the kitchen, examining two different jars she held up to a candle. She was making soup, and the aspirin and the bouillon tablets she bought came in similar bottles. She was trying to read them in a room full of burned-out bulbs neither of us could bring ourselves to replace. It had been four years since he had begun doing drastic things to provoke her, staying out late night after night and buying a gun and making up lovers, and now there was this.

"Why don't you ever get angry?" I said.

She kept looking at the jars, but she stopped turning them in the light. Maybe it was surprise at the first verbal acknowledgment between us that there was anything wrong with him. Or maybe it was just the first time it had occurred to her that she might get angry. After a few seconds, she turned to me. "Some people need to see your love more than you need to see theirs."

Although at the time I would never have admitted this, even to myself, it was a relief to leave her. I stayed away as much as I could, with the excuses of money for travel and commitment to my studies, until I relied so thoroughly on my detachment for happiness that even a phone call from her felt like an invasion. By the time she called me in May of my sophomore year, the feeling of guilt and sorrow her voice stirred in me was familiar.

"How's school?" she said.

"Good. Exams are coming up next week—"

"I should call back then."

"No, no . . ." Through the wires, I heard the Austrian clock tolling. She was sitting in my father's chair, I knew. I said, "How are you? How's your sewing?"

"I'm making a dress for Aunt Lynn."

"Oh?"

"It's like the one I made for Jenny."

"And Dad?"

"Not good."

I didn't know what to say to this. Just before I left home two years before, I had seen her break something intentionally. He had passed an entire dinner without speaking a word to either one of us, and afterwards, when she was alone in the kitchen with her back to the hall door, she held a plate at shoulder height over the kitchen sink for a few seconds, her arms outstretched, and just let go. Then she put on a pair of rose-pruning gloves and wrapped the pieces in newspaper and took them to the garbage can at the curb. There was that memory to turn to, but this was the first time I'd ever heard her express her pain with words. "I'm sorry," I said.

"Actually," she said, and stopped. The clock had finished. There was a click in my mother's throat. "Actually, he had a heart attack, Luther."

"He what?"

"He's dead."

There was a moment of silence then, during which, to my surprise, I felt the beginning of tears. I covered the mouthpiece on the receiver with my hand until the feeling passed. Then I said, "I'll be home tomorrow."

"Thank you," she said.

When I arrived, I found the front door unlocked, and a small stalagmite of sodden plaster obstructed the entryway. Rain had leaked through the light fixture, and he had not fixed it. My mother was in the kitchen, making deviled eggs by candlelight. I set my suitcase on the floor and took up a pastry tube full of the cooked yolk to help. She placed pimentos after me. She wanted to know what of my father's things I wanted to take with me for sentimental reasons, and it's a clear failure of character that I did not pretend to want anything. I forced her to make suggestions: his watch, his good winter coat, his tools. She asked me several times that first day, and I could only tell her I would think about it, but in my mildew-scented room that night, I could think of nothing he had owned that did not make me angry.

The following morning, she told me she was going to the grocery store to buy more food for the funeral reception, and four hours later, I found her there in the frozen-food aisle, a glass door propped open by her body, her breath and the steam off her coat clouding the glass. She was holding a frozen spinach soufflé in one hand and her purse in the other. "What about his pocket knife?" she said, and it is a dark secret of mine that what I felt at that moment was a fear mixed not with sympathy but with irritation. How could she mourn him? I led her to the cash register, her wool coat cool from the freezer, and when I took her wallet from her purse, I saw that beneath it lay my father's gun.

This, then, was what I asked for. It is a sign that I'd judged the severity of her mental state correctly that she did not even worry over why I wanted it myself. We buried him the next morning, and I stayed two more weeks to move her things to her parents' house in Princeton, and when I returned to school, I spent a restless night getting out of bed to flip on the fluorescent lights and reposition the pistol. First I hid it under the mattress at the head of my bed, but in that state between half-sleep and dreams when worry is still active but the line between reality and fiction is gone, I imagined the gun misfiring into the base of my skull. It kept me from sleeping. I sat up in bed and rested my hands on my knees. I moved it into my desk drawer. Then I worried about someone finding it there—a fire inspection. Surely it was against university regulations to keep firearms in the dorm rooms. I checked its chamber again for bullets. Finally, I put it in a small square biscuit tin and slipped it in the deep pocket of the winter coat my mother had insisted I take with me. This is where it stayed, untouched in my closet, until that strobe of police lights on my ceiling in Sacramento two years later. Funny; a burglary in the building might have made me want to keep a gun in my apartment, to protect myself, but instead I wanted only to hide it. When I examine the impulse, it seems there were two emotions behind it.

One was fear of loss, and the other was shame at the way my attachment to an unloaded pistol marked me as my father's son.

When I arrived to open my account, Liz was sitting behind a wooden desk in front of the vault, trifolding sheets of paper into envelopes. The Wells Fargo Bank on J Street had large windows, and when I entered the bank for the first time, the room was warm with early sun. I was wearing the winter coat, and when I approached her desk, I was sweating. She licked her finger before she separated another page from her stack. Although she seemed a businesslike distance from me when seated, she stood as I cleared my throat to speak, bringing her face startlingly close to mine.

"Yes?" she said.

"I want to rent a safe-deposit box."

She opened a drawer in her desk and pulled out a form. When she sat, I did too and began to fill it out, my pulse racing. I could feel the weight of the gun on my hip. I said, "Who besides me will have access to the box?"

"Nobody. It takes two keys to open, and you've got one of them."

"The bank doesn't have copies of the customer keys?"

She cocked her head. "Well, sure, but we can't open it without your permission."

"Who has access to those keys?"

"Without a signature from you? Just the bank president, I'm guessing." She smiled at me. "But then again, my dad's the bank president, so I could cop it while he's sleeping and snoop through your drawer no problem."

I must have looked stricken because she said, "Relax! I'm only kidding!"

When I went back to my apartment that night, I regretted leaving the pistol in the vault. Between the sweating and the interrogation and the panicky looks, I had acted so suspiciously, I was sure that she would open the box to see what I had been so eager to protect. I might simply have retrieved the gun and closed the account the next morning, but I'll admit already I was drawn to her, and somehow the solution of going often enough to become something less than a lunatic to her compelled me.

The next day, I stopped by a pawn shop and purchased four rolls of wheat pennies and set them in a biscuit tin similar to the one that contained my father's pistol. I did this half-a-dozen times, until finally, with the boldness I was counting on, she asked me what was in the tin, and I lifted the lid, printed with a scene of snowy New England, to let her see. I think it was then, after a bell's peal of laughter that made heads turn in the teller line, that she asked me out for that dinner.

Now, standing alone on my front lawn waiting for the sewer smell to dissipate, I had the strange thought that were it not for my father's pistol, I might have lived alone in this house, without dread or confusion about the way my crimes of emotion were yielding results so similar to his own.

I went inside and closed all of the windows. The smell was gone, but as I began to puzzle through the evidence again, I felt a sort of exhaustion. Hiring a plumber to repeat the time-consuming battery of tests I'd already performed was very unlikely to yield a better answer than I had been able to come up with myself, and seemed a concession of defeat. And finally—of course it no longer seems strange now—I thought of the one person to whom I felt I had nothing left to concede.

When I arrived in the parking lot, I stood outside for a moment, looking in. Larry's wife stood at the counter watching her television. She had dumped the contents of her purse on the counter, and she was pawing through them without looking. When her hand found a container of Tic Tacs, she flipped it open, shook one into her palm, and popped it in her mouth. I pushed through the door, and she gestured at the screen as if I had been there with her watching all along. "Sisters who're best friends, what do you think about that?"

"Excuse me?"

"These are my favorites. They do it all the time. Happy people who

love each other silly. By the end, they're holding them in their chairs."
She rolled her eyes. "How's your boy?"

"He's fine."

"What did I tell you?" She winked. "So what's the problem. Another clog?"

And here I surprised myself. Although I would have expected it to embarrass me to do so, instead of answering her, I looked down at the counter at the contents of her purse—a dirty pink wallet, a pack of Juicy Fruit gum, Chap Stick, Tic Tacs, a brush fleeced with a mat of her hair, dental floss, a wrapped tampon, some change. I am sixty-five years old and I think I have a glimmer of understanding now, but for many years any memory of this meeting with Larry's wife made me feel some combination of discouragement and vertigo—a brief panicky glimpse at the unfathomable Rube Goldberg workings that controlled my mind and heart. I had come for her help, and although every element that had so annoyed me in our previous encounters was magnified here—her inappropriate familiarity, her condescension, her vulgar jokes about human nature—somehow under the very circumstances when they should have unnerved me the most they did not bother me at all. They were almost a comfort.

"Tic Tac?" she said.

"Sure."

She picked up the box and shook one into my palm. I put it in my mouth. She took a second one for herself and said, "So what kind of trouble have you got yourself into this time?"

"A little case of trap-seal loss," I said.

She cracked the mint between her molars. "Could be an arm-over vent in the attic full of water. Larry's brother saw that once."

"I already opened the wall to check for sagging."

"Yikes. You have been busy. Well, it's one of six things. Design error, which is my bet. Or if the design is decent, somewhere in there you probably jimmied something."

"I don't think—"

"Well, how old's your house?"

"Twenty-two years."

"That's a lot of time for mistakes. A repair or a new sink or something. You're in here a lot after all." She smiled slyly. "I could come take a look if you want."

"What are the other five?"

She counted them off on her fingers: "Piece of string drawing water down the drain. Evaporation, which isn't likely. Clogged vent, like I said. Cracked drain pipe. You've done the smoke test already; where'd the smoke come out?"

"Just the vent."

"You could've missed some spots."

"What's the sixth?"

"What?"

"You said there were six."

She looked at her fingers. "Oh, yeah. It never happens. I've never heard of it once. It was just in the book we had to read for the boys' licensing exam."

"What is it?"

"Wind effect." She shook her head. "Supposedly wind can get channeled down the vent and suck the trap empty. But I think the botched repair's more likely. It said the wind thing was rare, and it doesn't seem like the type of thing that would just start happening all of a sudden. Something about the roof design has to whip it down there."

My chest filled. "Actually, I added two dormers last summer."

"And a do-it-yourself bathroom maybe?"

"Let's say it was wind effect. . . ."

She rolled her eyes.

I said, "Is there something simple that can be done to stop it from happening again?"

She laughed.

I said, "Maybe something you can sell me?"

"Now you're talkin'. How about trap primers?"

"Trap primers?"

"They use them mostly in public bathrooms on the traps under floor drains. The drains are required, but they don't get much use unless a toilet overflows; so the seal evaporates. The primer taps the supply line for a little water whenever it gets low," she said. She picked up the box of Tic Tacs and handed it to me. Then she stepped around the counter to lead me to the back of the store.

It would be difficult to characterize the relief I felt except to say that it's the kind I've experienced only a few times in my life, a kind of flight inside the chest and a buzzing in the skull that even in a person driving alone in a car can produce a sudden, irrepressible bubble of laughter. I switched the radio on, and when I found something vaguely triumphant, I turned it loud. All week a sense of loss I'd been channeling unexamined into paranoia had me imagining Liz greeting other people's children at some preschool or whispering over a table in a bistro to a man named Rudy. It held me back from any kind of action, and something in me knew that whatever the truth was, an affair or a job, the only path towards eliminating these secrets began with conversation. I had resolved sometime in the middle of last night to try to initiate more of this, and now when I parked outside the Crisis Center and looked up at the window above, I tried to picture her there, listening to a stranger's worries across the telephone lines because I would not share my own. A pigeon lit on the brick sill outside the window and struggled for balance. A boy spilled a bag of fried chicken on the sidewalk and birds swarmed around him, a cloud of dark wings. In the end, it was simply the sudden thought that Liz might not be there at all—might be pursuing her own secret life—that made me lose my will. It seemed more than my fragile excitement could bear.

Instead, I drove to the bank to withdraw the money Elliot had said he needed. Over the last two days, I had given it some thought. He was a smart boy, and although we had never discussed it directly, I was pretty sure that if asked he could make a fair guess about the size of my savings. In hindsight it seemed much more likely that his impulse to get a job had stemmed from a genuine feeling that I was too far removed from his life now to be able to imagine the urgency he attached to his new social expenses. I will admit that it was mostly competitive insecurity about the implications of this that made me want to surprise him with a crisp one-hundred-dollar bill.

He was home when I got there, eating a bowl of Cheerios at the kitchen table. He looked up at me when I came through the door.

"Hi," he said.

"Hello." I put my hand in my pocket. "I've got that money for you."

"What money?" he said.

He has grown into a kind and respectful man. He has two small children of his own now, both of whom will consent to being comforted by him when injured even if their mother is also available. I wish I could by some miracle have known this then. It might have given me better access to my sympathy for him, because as it was, within seconds any tenderness I felt was obscured almost totally by anger. I closed my eyes for a second. *Behind the walls of a house,* I told myself, *pipes do not always run straight. . . .*

I said, "The money you needed a part-time job to earn."

"Oh, right," he said.

It wasn't until then that it occurred to me that he didn't really need the money, and in retrospect, what amazes me most is not his lie, but that it took me so long to identify it. I can, I suppose, claim some counterbalancing shrewdness in the fact that by two thirty that morning standing barefoot on my lawn listening to the strangely stressful pulse of crickets, it had occurred to me that it was not the only lie he had told me.

The next morning, I stopped by Nathan's office unannounced. He was eating breakfast from McDonald's: hash browns fried into an oval and served in a paper sleeve. He had just taken a bite—too hot—and he made a little "o" of his mouth to cool it.

I said, "Listen, I won't stay long, but I wanted you to know that I feel I've made a mistake."

He finished chewing and swallowed. "What?"

"I'm embarrassed by my vacillation, but all I can say is my son has

221 THE TESTING OF LUTHER ALBRIGHT

been going through a tough time, and I overreacted worrying about the travel. If you've still got an opening, I'd like to reapply."

He set his hash browns down. "You're killing me, Luther. We offered it to the guy from L.A. the day after you turned us down. He starts next week."

"I understand. I figured that was probably the case."

"And he's a good guy, too."

"I'm glad," I said.

"He turned down Bechtel for us."

I nodded. Outside, rain had just started. It had been so dry lately, the soil in the empty median planters had turned to dust, and the big drops stirred it, little plumes of red smoke. It was a strange sight.

He said, "Candidly? I'd rather have you because I've worked with you before. You're a known quantity. That's why I offered it to you first. But I can't back out of the offer."

"I understand."

"I mean, technically? I could do it, but I won't."

"I respect that."

The rain was loud, and he looked over his shoulder to see it. "Looks like a big one."

"Yes."

We both watched it a minute. Over the last few months, even the sight of clouds had made me tense, but last night I had installed the trap primers while Elliot tinkered with the drive train for a go-kart in the basement. Then I had closed all the windows. I used the thought of this to soothe myself—to slow my heart.

"Shoot, Luther," Nathan said.

"I know." I wiped my palms on my thighs. "I don't suppose you could use two people."

He laughed. He shook his head, eyeing me. "It's just not in the budget."

"I could work for a percentage of the business I bring in for a while."

"You're killing me again."

I held up a hand. "I understand."

He took another bite of his hash browns now, cool enough to allow him to consume half the oval in a single bite. My heart fluttered inside my chest. Something about the way he chose to take a bite then instead of thanking me for stopping by. I could tell he was thinking about it. "The truth is we probably *can* use the help."

I waited.

"There's this big job we're about to land. I never thought they'd give it to us, but if they do, we're going to be stretched really thin."

I said nothing.

"You could have a job with anyone looking, Luther. You really want me to call you if we get the contract?"

I scratched my chin in an effort to make it appear I was weighing this, but the truth is the odd carrel of loneliness I had erected for myself in the busy front-room of my family life made me yearn with unreasonable urgency for a second chance at a job with him—a man who could not inhibit himself even from eating fried potatoes to keep his heart from bursting. It seemed best to hide this.

"Sure," I said. "I want to take the right thing with the right company. I'm going to keep talking to people, but call me when you know, and we'll see where I am."

"Okay." He lifted the empty white paper bag and peered inside as if looking for more food. The meeting was over, and a stronger man might have risen and left at this point, but my curiosity overwhelmed me. I told myself it would be useful in my dealings with Elliot to know for sure.

I took that box of Tic Tacs from my pocket and opened it. I put one in my mouth and set the box on his desk. Then I said, "I ran into Robert yesterday."

He reached across the table for the Tic Tacs. "Who?"

"Belsky."

He put a mint in his mouth and furrowed his brow, thinking. "I'm terrible with names."

"He worked in Design with us at the Department."

"The guy with the limp?"

"No, that was Burt Sage. He left a while ago. Belsky's the one with the red hair and the really loud laugh."

"Loud laugh," he said. "I guess I don't remember him."

8 The Gun

Two months later, I had my last chance with both of them. Maybe if I had been better at imagining the future, I might have seen the moments for what they were and made different choices. I think about that sometimes. I think of my parents, and I even begin to feel sorry for my father, who for all his mistakes, I finally understand, was merely trying to wrench from my mother the same depth of intimacy Elliot was trying to wrench from me. After that year, Elliot would get some of what he needed from Belsky, who invited all of us on winter ski trips I tactfully declined but let Elliot attend. Then he would go away to college and fall in love with a woman so frank that when she first met us she confessed she'd dreamt she showed up for our dinner wearing nothing but the tam-o'-shanter from her old Brownie uniform, and half an hour later, in a fish restaurant not far from campus, she asked me how I'd really felt all those years ago when Elliot had shaved his head. Her manner caught me off guard, and I changed the subject quickly, but in my better moments I was happy that my son had found someone with whom he could share his secrets.

As for Liz, she would grow happier in most ways than I had ever seen her, and maybe it was this that would for a time confuse me into thinking my evasions had done no permanent harm. Her volunteer work gave her a confidence about her abilities that our family life never had, and it transformed her into a more sure-footed version of the bold and expressive woman I had known at the bank, so that briefly I was able to fool myself that in driving her to the Crisis Center, instead of hurting her, I had given her some kind of gift. Her sisters sensed the change in her over the telephone wires and began to turn to her in times of trouble. Eleanor got divorced a second time, Pam lost a child in a traffic accident, Charlotte went through a painful bankruptcy with her husband, and each of them in turn showed up at our house to stay awhile in Elliot's attic bedroom and receive Liz's comforts. She always knew just what they needed. Eleanor she sat up with until two in the morning drinking wine and exhausting her stores of both tears and laughter, and with Pam she read silently on the patio, sipping tea.

From time to time, she would lash out at me in the way that she had early in our marriage: the night Elliot's girlfriend asked me what I'd felt about the head shaving, for example, when surprise and a decade of distance made me answer more honestly than I ever had for Liz ("I was terrified," I said); one anniversary when some uncomfortable mixture of hopeful humor and morbid curiosity drove her to give me a set of proof Eisenhower dollars, and despite the obviousness of the unspoken lie my old collection represented by then, I still feigned a collector's excitement about the gift; and once when I would not join her in a conga line on the last night of a cruise to Acapulco. It was a cruise she'd tried to persuade Elliot and Gina to take with us, and she was probably just exhausted by the strain of passing the week without blaming their gentle refusal to come along on me.

But mostly she treated me with a tender remove, as if I were a terminal patient whose condition she regretted but had long since accepted with sympathy and peace. I haven't been able to fool myself that giving up on that intimacy with me did not cost her anything, though. Ten years later she was diagnosed with the cancer a yearning for children had once helped us skirt, and in her last weeks, our house filled with the people who loved her. Elliot and Gina slept together in the attic in his narrow bed, and Liz's sisters and mother took rooms at the Marriott in Rancho Cordova. Trish had just found out her husband was having an affair, and she slept on the couch in the living room next to the hospital bed we'd rented from Hospice and talked to Liz, whenever she woke, about what a painful combination fury and nostalgic longing proved to be. I was glad they'd all come, especially Trish, whose needs seemed to move Liz past her own suffering, but as I sensed the last day coming I wanted very badly to be alone with my wife.

One night while Trish slept, I carried Liz outside and laid her on the chaise next to the unused hot tub beneath the stars. She still looked so beautiful. She had lost her hair, but she was wearing a red wig she had chosen from a catalog and pinned with silk daisies to amuse her unhappy sister, and against the bodice of her nightgown lay a necklace of painted macaroni Elliot had made as a child.

She raised her arms up behind her red hair and crossed her thin legs. "Skinny-dipping?" she said.

I laughed.

"Or maybe just a little nooky?"

I started to cry.

"No . . ." she said softly. She took my hand. "Shhh."

I closed my eyes, but I could not stop. She rubbed my knuckles with her thumb.

"What is it?" she said.

"I was remembering what you said about Trish after that fund-raiser in San Francisco. That she lived such an important life. Do you remember that?"

"Yes."

"And here she is now, getting help from you while you're dying."

She shrugged, but I could see that her lip was trembling.

I said, "It's you who's important," I said.

She shook her head.

I said, "Everyone comes to you. You help everyone you touch."

She shook her head again. She was crying now too, but quietly, and I knew with bitter clarity why. I tried to make it funny, although I knew it wasn't: "Even me," I said.

Her whole body shook at this.

"Yes," I said. "Yes, you did. You helped as much as anyone could have."

She covered her eyes with her thin hand.

I said, "You're the most important person I know."

But days later she was gone, and then there was a funeral, and a dinner, and the emptying of my house of needs and noise, and going over that conversation in dark rooms at night, revising it, straining for words I might have found to persuade her of her worth, it is then that it became clear to me that the chance I'd missed had really come years ago.

The first Sunday of that summer vacation, Elliot asked me to meet him in the field behind our house—the acre of scrub brush that separated our yard from the Fair Oaks Power Plant. When he approached, he was carrying a box, and his stray dog followed closely, her leash dragging and catching at times in the weeds. On the last day of school, he had found her on the shoulder of the frontage road with a bad cut on her leg. In her panic, she tore up the backseat of his new car on the way to the clinic, and then turned on a veterinary aide, but instead of taking her to the ASPCA, he had purchased a full round of shots, a forty-pound bag of kibble, and a big plastic dome called a Dogloo. At night, when she wasn't asleep inside it, she crept as close to the house as her tether allowed and barked until he opened his window and called softly to her. Not long after her arrival, I noticed three fine furrows of dried blood on his forearm. Still, he checked out a book on dog training at the library and spent hours with her each day in our yard.

He set the box down, and the stray sniffed between my legs.

"Down," Elliot said calmly, and to my surprise, she dropped to the dry grass, her nose resting on my shoe.

"Wow," I said.

"It's amazing what they can learn," he said.

"No kidding."

"They want to be part of a group with rules."

"Pack animals."

"Right."

He was spreading out a blanket on the rough stubble of weeds. He gestured for me to sit, and I did.

He said, "I can't stay very long."

"Okay."

He pulled back the flaps of the box. "Tim's dad is taking us to a monster truck race before work." I had finally floated the idea of spending the summer expanding the garage, but in the end he and Tim had found jobs together at the McDonald's in Arden Fair Mall.

The dog stretched and pressed a paw into my thigh, and I started.

"No," Elliot said, and the dog retracted.

"I'm sorry," I said.

"It's not your fault."

"Maybe I should—"

"Relax, Dad. I'm just training her." He pulled the box towards him over the blanket. "Ham or tuna?"

"Tuna," I said.

Then he opened the box and withdrew two sandwiches wrapped in waxed paper, a red apple, a bruised Bartlett pear, and two cans of root beer.

He also took out his plumbing notebook, a torque wrench, and my father's gun.

"Bon appétit," he said, and he reached for his sandwich.

In going over this ground in memory in the last twenty years, I have been able to isolate two separate and distinct areas of regret. First is that although the sight of a gun in my son's hands ignited a quick flare of panic, it was quickly extinguished by the memory that I owned no bullets and replaced by a familiar and infuriating certainty that he was simply testing me once again. It did not even occur to me to worry that he might have purchased a box himself, and given the willingness to take reckless action to torment me that he'd displayed in the last six months, this seems almost incredible. Second is that when faced with the audacious bluntness of this final provocation, I did not just finally break down and ask him why the hell he was so angry with me. But by then he had me so well conditioned to the fire-drill rigors of recognizing and responding to his challenges that hiding my emotion at another was almost a reflex. At that point, as desirable as it would have been for both of us, I'm not sure it was even possible for him to break me.

I picked up my sandwich and unwrapped it carefully, raised half of it in a sort of lame toast, and took a bite.

He laughed bitterly, his tongue dotted with pink bits of ham. "You're not even sweating."

"It's not very hot out," I said.

"Weird things to bring to a picnic, eh?"

"A little unusual."

"Nice wrench, don't you think?"

"I've always liked it."

"Feel like reading some of my notes?"

"If you want me to."

"Where'd you get the gun?"

"It was my father's."

His sandwich was limp in his hand. A bit of ham escaped it and fell on the blanket. The dog snapped for it, her long tongue lashing out.

Elliot said, "That's all you're going to say about it, isn't it?"

"Unless you have more questions."

"You don't want to ask me anything yourself?"

"No."

"Not even about the wrench?" he said.

How can I explain it? I thought he was simply giving me one more opportunity to fail him with my anger, instead of the last to win.

I said, "I trust that you tell me what you want me to know."

He looked at me for a moment, and then he turned to his dog and held his sandwich at arm's length. She took the whole of it in her dexterous mouth and watched us as she chewed. Then she swallowed and dropped a slice of sweet pickle from between her lips, whole. Elliot started putting things back in the box, first the wrench, then the plumbing notebook, and finally the gun. He closed its cardboard flaps, touched the dog on the head, and they walked off towards our house together. He didn't say good-bye, and for reasons I can't understand, I didn't say it either. I was watching him go, and this preoccupied me so that I was more like another person observing myself watching my son depart. Elliot held his head upright, but in a way that he had that suggested disappointment. I had studied it before. Maybe his shoulders sloped more than those of other boys. Or it was the elongation of the neck; it made his head look like a burden to support. He crossed the fiery line where the sand-colored scrub brush met our malachite lawn, and then passed through a small opening in our hedge and disappeared from view until I could see him over its top, trudging towards the elm on the high ground in our yard to tie his dog. He kneeled and kissed her on the bridge of the nose, which she bowed for like a pauper being knighted. He held her dark nose to his forehead. The dog was still. It was as if she knew how she had been blessed to be the recipient of my son's least guarded advances, and, ridiculous as it was, I felt a quick jealousy. The kiss lasted no more than a second, and the feeling passed almost as quickly, like a match blown out. Then my son stood, picked up his box of questions, and walked into my house.

I was left sitting on the blanket, and for a moment, I pretended it was thoughtful—his leaving it for me—but I knew he had intended no consolations. It was hot, and the sun drew last night's rain from the dry yellow stalks, making them smell green. The power lines to my right and left crackled with electricity. My plot had been priced well below market for the area because no developer could conceive of a design that would avoid views of these transformers without sacrificing so much natural light that no buyer in the Fair Oaks market would want to live in it, but I'd designed a two-story L-shaped ranch with two skylit wings facing southeast, and no windows at all along the southwestern wall. To the tricks of architecture, I had added the screening of a thick row of Leyland cypress, which I now had to stand on a ladder to trim. But still, if you stood at the edge of the yard, you could hear the humming.

When I finally came back to the kitchen, Liz was calling out to me from the basement. I found her at the base of the wooden steps standing on a steamer trunk, flashlight in hand, peering through a hinged door in the beam I'd built to enclose the soil pipe. The plasterboard above her was darkened and dripping, and her hair was damp with sewer water. As she pushed it aside to see me, she paused to steady her voice. "I've been trying to fix it myself, but I can't find the key."

"What key?"

"The key to the mechanical closet. To switch off the main."

I reached above the doorsill then, but the key was not there. I ran the length of it with my fingers. Dust. A patch of wood I might have sanded more. I tried the knob, but unfortunately he had not forgotten to relock it.

I stepped onto the trunk next to Liz. When I built the house, I had joined each length of drainage pipe with a neoprene sleeve and a stainless steel shield I tightened to sixty inch-pounds with a torque wrench. What I saw when I looked inside the hatch was a welt of water leaking out both ends of the sleeve. The screw clamps had been loosened so much that the edges of the shield didn't even touch. Drainpipes are empty until plumbing is used;

to get this volume of water to leak from the pipe, he would have had to run a tap for a very long time. Liz was quiet next to me, and it was her hair as much as the pipe itself that smelled of sewer water now. Oddly enough, I think it was this, finally, that moved me to rage.

As I climbed the stairs, I took two at a time. The door to his bathroom was closed, and I could hear the water running. I could not think of words I would say because I was both bewildered and angry. I could imagine only holding both shoulders firmly as I did when he swung his young body out over our roof. Maybe I would lose my will. Maybe I'd make another sound he would mock. I banged on the center of the door with my fist, but inside the bathroom the water didn't stop, and it was only then—remarkably, finally—that I thought how easily he could have purchased bullets for my father's gun.

I'm not sure I can even characterize the feeling I had at that moment. It has invaded a handful of my dreams in recent years, and the loneliness of waking up a widower, my son a five-hour plane flight away with a wife who knows him better than I ever have, is such a comfort by comparison that I am briefly grateful to wander around the house in the dark and visit all those things that haunt me by day: photographs, empty dresser drawers, a full-sized kitchen. It was the feeling that if I could take back all the years of joy, all his smiles and shy looks of pride, snatch them back and have lived an immeasurably smaller life of television watched alone and risks avoided inside a small apartment, I would have done so without hesitation; not to spare my son his adolescent anguish—it was much weaker and more selfish than this—but to spare myself the life that would begin when I looked at the scene he had left for me on the other side of his bathroom door.

For a moment, things got very slow. Steam seeped out beneath the door. The grandfather clock below me tolled. I did not go for a screwdriver to remove the knob, as I might have. I rammed my shoulder against the door, so hard that for the next week I could not raise my arm to take a cup from the kitchen cupboard or shave my face without pain, and as I leaned back to do it again, the water stopped. There was a sound of wet feet slapping the tile and a towel pulled from the bar. He opened the door and stood there dripping water. Steam kissed my face. "What?" he said.

He was leaning towards me, his face red with heat and righteous anger. Water dripped from his nose and ears onto his clavicle.

"What is it?" he said.

Sometimes I look back on this day, and I think, *What mysteries are so many of a human being's most important choices?*—mongrels of a hasty copulation between body and soul. I was so full of things at that moment—bloodrush, fury, sweat, habit, adrenaline, confusion, shame, and, maybe most potent of all, the invisible misfires and wire-pulls of memory—that despite the pain of an unbearably complex fullness, almost a bursting, I cannot say I had any clear thoughts at all. There was just a tidal swell of mind-noise and corporal discomfort through which my indescribable relief that my son was alive passed quickly into something else.

"I know what you did," I said.

"It's not the first time."

"I know."

He stood, dripping. Despite months of work with those weights, his bare chest looked small.

"I forgive you," I said.

"I did them all."

"I know that."

"Even the clog. Even the trap seals."

"I know."

His glasses clouded over with steam. Although he was half-naked and sixteen, it occurred to me that he might not believe me without a larger gesture, and without hesitation, I rested a hand on his bare shoulder. He looked at me, waiting, and my strong impression is that at that moment he still had enough hope to believe that I might summon the insight and courage to stop short and call a halt to it—that instead of reaching up my sleeve for another ace from a conjurer's deck of bland emotions, I might, finally, for once in my life, say something completely honest. A breeze stirred the papers in the attic behind me and made paper noises. They settled. But then I saw that key on the counter next to his sink, and in the wake of my horror at having made room for mortal danger in his life, the sight of this went straight to simple reflex. I took my hand from his shoulder as if from a hot stove and picked up the key. He studied my face after this withdrawal with something like the mixture of contempt and longing Liz had displayed in the radiologist's office. Then he took off his cloudy glasses. He rubbed his eyes. I'm sure now that this was a prelude to tears I should have stayed to witness, but before they came, I had turned for the stairs to hide my own.

It would take a long time for me to realize that his tests of me were really over. In the years to come, at those moments when I expected an upwelling of disappointment might move him to words of judgment, he would offer only those gentle physical gestures of respect and affection that in time seemed the saddest condemnation of all. At his college graduation he would shake my hand, in Liz's hospital room he would hold it, and when the band stopped playing at his wedding reception, he would lead me alone to my car.

When I got back to the basement, the pipe had already stopped dripping. Liz had gone upstairs to change her clothes and rinse her hair—in the bathroom later I'd find an empty bottle from the liter of club soda she'd used so she wouldn't have to run the taps—and I took the opportunity afforded by my privacy and enlightenment to open the door to the mechanical closet to make sure that Elliot had not kept the gun. The tin had the right heft, but I knew better than to trust this. I took it out of the wall and opened it to make sure, and looked inside the empty chamber. Then I put it back, and when I locked the maintenance door, I pocketed the key.

After I finished retightening the seam on the soil pipe, I found Liz in the kitchen, cutting cookies shaped like stars and moons.

"Sorry about the mess you stumbled on," I said.

She waved away my apology with her free hand. "Will it be hard to fix?"

"Just a little Sheetrock patching," I said.

I reached out for the bowl of cookie dough, and she passed me a scrap between her fingers. It seemed to me a foregone conclusion at this point that she wouldn't ask me about the banging she'd heard when I tried to break down Elliot's door—she'd ask Elliot instead—and although a year ago she would have, it did not occur to me that if I didn't bring it up myself, we would never go back to that place. Outside, Elliot's dog began barking. I heard Elliot's window slide open, and the soothing tones of his voice, although I could not make out his words. Liz heard him too; I could tell from the way her eyes glanced at the ceiling and her shoulders relaxed. Something about it. I said, "Last month I came across a help-wanted section in the paper you had marked up with a pen."

She turned and went back to rolling the dough. "Oh, that."

My heart was beating fast.

"It was silly," she said. "I was just— I was just thinking about what jobs I could get if I wanted to."

"Why would you want to?"

She looked up at me and raised a hand, palm out, and then turned it and pressed it to her lips. "Oh, no," she said. "It's not— Really, I just, I haven't had a real one since the bank—you know, one with an interview and a paycheck. It was fun to think about what I was qualified for."

"But it looked like you called some of them."

She set the rolling pin aside now. "I did. I went for an interview even. Two actually. Just to see if I could get the job."

"And did you?"

"Yes. But I turned them down because I didn't need them." She picked up a star cutter, but just held it. "It was just for fun, Luther. I know it's silly, but working at the Crisis Center made me feel useful."

"You are useful," I said. But I sensed vaguely that I had robbed her of this feeling in the domain where it would have meant the most to her. She could see this in my face, I think. Before I could dwell on it and begin to fathom the damage radius of my secrecy, she obscured it with lines and gestures cribbed from days when our conversations still seemed pregnant with the promise of some future revelation.

She said, "How about you? How was work?"

"Oh, fine."

She smiled. "Tell me."

I had started with Nathan just a week earlier, and each night she had found a different way to celebrate—champagne, a cake, an office nameplate hidden in the butter dish.

I said, "I got assigned my first project."

She held out another scrap of dough. "Details," she said.

Upstairs, I heard the toilet flush and pictured my son disguised in pajamas, a man. I set the torque wrench on the counter and took the piece of dough from her hand.

I said, "It's a six-week evaluation of a prospective dam site on the Pak Mun River in Thailand. They interviewed three firms, and when they picked us, they asked specifically for me."

"That's fantastic," she said.

And in some ways, it was. I did well at Nathan's office, traveling to six different countries in my first year. Liz got promoted, becoming Counseling Trainer and then Volunteer Supervisor, and after a while I stopped bracing myself for questions she would never ask about the pieces of the story Elliot had chosen to share with her—his mischief with the trap seals maybe, or the secret of my father's gun. By the end of Elliot's freshman year in college we spent half our evenings separated by work we enjoyed, and most of the others at tables for four in downtown restaurants, where she listened to the troubles of her fellow volunteers and their husbands with a bright intensity that I loved, I see now, because it was an unearned window on the passion she had tried so hard to devote to me. Elliot chose a school in New Hampshire, but he came home for every holiday, so that I could almost imagine there was no significance to the distance. Then after Liz died, he began to eliminate annual visits home with a tender restraint—his birthday one year; the next year mine; the first Christmas he spent with his in-laws in Vermont—until finally he brought his wife and sons out to visit me only once a year, for Thanksgiving.

But that day twenty years ago, with the threat of the plumbing and the job and Elliot's research topic behind me, I was reasonably optimistic that I could start fresh, building intimacy into our exchanges on the bedrock of my secrets. It was another two weeks before I left for Thailand, and in that time, I opened a safe-deposit box and gave up my father's gun. I checked the function of the trap primers daily, and gave Liz her own maintenance closet key. A few times I thought of driving to tell Larry's wife the punch line to my plumbing problems, but I think I already knew I would never tell Liz, and for all my myopia I was at least aware enough of the betrayal this small temptation represented to resist it.

The night before my flight, Elliot was at the far end of the yard teaching the dog to wait for his release before fetching a tossed ball. Liz stood at the kitchen sink snapping the ends from beans. I went upstairs to change, and tried to imagine the life they would lead alone together during my six weeks on the other side of the world. A hint of the missed chance this kind of travel would come to represent flickered through me, although it would be years before I really understood it. Just then I felt relieved. Even a little victorious.

I opened my wallet, and inside it was that picture of our family standing in front of the Grand Canyon. I had taken it by positioning the camera on a rock and setting the timer for thirty seconds. I walked to the canyon wall where my wife and son stood and tossed a stone out into the shimmering air, and we watched it fall past the rose-hued record of one hundred million years of geologic time. A bird flew by. A chipmunk passed us on the path. Silence. The stone struck the wall for the first time a mere two seconds before the aperture opened, and into the hush of their held breath I whispered "Smile" and captured for all time on both of their faces that mixture of awe and surprise that is wonder. On my own is a different thing. I used to think of it as a father's joy, but just recently it has begun to strike me as the lonelier joy of a magician.

Acknowledgments

A number of people were important to the writing of this book. I was helped daily by the long reach of three teachers, Mr. Sloan (sixth grade); my high school English teacher, Blair Torrey; and my thesis advisor, Toni Morrison, each of whom sometimes found a few things worthy of praise in my homework assignments and always respected me enough to point out a great deal that was not. For various invaluable contributions, including encouragement, candor, technical information, geographical perspective, critical insight, editorial advice, and unstinting gifts of time, I would like to express my deep gratitude to all of the following people: Robert C. Allen, Clay and Amy Brock, Laurel Canan, Ethan Canin, G. Scott Cuming, Suzanne Dresdner, Carole Glickfeld, Courtney Hodell, Alan Locker, Amy Loyd, Melanie Rehak, Chandler Tuttle, Amanda Urban, Steve Verigin, Joshua Weinstein, and Dottie Zicklin. I would also like to thank all those friends and family members who rendered emotional support in the form of comfort, distraction, or childcare; my children, for countless small and priceless things; and Jeff, my best reader and best friend, whose company was itself the most frequent aid.